Hardback ISBN 978-1-80483-217-2

Ebook ISBN 978-1-80483-215-8

Kindle ISBN 978-1-80483-216-5

Audio CD ISBN 978-1-80483-223-3

MP3 CD ISBN 978-1-80483-220-2

Digital audio download ISBN 978-1-80483-214-1

Boldwood Books Ltd
23 Bowerdean Street
London SW6 3TN
www.boldwoodbooks.com

MURDER IN TUSCANY

T.A. WILLIAMS

B

Boldwood

First published in Great Britain in 2022 by Boldwood Books Ltd.

Copyright © T.A. Williams, 2022

Cover Design by CC Book Design

Cover Photography: Shutterstock

A CIP catalogue record for this book is available from the British Library.

Paperback ISBN 978-1-80483-222-6

Large Print ISBN 978-1-80483-218-9

To Mariangela and Christina with love, as always

1

SUNDAY AFTERNOON

I've never tried it, and I have no wish to, but I imagine there's a moment when you're about to do your first parachute jump and you find yourself standing at the open door of an aircraft thousands of feet off the ground, when all that's going through your head is, *What the hell am I doing here?*

That's the way I felt that day.

I'd stopped the car right in front of the rusty iron gates. It's not that they were closed. In fact, from the look of them, almost submerged beneath ivy and tortuous climbing weeds, they'd been open for decades. I'd stopped to consider my options and they were, quite simply, binary: stay or go.

The white gravel drive curled gently upwards towards a big clump of cypress trees higher on the hillside. Partly hidden in the midst of them I could just about make out the villa, which the website described as a *stunning piece of Renaissance architecture*. It was a large building with what looked like a little tower rising from the centre of the roof. The walls were a sun-scorched ochre colour, not dissimilar to the bone-dry earth surrounding the dusty olive trees on both sides of the drive, and from here it looked as though most of the faded green shutters on the windows were closed – presumably against the baking heat of the July sun. There was no escaping the fact that it was a charming view and a beautiful building, but my heart sank all the same as I stared at it.

What the hell was I doing here?

I was still seriously considering whether to turn around and head back to the airport when there was a strident toot of a horn. Glancing in the mirror, I saw the long, sleek shape of a flashy-looking sports car behind me. If the raging bull on the bonnet had been real, it would have been pawing the ground in frustration. Selecting first gear, I hastily drove in through the gates and pulled over so the bright red beast behind could overtake my little rental car. As the other vehicle drew level, it slowed and the window on the passenger side opened. Considering the roof was down, this hardly seemed necessary, but the driver was clearly keen to be heard. I opened my own window to hear what the man had to say and flinched at the impact of the hot, dry air on my face after the air-conditioned interior. Tuscany certainly gets hot in July.

'Can I help you?' The man addressed me in Italian and one thing was immediately clear. From the acerbic tone and the autocratic expression on his suntanned face, this wasn't a man who was used to helping people.

I mustered my best Italian, the result of having an Italian grandmother and having done A-level Italian many years ago, topped up by three years of intermittent attendance at night school classes at Dulwich College more recently.

'I'm here for the writing course. Up at the villa...'

The Lamborghini driver immediately became

less aggressive – not friendly by a long chalk, but noticeably less confrontational.

'Excellent. Follow me.' The words were delivered in English in the clipped tones of a member of the privileged upper classes and I felt myself groan inwardly once more, but before I had a chance to respond, there was a snarl from the engine alongside me and the supercar, which had probably cost more than I've earnt in the past five years, set off up the drive. The car and the track all but disappeared from sight in the dust cloud produced by the spinning wheels and I hastily scrabbled to close the window, but not before a choking cloud of Tuscan dust had blown in and started me sneezing. Mouthing a few choice expletives, I blew my nose and waited for the dust cloud to subside before accepting my fate and setting off up the drive.

As the track climbed ever higher, I had to admit, albeit grudgingly, that this was a rather fine place in which to spend two weeks. The views opened out over the surrounding hills and that might even have been Florence itself in the far distance, but in the heat haze it was impossible to tell. Of course, it wasn't the place that was worrying me. It was what I was going to be expected to do here and with whom.

As I was almost up at the villa, my phone started ringing. Old habits die hard so I pulled over and stopped before answering it, although the only accident this distraction might have been likely to provoke would have been to make me run over one of the numerous lizards who for some reason known only to themselves felt obliged to shoot across the track just as the car approached. A glance at the caller ID told me that it was my daughter, Tricia, and my spirits rose – a bit.

'Hi, sweetheart, how's the weather in Birmingham?'

'It's sunny for a change and I'm fine thanks, Dad. What about you? Have you got there yet?'

'I'm literally just driving up to the villa now.'

'And is it as gorgeous as it looked on the website?'

'I suppose it's pretty enough, if you like that sort of thing...'

'Do try to sound a bit more cheerful, would you, Dad. They aren't going to eat you, you know.'

'I'm not so sure about that.'

'You'll love it, you wait and see. Just think, you a writer, in there among all those other writers.'

'There's writing and there's writing, Trish. I shudder to think what sort of weirdos I'm going to find myself surrounded by.'

'They're probably perfectly normal people who just happen to like...' She was trying hard, but I heard her voice crack as she attempted, unsuccessfully, to stifle a giggle. '...erotica.'

'Oh, God...'

'Come on, Dad. From the website it looks like it should be fine. Sponsored by a bestselling author, taught by professional creative writing tutors, it isn't just going to be a bunch of dirty old men in grubby raincoats, you know.'

'Those bastards...'

'That's unfair, you haven't met them yet.'

'I wasn't talking about them. I was talking about the bastards, my so-called colleagues, who came up with this crazy idea. I'd have preferred it if they hadn't given me anything at all!'

'I think it was a lovely gesture as a retirement present. It's perfect for you – well, almost.' I could hear the mirth in her voice again. 'They just didn't check the small print until it was too late. And they have apologised, after all.'

'Oh, they apologised all right. Once they'd stopped laughing. I don't know why I let you bully me into coming. So the course organisers wouldn't give a refund. So what? Why put myself through this?'

'Dad, we went through all that last weekend. I'm sure it'll be fine. Just give them the benefit of the doubt and try to enjoy yourself. Like I've told you time and time again, think of it as a free holiday in a place you've always wanted to visit – after all, that's what it is.'

'Yes, I know, it's just that the last thing I need is a course teaching me to write smutty books...'

She was right. We had been through this already and I had promised her I would try to fit in, however potentially embarrassing it was likely to be. The fact that it was free and in Tuscany sweetened the pill but didn't do much for the feeling of dread I'd been nursing. Doing my best to sound more positive – if only for my daughter's sake – I tried to adopt a slightly cheerier tone.

'I promise I'll be good. Besides, it said that all

my afternoons will be free so even if I'm bored stiff in the mornings I can always get out and about and do some sightseeing. I rented a car at Pisa airport, so I've got transport. And it's only for two weeks...'

'That's the spirit. And you are in the historic heart of Tuscany, if not Italy, after all. Just think of all those wonderful old churches and castles and stuff for you to poke around in. Didn't you say you'd got a list of places you needed to check out? You wait; you'll have a great time.'

'I wish I shared your confidence.'

'It'll be great. Anyway, enjoy yourself and stay in touch.' There was a momentary hesitation before her final words. 'I spoke to Mum earlier and she sends her love.'

'Bye, sweetie. Thanks for the call.'

As I slipped the phone back into my sweaty breast pocket, her words were still echoing in my head. Was that really what Helen had said or was that the invention of a daughter who wished things could go back to being like they used to be?

There was no further time for conjecture as a glance in the mirror revealed a VW minibus coming up the drive some way behind, so I hurriedly set off up the track again before I found myself on the receiving end of another dust storm. As I reached the top of the olive grove, the drive took a sharp turn to the right and led into the trees where the shade made a welcome change from the relentless sun. Another slight bend in the road and I emerged onto a circular gravelled parking area surrounded by bushes covered with beautiful pink and red blossoms. In the middle of the circle was an elegant old fountain, which wasn't working. Pretty obviously it needed a drink as badly as I did.

I parked the car a healthy distance from the Lamborghini – the last thing I needed was a claim for damage to a Lambo – and opened the door. Stepping out into the heat, I saw the minibus arrive and pull up between my car and a flashy-looking BMW with UK plates. I was just retrieving my bag from the boot of the little Fiat when footsteps in the gravel behind me made me turn. A dark-haired woman maybe four or five years younger than me gave me a smile that lit up her face but didn't extinguish the lines around her eyes.

'Hello.' She addressed me in excellent English

with just the slightest Italian accent. 'Are you here for the writers' course?'

I straightened up and held out my hand, feeling like I was about to be led to the stake. 'That's correct. My name's Dan Armstrong.' It still felt strange to introduce myself to strangers as anything other than DCI Armstrong.

The woman shook my hand and introduced herself in her turn. 'I'm Maria, Maria Moore. My husband is Jonah Moore, the author. Welcome to Villa Volpone.' She indicated the assortment of people emerging from the minibus behind her. 'I've just been picking up some of the other participants.' Raising her voice to attract the attention of the group, she pointed towards me. 'This is Dan, everybody. He's joining us for the course.'

There was no escape now, so I dropped my bag and gave a self-conscious wave, bracing myself for a bunch of weirdos, perverts, and degenerates. There were four people in the group and to my surprise and considerable relief, none of them immediately appeared to fall into any of those categories. There were two elderly ladies who wouldn't have looked out of place in a parish council meeting, a very intense-looking woman with stunning ebony skin and an amazing mass of grey and black striped dreadlocks, who looked fifty but might well have been ten years younger, and a very attractive auburn-haired woman with freckles who probably was fifty but was doing a pretty good job of trying to look ten years younger. I was also pleasantly surprised to find that the course participants were all female. As my eyes surveyed them, I felt a little wave of relief. They looked remarkably normal and several of them appeared to be as apprehensive as I felt.

'We're so glad to have some men on the course this year.' Maria Moore gave me an appraising look and the others followed her example, making me feel a bit like a prize bull (or, more likely in my case, a scruffy old steer) in a show ring. 'It does make such a difference to the dynamic. Now, let me show you where you're going to be living. Agatha, Elaine, do you want a hand with your bags?'

The two older ladies shook their heads in unison and reached for their suitcases. 'We're fine, thank you, Maria.'

The taller of the two spoke on behalf of both of

them with the sort of precise, confident tones of somebody who knew her own mind. Together with her fragile little companion, they lugged their bags up the steps to the main entrance without protest. I thought about offering to help but had a feeling the tall lady would have taken it as an affront to her dignity.

I let them all head for the villa before following. While waiting, I looked around more closely and a couple of things caught my eye. Although I know precious little about supercars, it looked as though the Lamborghini wasn't in the first flush of youth so I revised my earlier estimate. It was probably only worth a hundred grand or so. Not that this made it much better. That's still a hell of a lot to pay for a car. The villa looked very well maintained and the gardens meticulously cared for. Either Mr and Mrs Moore spent the rest of the year working twelve hours a day in the garden or they had help – and help doesn't come cheap.

The main entrance was through a pair of exquisitely carved wooden doors about twice the height of normal doors, and inside I found myself in a massive, marble-tiled hallway lined with mirrors in gilt frames that reflected the light from the huge chandelier hanging in the middle of the ceiling and presented us with disconcerting images of ourselves from the side, front and back. It was a bit like being in a huge changing room. I instinctively straightened my shoulders as I caught myself slouching – Helen had constantly nagged me about this – and of course that made me think of her yet again. My mind was still on her when I felt a tap on the arm.

'Hello, Daniel, was it? My name's Agatha. I write straight sex.' It was the taller of the two septuagenarians and she used the words without a hint of embarrassment while I had to struggle to keep my cheeks from colouring. Interestingly, her blue-grey eyes perfectly matched her hair colour and I wondered if this might be intentional. These same eyes were studying me closely and I realised that in spite of her advancing years, this was a canny lady.

An answer to an introduction like this coming from a lady who could have been my mother didn't readily spring to mind so I just held out my hand. She took it and shook it so hard I couldn't help wondering if she cracked walnuts for a living.

Nursing my aching hand, I reflected that with a name like Agatha, she might have done better to write murder mysteries rather than 'straight sex'. Ignoring the hand-crushing, I answered politely, 'I'm pleased to meet you, and it's just Dan.'

'And what's your genre, Dan?' Just in case my education wasn't up to par, she added a translation. 'What sort of stuff do you write?' She was still studying me closely and before I could answer, she made a remarkably astute observation. 'Do you really write erotica? Somehow I have my doubts. You don't have the eyes for it.'

I shook my head, keen to have a chance to explain what had brought me here. 'You're dead right; erotica's not my thing. I do write, but I'm halfway through writing a historical mystery – no sex.'

It felt important to make that clear. I wondered vaguely what she'd seen in my eyes and how the eyes of a writer of erotica are supposed to look – out on stalks, maybe? Of course, it could just be that thirty-three years in the murder squad had left their imprint on my face as well as on my failed marriage. I quickly went on to give her a brief summary of the chain of events – whether cock-up or conspiracy on the part of my former colleagues – that had led to my being here and her stern expression mellowed as she guffawed with laughter.

'Elaine, do come and say hello to Dan. He's here by mistake.'

The smaller of the two ladies came over and shook hands with me far less aggressively. She barely came up to her companion's shoulder, her hair was snowy white, and she was wearing a grey cardigan in spite of the thirty-degree-plus temperature. All she needed were a couple of knitting needles sticking out of her bag and she would have been a dead ringer for Miss Marple. 'Really, you'll have to tell me how that happened, Dan. Is this your first?'

'My first?'

'Your first summer school here at Montevolpone. It's my first time, although Agatha's been here twice before.'

I nodded. 'Yes, it's all new to me.'

Introductions completed, Agatha took over the conversation once more. 'Elaine and I've been friends for years. She writes BDSM erotica.' She shot a look of admiration in her frail-looking companion's direction. 'She's been very successful.'

I did my best not to let an expression of amazement spread across my face. What did those letters stand for again? If I'd been in the vice squad, I would have known straight away. I knew the S and M stood for sadism and masochism, but the other letters? B for bondage, probably, but what about the D? One thing was for sure: I wasn't going to ask. Appearances can be deceptive. Either this timid little woman had a chequered past and a good memory or her imagination was remarkable. It certainly sounded as though older people had moved on since my mum's time.

I found myself repeating the mantra I'd always drummed into my staff: don't judge people on their appearance alone. Over the years on the force, I had come across professional-looking doctors who could kill, smiling priests who could molest and rape, and charming urbane lawyers who could cheat and lie, and up till now I had truly believed I had heard it all. Now it looked as though I might be wrong after all. I viewed mild little Elaine with renewed interest and just murmured, 'Good for you.'

'Dan, this is Diana.' Maria Moore materialised among us, leading the forty- or fifty-year-old lady with the amazing hair. Diana looked as uncomfortable as I felt, and I immediately warmed to her. 'She's a first-timer as well.'

'Hello, Diana.' I gave her a smile and held out my hand. 'Looking forward to it?'

'Hello.' Her handshake was the proverbial wet fish, but she did manage to muster a hint of a smile. My suspicion that she might be younger than she looked gained momentum. 'Are you as nervous as I am?'

Before I could reply, Agatha cut in with her imperious air. 'And what's your genre, Diana?' Clearly, she was on the quest for information again. I wondered idly if she, too, had once been in the police force. In a 'good cop, bad cop' situation I could well imagine her as the steely-eyed interrogator. Personally, I've never been one for that sort of thing. I've usually found that if you pick your moment and make sure your questions keep the suspect on the back foot, you get results without having to bring out the thumbscrews.

Diana answered freely. 'Historical erotica. I'm a

professor of ancient history at Bristol University and I'm just finishing my first novel, which is set in ancient Rome – you know, orgies and all that.' There was just a hint of a lovely Jamaican twang in her voice. 'There was no shortage of that sort of thing going on back in ancient Rome.'

'Excellent, excellent.' I couldn't help noticing that Agatha, as well as looking like Marge Simpson, had a tendency to sound like Mr Burns from the cartoon series. 'Dan's here by mistake.' She giggled again. 'He's historical as well.'

'Steady on, Agatha, I'm younger than I look.' My weak attempt at humour even brought a smile to their faces and I began to feel a little less apprehensive. Maybe my fellow students weren't going to be too objectionable after all.

I told them that my area of interest was the Renaissance and had just finished explaining yet again about my retirement present and the misunderstanding, when the last of the new arrivals joined the group. Close up, this confirmed my first impression that this woman was very good-looking. She had beautiful red hair – either natural or out of a bottle, I'm no expert on hair – and if it hadn't been for the same stress lines I'd spotted on Maria Moore's face, she probably could have passed for forty rather than fifty. Mind you, I reminded myself, I was a fine one to start judging people for trying to slow the ageing process. Although I'd just retired at the ripe old age of fifty-five, the very thought of describing myself as retired was anathema to me and I'd taken to referring to myself as an author, although I'd yet to finish writing my first book.

'This is Charlotte.' Maria, the wife of our illustrious course leader, introduced her and as I shook hands with Charlotte, she caught my eyes for a fraction of a second and I was mildly surprised to feel a little shot of what might even be attraction run through me. This was a surprise because for the past thirty years of my life there had only been one woman for me, and maybe there still was, in spite of her now living alone in the family home in Dulwich with our two ancient and very grumpy cats while I was squeezed into a microscopic flat in Bromley.

'If I can have your attention. Please!' Any further conversation was interrupted by the strident tones of another female voice and all eyes turned towards the beautiful, sweeping marble stairway that led to the upper floors. Standing on the bottom step was a minute lady, even smaller than Elaine, probably well into her sixties and wearing the sort of high-necked lacy blouse and long skirt that wouldn't have looked out of place in *A Room With a View*. Realising that she had our attention, she addressed us. As she spoke, I couldn't help noticing the similarity between her patrician English accent and that of the driver of the Lambo.

'Welcome to Villa Volpone, everybody.' In spite of her words, she didn't look particularly welcoming and I was reminded of my old headmaster, Bumface Burgess, who had shot fear into the hearts of even the most recalcitrant bullies. In spite of her tiny stature, I almost felt as if I should stand to attention. 'My name is Millicent. My brother is the author Jonah Moore, who of course needs no introduction.'

The way she referred to him was odd. Although there was reverence in her tone as she mentioned his name, there was an undercurrent of something else – disapproval maybe? I glanced across to Maria Moore's face as she watched Millicent and for a second or two I felt sure I could spot dislike, or worse. Pretty clearly there was no love lost between wife and sister-in-law.

'If you would all like to follow me, I'll show you to your rooms.' Quite clearly, this wasn't a suggestion, it was an order, and we all obediently picked up our bags and started moving. Before setting off, Millicent pointed across the hall to a corridor leading to the left. 'Drinks in the lounge at six thirty. Dinner in the dining room at seven thirty. Dress code informal. I hope you all remembered to inform us of any allergies. We can't be held responsible if you didn't. Now, come along.'

Brusque, that was the word. It came to me as I followed the others up the stairs. Yes, her manner was decidedly brusque. Five out of ten for customer relations. Should try harder. I couldn't vouch for the others, but I was looking forward to a relaxing break rather than a forced labour camp, and I hoped the other course leaders would be more like Maria than this little tyrant. My feeling of apprehension, which had been starting to wane, now returned with a rush and I hoped this wasn't an omen.

We were all housed on the second floor. Presumably the first floor was reserved for the family. Corridors led off on either side at the top of the stairs and a quick count told me there were probably a dozen guest bedrooms up here. Millicent caught my eye and pointed to the right.

'You're along there in Dante. Third on the left. See you downstairs at six thirty. Please try to be on time.'

Her tone remained autocratic, and I toyed with the idea of giving her an ironic salute but, remembering my promise to Tricia, I just murmured my thanks and watched as the four female guests were led off in the opposite direction. Whether this was sheer chance or deliberate segregation remained to be seen.

I walked past rooms labelled 'Botticelli' and 'Michelangelo' before reaching the door with 'Dante' on it. Turning the handle, I went in to find it an enormous, high-ceilinged room, quite a bit bigger than the whole flat I was currently renting in Bromley and with a marble-clad bathroom the size of my English bedroom. Dropping my bag on the floor, I went across and opened the windows, pushing the louvred shutters apart to reveal the view, and it was pretty damn good. The room looked out over red-tiled outhouses and formal gardens and onwards into the Tuscan hills. Clearly this was the back of the house and the gardens here were well maintained and extensive, with an inviting-looking swimming pool partly concealed behind an immaculately clipped hedge at the far end.

After standing there for a few moments, I slowly felt myself beginning to relax. So far, the other people on the course looked fairly normal – depending on your views on sadomasochism – and I was pretty sure I'd been able to explain the mistake that had led to my presence here. Being objective, I now admitted to myself that my fear hadn't been of finding myself amid a bunch of pervs so much as people thinking I was also equally depraved. In fact, it was beginning to look as though writing erotica wasn't the preserve of dubious men in grubby attics surrounded by pornography, but maybe a genuine literary genre and, from the look of it so far, one chosen predominantly by women rather than men. All the same, I thought it best to withhold judgement until I saw the rest of the participants.

A glance at my watch told me that it was almost five. Millicent had made it clear that we were expected to be on parade at six thirty and that gave me time for a quick walk around the grounds first, so as to get my bearings and get a breath of air. I went out into the corridor, closing the door behind me, and toyed with the idea of locking it, before deciding to leave it open. This was somebody's private house after all and the only item of any value left in there was my old laptop, which was probably worth considerably less than any one of the succession of paintings lining the walls, mainly of austere men with outrageous facial hair.

On the broad landing at the top of the stairs, a narrow door set in the opposite wall attracted my attention. I've always had an inquisitive streak so, since I was alone and couldn't hear sounds of anybody coming, I went over and opened it. I peered inside to find a spiral stone staircase, presumably leading up to the little tower I'd spotted as I came up the drive. There was nobody around so my natural curiosity tempted me to slip up the stairs and check it out. The stairs were steep and narrow but the room at the top was fascinating: perfectly square and flooded with light. It took me a few moments to realise what its original purpose must have been, even if it was now clearly a panoramic lounge. The host of holes in the walls, their diameter just a little bigger than a wine bottle, provided the clue. Now they had been masked off on the outside or replaced by windows but once upon a time they would have been open to the elements. I was in a dovecote.

I stood and stared out of first one window, then the next, enjoying the three-hundred-and-sixty-degree views they presented. The city in the distance to the east was almost certainly Florence and all around were olive groves and vineyards, the vines laid out with mathematical precision. In the garden down below, I saw a couple emerge from the villa and head for the pool. The man was tall and even from up here I could see that the woman with her long blonde hair and longer legs looked good. It was very hot up here and the idea of a swim was suddenly very appealing. The two figures were walking hand in hand and looked as though they were happy in each other's company – like Helen and I used to be back in the good old days. Then the woman suddenly stopped and turned back, leaving the man alone – just like Helen and me.

Rousing myself from my introspection, I decided I'd better clear off. After all, as I'd just been reminding myself, this was somebody's private house, so I abandoned the panorama and set off down the stairs. I almost went back to my room to change into my swimming shorts but decided to delay exposing my pale English knees until I could be sure there wasn't a group of ladies waiting to giggle at them.

I met nobody on my way down and found the hallway also empty. Outside it was still hot but, by choosing a route that led in and out of patches of shade cast by the trees, bushes and the building itself, I managed to avoid the worst of it. I walked around the side of the villa and down a gentle slope onto a flat lawned area where the grass had been mown to perfection. The lush green colour pointed to the fact that there had to be a very efficient irrigation system here. Hoops set in the lawn indicated that this was used for croquet – not a game I've ever played – and a sudden image came into my head of how it must have been back in the belle époque when the English aristocracy discovered Tuscany. I imagined ladies in long skirts protecting their lily-white complexions with parasols while men in stovepipe hats played croquet, smoked cigars, and indulged in refined conversation about the empire. Although some sort of hat would have been welcome today in this still scorching late afternoon sunshine, none of these other pastimes are my thing so I didn't feel I was missing out.

A gravel path led along the side of the lawn, through a rusty metal archway festooned with fragrant roses, to an area with seven or eight ancient olive trees to one side and a kitchen garden on the other. There were huge-leaved artichoke plants around the feet of lemon trees laden with fruit. Salad beds, tomato plants, and raspberry canes jostled for position among peach and apricot trees, also covered in ripe fruit. The air was filled with the constant buzzing of bees and I could see four hives a bit further along, just before the hedge surrounding the pool. My senses were assaulted by a delightful cocktail of scents and I had to admit that this place took a lot of beating. Maybe it wasn't going to be so bad here after all.

I pushed open a quaint wicker gate and wandered through what was almost a tunnel of aromatic rosemary bushes until I emerged by the poolside and received a shock. Out in the middle of the water, floating face-down, was a body.

Instinctively I ran to the edge and was on the point of diving in to rescue the man in the hope that he could still be revived when the body started moving and swam lazily towards the side. I relaxed and gave myself a mental telling-off. This was yet another example of what Helen described as my obsession with death. According to her, any other normal human being would have accepted the scene for what it was: a man floating about in the cool water on a hot sunny day. I, to use Helen's words, stubbornly continued to see life through a depressing, pessimistic veil of suffering and death, even though I had now given up the day job. Was that true? Maybe. I defy anybody to spend thirty years in the murder squad and not emerge unaffected. Although my wife would have been horrified at the thought, there was no getting away from the fact that I still missed it – bodies and all.

When the man spotted me, he climbed out of the pool and came padding around towards me, his hand held out in greeting.

'Hi, I'm Gavin. Are you another lamb for the slaughter?'

'If you mean the writing course, the answer's yes.'

I sized him up as he answered. This is something I've always done and it was yet another of those things Helen had on her list of my habits that annoyed her. He was young, probably late twenties, and he was tall and slim. He had a lush head of dark hair on him that parted naturally down the middle. I envied him that. Mine has always been unruly and now as it inexorably turns grey at the temples, I look more and more like a scarecrow. On his wrist was a steel Rolex Submariner watch and I was pretty sure this wasn't a cheap knock-off. It, along with its owner, looked like the real thing. Even without his plummy accent, he was almost certainly another member of the privileged classes. Of course, I reminded myself, my colleagues on the force had had to stump up several thousand pounds for this two-week residential course for me so it was inevitably going to be limited to those with considerable means. Still, the guy looked friendly enough, so I borrowed one of Agatha's questions and used it on him.

'My name's Dan. Glad to meet you. What's your genre? I'm writing a historical novel.'

'I'm not totally sure, to be honest. I've been trying my hand at writing Gothic horror: you know, loads of blood and gore and so on. Apparently there's a market for it but it's pretty hard going trying to write about gruesome torture, mutilation, and people being chopped up and fed to the pigs, that sort of thing.'

A shudder ran through me. I'd covered a case once when the unfortunate victim had been chopped up and fed to an East End drug baron's dogs, and the memory still sickens me to this day. Interestingly, the dogs evidently didn't find the unfortunate victim to their taste and there were enough bits of him left over to make identification possible – not easy, but possible. 'So you don't enjoy that sort of thing?'

Gavin grinned and shook his head. 'God, no. I thought I'd try it, but it's no good. I need a different direction.' His expression became more serious. 'To be honest, that's the reason I let Emily drag me along to this course. Hopefully it'll help me find my niche.'

'Well, I wish you...'

I was unable to finish the sentence as a black flash appeared in the corner of my eye, but it was too late. The beast came charging down the path amid the rosemary bushes, ricocheted off Gavin's legs and caught me around the knees. With hindsight, I was probably standing a bit too close to the water's edge and I didn't stand a chance. As the dog skidded past me and flung itself enthusiastically into the pool, I wobbled, windmilled my arms wildly and almost regained my balance before toppling sideways into the water. I was vaguely aware of a spectacular splash ahead of me as the dog hit the surface and disappeared underwater. A split second later, I followed it. When I emerged, coughing and spluttering, it was to find myself face to face with a very happy Labrador with a broad canine smile on its hairy features. From above me came sounds of somebody having hysterics and I looked up to see Gavin in paroxysms of laughter.

Doing my best to affect a grown-up air, I started treading water and tried the blasé approach.

'The water's very refreshing.'

Gavin collected himself and leant down to offer a helping hand as I hauled myself out of the water. At least he'd had the decency to stop laughing by now. The question going through my head was whether my new phone really was waterproof as advertised. I stood there, water pouring off me onto the hot flagstones, while Gavin explained what had happened and it turned out that it was my own fault.

'You left the gate open, didn't you?' Seeing me nod, he explained. 'Antonio told me to make sure I kept the dog away from the pool. He's a Labrador and they're notoriously obsessed with water, but this pool's reserved for humans.' He grinned. 'But preferably not with their clothes on.'

'Indeed. And who's Antonio?'

'You haven't met him yet?' Gavin's grin broadened. 'You're in for a treat. I'm not totally sure what his official position is, but he looks like Count

Dracula minus the cape. You know, slicked-back jet-black hair, cadaverous face and the sort of hook nose that could be useful for opening tin cans. He was here to greet us when Emily and I arrived a few hours ago. He scared the pants off her, by the way. He's Italian but he speaks pretty good English, which is just as well, seeing as my Italian doesn't go much beyond *vino* and *gelato*. I imagine he's the butler or general factotum.'

I filed away his use of such an archaic term as further proof that this young man came from a privileged background. 'I look forward to meeting this character.' I could feel cold water running down my back, into my boxers and out again down my trouser legs and it wasn't a comfortable sensation. I shuffled my feet and shrugged off my shoes, which, predictably, were full of water. 'And Emily? Is she your wife?'

Gavin shook his head. 'Girlfriend, as of a few months now.'

'And she didn't fancy joining you in the pool?'

'She was going to, but she had to go back and get her phone from the room. For me it was a toss-up whether to go for a swim or a snooze. We've been in the car all day and in this heat it's not easy to keep your eyes open – particularly me. I've always been able to fall asleep at a moment's notice. In fact, I think I might go and have a lie-down now.'

'Have you driven all the way from England?' Presumably Gavin was the fortunate owner of the swish BMW in the car park.

'Yes, but we've taken a few days over it. We stopped off in Paris and a little place in Burgundy on the way and spent last night in Geneva. What about you?'

'I flew over from London today and rented a car.' I looked down at the Labrador, who was doggy-paddling happily about in the pool, snuffling to himself. 'I suppose I'd better try to get the dog out of the water, seeing as it's my fault he's in there. Any idea what his name is?'

'Oscar, I think. Hang on, I'll try it.' Gavin raised his voice. 'Oscar, come here, boy. Come on, Oscar.'

I was impressed to see the dog turn his head towards us and start swimming in our direction. Seeing the logistical problem of hauling a big, wet animal out of deep water, I glanced around and saw steps at the far end of the pool. Calling his name and making encouraging noises, I made my way in that direction, my soggy socks making sinister farting noises as I squelched along the poolside. The Labrador obligingly swam next to me until he reached the shallow end and was able to climb out of the water up the steps. Then, less obligingly, he proceeded to shake himself, sending a malodorous shower of water all over the place, much of it landing on me, but by this time it didn't really matter. Brushing my hair out of my eyes, I looked down accusingly.

'You horrible animal!' I didn't really mean it and the dog could tell. I've always loved dogs but Helen's a cat person so we never had one. I crouched down beside him and ruffled his ears. 'Feeling a bit warm, were you? I don't blame you for going for a swim but you're going to have to be more careful.'

The dog looked totally unrepentant and gave my fingers a friendly lick. I was just straightening up again when that same very pretty blonde woman I had spotted from the dovecote appeared along the path through the rosemary bushes. She was wearing short shorts and a tight top and there was no doubt about it: she and Gavin made a good-looking couple. She stretched up on tiptoe and kissed him affectionately before both of them set off, presumably back to their room. Just before disappearing, Gavin gave a lazy wave of the hand and I waved a still dripping hand back at him.

After waiting a few moments a safe distance from Oscar, who had decided to shake himself again, I pulled out my phone and was heartened to see that it was indeed still working. After fighting my way out of my wet shirt and wringing the worst of the water out of it, I wondered whether I should do the same with my trousers but decided against it just in case any of the other guests should pitch up and find me in my wet underwear. Definitely not the sort of first impression I wanted to present.

After struggling back into my shirt and squeezing into my shoes again, I caught hold of the dog's collar and headed for the gate, keeping a tight grip in case he should choose to dive back into the pool. Once we were both safely out of the pool area, I closed the gate behind us and pushed the bolt across. What's that old saying about shutting the stable door...?

I stopped and took stock. Although soaking wet,

I was far from cold and could feel the hot sun already starting to evaporate the water, so there was no need to head straight back to my room; not least as wet footprints and puddles all the way across the marble floors and up the stairs to my door could have been embarrassing. Instead, I decided to take a little walk and allow the dog and myself to start to drip-dry naturally.

A path disappeared into woodland on the far side of the kitchen garden, so I set off in that direction. The dog trotted affably along with me, apparently happy to go for a walk, and I enjoyed having company. In among the trees, it was noticeably cooler and there was a strong smell of resin. The path meandered through the wood until it reached a high wire fence where I saw a padlocked pedestrian gate. Clearly this was where the estate ended. Beside it was a wooden bench and sitting on the bench was Charlotte, the fifty-year-old-who-looked-like-forty, who was instantly recognisable by her red hair. She took one look at me and her eyes opened wide.

'Oh, good Lord, have you been swimming with your clothes on?'

'Look out!'

My warning came too late. The sociable dog had already spotted her and charged across to say hello. His greeting included an attempt to climb onto her lap and within seconds, her skirt was soaked. I squelched over and pointed to the bench beside her.

'Mind if I join you?'

'Be my guest.'

I sat down and glanced across at her. She had managed to calm the dog down by this time and he was rolling about in the dry grass at her feet. Her wet skirt was plastered tightly against her thighs and she was clenching her hands together on her lap. Being an observant sort of person, I noticed there was a wedding ring on her left hand and I wondered for a moment why her husband hadn't chosen to accompany her to Tuscany before reminding myself that the man probably had had the same reservations about weirdos that I had. She looked up from the Labrador and it was a relief to see her smiling.

I hastened to apologise as Oscar sat up, tongue out and panting. 'I'm sorry about that. He's a very exuberant sort of dog. He's just pushed me into the swimming pool, hence the wet clothes. Unfortunately, I didn't see you sitting here until it was too late.'

'Don't worry about it. I'll dry out. He's a lovely dog. Is he yours?' She was stroking the dog's head now as he rested it affectionately on her lap.

'No, he belongs to the house, I believe. By the way, I'm Dan.'

'I remember. I'm Charlotte.'

Her eyes met mine for a moment and that same frisson of attraction ran through me and I found myself momentarily without words. I finally took refuge in the standard question. 'What sort of thing do you write?'

She shook her head ruefully. 'I'm just a novice, I'm afraid. I've been thinking about writing for years and it's only now that I've finally decided to see if a writing course could give me the kickstart I need.'

'And you're going to write erotica?'

'It seems as good as any. Look at the money that woman who wrote all the *Fifty Shades* books must have made.'

'How did you hit on this course?'

For a second or two she looked unsure before her face cleared. 'Somebody recommended it, but I honestly can't remember who. What about you? Have you written lots? It's unusual to find a man writing erotica.'

'Is it really? I don't write erotica; I'm here by mistake.' I went on to tell her how my former colleagues had given me the course as a retirement present but hadn't read the small print – or so they said. She giggled in response.

'I bet it wasn't a mistake. I bet they did it for a laugh; you know, like chaining people to lampposts in their underwear on stag dos and so on. You men are always playing practical jokes.'

'You might well be right, but I have to admit that this is quite some place. Mr Jonah Moore must be doing all right for himself.'

Her smile faded for a moment, to be replaced by a look of envy or more. 'How the other half live!' Then she made a visible effort and her face cleared. 'Well, good for him. Wish I had a place like this...'

We chatted for five minutes or so before I began to feel increasingly uncomfortable as my wet underwear had decided to shrink into what felt like a tourniquet around my nether regions, so I stood up – gingerly – and took my leave. Seeing me rise to my feet, the Labrador did the same and then immediately shook himself, sending yet more drops of moisture flying about.

'I'd better get back to my room and change before the drinks thing. See you later. Come on, Oscar, you need somebody to dry you.'

Just as we were approaching the villa, my phone bleeped to announce the arrival of a text. I glanced down and as I saw that it was from Helen, my heart gave a little involuntary leap. But I immediately discovered that any optimism was misplaced.

Hope you have a good time. I'm going away for a few days myself so if you need me, call me on the mobile.

No little *x*, no signature. Nothing.

2

SUNDAY EVENING

Now wearing clean, dry clothes, I arrived downstairs again just after six thirty and got my first sight of Antonio (aka Dracula). Gavin hadn't been joking. The general factotum was dressed in a formal black waistcoat and an immaculate white shirt and he could have come straight out of *The Addams Family*. When he spotted me, he inclined his stringy body in a formal bow and as he did so the light actually reflected off his oiled hair. His complexion was remarkably pale and if I hadn't learnt from Gavin that the man had been up and moving about earlier on, I might well have subscribed to the theory that Antonio normally spent the daylight hours lying in an open coffin in a crypt far below. Suppressing a smile, I walked over to him and held out my hand.

'*Buona sera.*'

Antonio looked at my hand uncertainly before shaking it.

'Good evening, sir. Do you speak Italian?'

'Sort of. I'm a bit rusty.' I was rather proud of this word that I had dredged up from my memory banks.

He nodded and continued in Italian. 'Drinks are down there in the lounge.' He extended a very long arm in the direction of the right-hand corridor. 'First door on the left.' His tone was as sepulchral as his appearance, but I was pleasantly surprised to see what could well have been interpreted as a smile materialise on his gaunt face. His Italian enunciation was clear and I was delighted to understand him quite easily. I smiled back and continued in his language.

'I'm Dan. You must be Antonio.'

'I am indeed, sir. You speak good Italian.'

'Gavin told me you speak much better English, but it's good for me to practise my Italian if you don't mind. As you will hear, I still make a lot of mistakes.'

'I'll be delighted to speak Italian with you as often as you like, sir.'

'Thanks, that's very kind, and it's Dan.'

'Yes, sir.'

At that moment, the sound of heels on the marble stairs attracted the attention of both of us. We looked around to see that it was Charlotte, no longer wearing her sodden skirt, and she had definitely scrubbed up nicely. She had chosen a stylish, light-blue dress that revealed quite a lot of skin and she had done something to her hair – as already established, I'm no expert on women's hair – making her look decidedly glamorous. I surreptitiously glanced down at my jeans, polo shirt, and trainers. Maybe I should have gone for something smarter in spite of Millicent's 'dress code casual' announcement, but I had only brought two pairs of shoes and my good leather ones were currently upside down on my window ledge, hopefully drying out in the evening sunshine. What state they would be in once they dried remained to be seen.

Antonio gave her a respectful bow and addressed her in English. 'Good evening, *signora*. Drinks are being served just down there: the first room on the left.' He really did speak it well – better than my Italian.

If she was awed by Antonio's appearance, she didn't show it. 'Thank you.' She gave him a hint of a smile and turned towards me, an apprehensive expression on her face. Clearly I wasn't the only one suffering from nerves. 'Hello again, Dan.' She gave me a wink, 'I'm pleased to see you brought a change of clothing. Are you on your way to the drinks thing as well?'

'I am indeed.' Together we went along to the lounge where we found long, tall Agatha, the 'straight sex' writer, and white-haired Elaine, whose chosen literary genre was a good deal raunchier than that. They were already clutching glasses of Prosecco and were talking to Maria and what had to be her husband, the famous author. This was the same suntanned man I had last seen driving the Lambo. He was about my age and the same height – just over six foot, give or take an inch – and he had probably been a good-looking man a few years ago. Now his jowls had sagged a bit and his paunch expanded to the extent that he looked seven or eight months pregnant, but he still had the air of a man who was confident – probably overconfident – in his own skin. When he saw us, he beckoned us over.

'*Buona sera* to you both. How lovely to meet you. Do come and join us.'

He sounded genuinely pleased to see us, but you didn't need to be a former detective chief inspector to see that his attention was firmly directed at Charlotte – or more particularly at her cleavage. She, for her part, surprised me by blushing like a schoolgirl. Clearly, underneath the femme fatale façade she was a sensitive creature. A swift glance at our hostess revealed that Maria, too, had noticed the orientation of her husband's eyes and just for a second I read real anger in her. This disappeared in a flash, to be replaced by a look of resignation, and somehow I had a feeling this wasn't the first time her husband had demonstrated interest in another woman.

Oblivious to his wife's disapproval, our host was still addressing himself to Charlotte.

'Jonah Moore.' He introduced himself with a

little too much gravitas and held out his hand towards her. 'And you are...?'

Charlotte was still blushing and still looking apprehensive. 'I'm Charlotte. I saw you at your book signing in Bristol last year.'

He affected a smile with just a touch of modesty, which he didn't quite pull off. 'It's always good to meet my fans.' Finally acknowledging that I was also standing there, he turned and held out his hand.

'Good evening. We met outside, didn't we?'

'Dan Armstrong, and yes, you almost asphyxiated me with the dust cloud thrown up by your car.' Realising that Tricia would not have approved of my tone, I was quick to change the subject. 'You have a delightful house. Have you always lived here?'

'I've lived in Tuscany for most of my life. Ever since my first major bestseller.'

His choice of words implied that he had had many bestsellers but I knew differently. Although one of Jonah Moore's early books had indeed sold well, none of his subsequent works had reached the same dizzy heights – or at least that was what Wikipedia said – and that probably explained why he was running this summer school for aspiring writers to help pay for the upkeep of this place. As far as I know, J. K. Rowling and Dan Brown aren't in the habit of taking in paying guests.

After shaking hands with the great man, I turned my attention towards Maria. 'I'm afraid I must apologise. I was inadvertently responsible for letting your dog into the pool earlier. I didn't realise I had to close the gate behind me. I promise I won't make that mistake again.'

She gave me a friendly smile. She had changed into a smart summer frock and she looked good – all except the worry lines around her eyes. 'That's quite all right. Antonio dried him off.' She shook her head sadly. 'I'm afraid I can't go near Oscar as I'm allergic to dog hair. Such a shame as he's so sweet.'

So why on earth had they got a dog, then?

'Dan and Oscar are the best of pals.' Charlotte had by now managed to drag her attention away from Jonah, although he still looked as though he was about to dive into her décolleté. 'They went swimming together.'

In response to Maria's raised eyebrows, I explained what had happened, ending with the words, 'But it was my fault, not his. He's a lovely dog.'

Just then a new face appeared at the door and Jonah managed to stop drooling over Charlotte, looking up and producing a beaming smile. 'Serena, darling, you made it. How wonderful of you to come.' He opened his arms wide and went across to kiss the newcomer warmly on the cheeks before catching her by the hand and bringing her back to the group. As he did so, I distinctly saw his free hand slide across her bottom and she recoiled. I spotted an expression on her face indicating that her reaction to Jonah's touch was far from warm, but she hid her distaste well. For his part, Jonah didn't appear to register her hesitation although I had no doubt his wife had witnessed the scene. 'Everybody, this is Serena, although you probably know her better by her nom de plume: Sabrina Butterfly.'

Serena (aka Sabrina Butterfly) was probably in her mid-thirties, so roughly twenty years younger than Jonah and me, and attractive in an understated way. She had short hair and was wearing no make-up but didn't need any. She was swathed in a caftan-style dress in an extravagant bright blue and green pattern and she had pendulous earrings, a series of ethnic-looking bracelets on her wrists, and a necklace made up of tiny conch shells. To my surprise, Maria didn't appear in the least bit fazed by the intimate greeting her husband had given her and she herself kissed Serena affectionately, without any hint of the disapproval his reaction to Charlotte had produced. The explanation for this unexpected tolerance was provided by her husband: unlike some other women, it appeared that Serena didn't pose a threat to their marriage.

'Serena writes the spiciest lesbian romance, don't you dear? Are you all on your own this time or have you brought the lovely... what was her name again?'

Serena's face darkened. 'Lihini, her name was Lihini. I'm on my own this year, Jonah. I don't see her any more.' She sounded civil but definitely not affectionate towards him.

'I'm sorry to hear that. She was such a beautiful little girl.' Jonah waved to attract the attention of everybody. 'Serena's an expert on self-publishing as well as erotica and she comes every year to help out on the course alongside my sister and myself.'

Agatha (aka Marge Simpson) presumably knew Serena from previous years and hastened to introduce her friend Elaine, who was standing timidly at her elbow, wearing a sack-like frock that, while no doubt refreshingly light and airy on a hot evening like this, probably wouldn't have made it into any designer's summer collection. 'Serena, hello. It's good to see you again. You really must meet Elaine. She also writes erotica. Tell her, Elaine.' She almost shoved Elaine towards Serena and I had to suppress a smile.

Elaine flushed shyly. 'Hello, Serena. I've read all your books and I'm delighted to meet you. You have a lot of talent.'

While everyone chatted and drinks were distributed, we were joined by Gavin and his girlfriend. The appearance of the young blonde immediately put another smile on Jonah's face and, as he headed over to greet her and Gavin, I could see that same look of resentment on his wife's face. Even Charlotte looked disapproving but what was fascinating was the scowl that appeared on the young blonde's face as the famous author ran his eyes over her. She was an attractive woman and she probably got a lot of that. Being subjected to lustful looks isn't something to which I'm accustomed, but I imagine when you're a twenty-something and a paunchy fifty-something surveys you like a piece of meat on the slab, it must be a distasteful feeling.

Over the next hour or so the course participants arrived and everybody was introduced. Diana, the ancient history professor, was looking a bit more relaxed and I very quickly found the way to get her talking. A couple of glasses of remarkably good Prosecco probably helped.

'Feel like telling me about your historical novel? Is it all imagination or is it based on fact?'

This was clearly the key to getting her to open up and she was soon in full swing, explaining the intrigue and in-fighting taking place in Rome in the years after the death of Christ and how she had structured her novel around it. Her knowledge of the Roman period was encyclopaedic and I felt sure she must be an excellent teacher. I began to feel less comfortable when she then went on to describe in considerable detail the sort of thing the licentious patricians got up to at their orgies and it was a relief when she finally turned the question back on me. I told her about my murder mystery, loosely based on the all-powerful Medici family who ruled Tuscany from the early fifteenth century for almost three hundred years. I also made a point of reminding everybody that there was no erotica in it – just saying.

I was still talking when we were joined by two late arrivals, who listened intently. Once I'd finished giving Diana a list of some of the places over here that I intended to visit for research, we turned our attention to the newcomers. They were a serious-looking man and a woman, probably in their early forties, and as the man started talking it was immediately clear that they came from the other side of the Atlantic.

'I'm Will Gordon. This is my sister, Rachel. We come from Vancouver, Canada.'

As if by magic, Agatha materialised alongside the siblings and subjected them to a battery of questions. They answered readily and explained that they were both budding authors, although neither of them appeared to have written a word so far. Will explained their situation.

'We've been trying to decide what to write. Rach likes the idea of erotica so maybe that's the way to go, but we're here to learn from all you experts before we make a start.'

I tried to dismiss the thought of what would happen if I were to suggest writing an erotic book to my own sister and shook my head. 'We're not all experts. I'm here to learn as well.'

Any further conversation was interrupted by the tinkling of a bell and Jonah's mousy sister, Millicent, appeared, still dressed like Maggie Smith in *Downton Abbey*. As before, her announcement was delivered with all the genteel grace of a regimental sergeant major.

'Dinner is ready *now* in the dining room! Follow me.' There was a pause before she added as an afterthought, 'Please.'

On the way through to the dining room, I took advantage of the fact that Agatha was an old hand and probably knew the household dynamic by now. Keeping my voice down, I quizzed her about Millicent, and the answer was informative.

'She's five years older than Jonah but she's spent all her life in his shadow. She idolises him and, to be honest, she and Serena do all the work on the course – with a bit of help from Maria.'

'So the great man doesn't participate in his own course?'

She shook her head and tut-tutted disapprovingly. 'Too much like hard work for our Jonah. He has other ways of spending his time.' She raised her hand to her mouth as if holding a wineglass and tipped her head back. 'A bit too much glug, glug, if you know what I mean.'

'He's on the booze?' I didn't like the sound of this – not for the effect it might have on him so much as the effect on his wife. I rather liked Maria and I'd seen with my own eyes the damage alcohol can do to people's lives. One thing was for sure: Jonah wasn't accumulating too many brownie points in my eyes.

'Oh yes.' Agatha sounded sure of her facts. 'Drinks like a fish.'

'And Millicent, his sister, is she retired or what?' I was half expecting to hear that she had lived a life of idleness and luxury as a member of this wealthy family but the answer wasn't what I was expecting.

'She told me she's spent thirty-five years teaching English somewhere in the Midlands. This is her summer holiday.'

'She's still working? I thought she might be retired by now.'

Agatha tapped the side of her nose sagely. 'She's younger than she looks.' Her expression became more serious and she lowered her voice to little more than a whisper. 'Mind you, having Jonah as a brother has probably aged her prematurely.'

'Because of his drink habit or has he been in more trouble?'

'Definitely the drinking but I've heard he was on the verge of bankruptcy when he met Maria.'

'Really? But this house...'

'Belongs to Maria. She's from an old Italian family and she inherited it from her parents. If it hadn't been for her, you can be sure Jonah wouldn't be driving around in a swanky sports car.'

'Well, well, well. And how long have they been married?'

'Ten years or so, I believe.'

This reminded me of my brief conversation with Jonah. When asked if he had spent all his life here, his answer had been opaque, saying that he had lived in Tuscany ever since his bestseller. So he must have met and married Maria while already living somewhere unspecified in Tuscany, presumably somewhere far less grand than here at Villa Volpone. The appearance of Maria in his life must have been providential if he had been broke, as Agatha said. From what I'd seen this evening of Jonah's evident interest in other women, he might do well to curb his carnal instincts if he hoped to maintain his hold on the goose that laid the golden eggs. And if Agatha was right, cutting down on his alcohol intake would no doubt help as well.

At that moment, we reached the dining room and had to separate, taking our seats according to cards bearing our names, written in immaculate script – no doubt prepared by Millicent – and I found myself positioned near the head of the table between Maria Moore and Rachel the Canadian.

There were two empty chairs at the opposite end of the dinner table and Maria explained that they belonged to the last course participant and her

partner, who had been delayed and would be ar-
riving very late. They were coming from America
and apparently there had been a problem with
their flight. By the sound of it, apart from the delayed American, there were only going to be two
other men on the course and I'd already met them
both. Will from Canada and Gavin the BMW driver
both seemed remarkably normal. I settled down to
my dinner with renewed optimism. It might be all
right after all.

The meal was excellent. It started with a selection of traditional Tuscan antipasti including br-
uschetta: slices of white bread topped with luscious
chopped tomatoes smothered in thick green olive
oil. Along with this was hand-carved cured ham
and orange-fleshed melon from the garden. I suddenly realised how hungry I was after only a cup of
tea and a Kit Kat on the flight over, and I tucked in
with gusto. This was followed by panzanella: a
salad made of a mixture of tomatoes, cucumber,
onions and what Maria told me was stale bread, all
soaked in olive oil and wine vinegar. Straight from
the fridge, this was pleasantly refreshing. The main
course was roast lamb accompanied by little cubes

of potato roasted with rosemary. Finally, Antonio presented us with a fruit salad made up of peaches, apricots, strawberries, and other fruits from the villa's own gardens, accompanied by succulent little meringues and sumptuous vanilla ice cream that tasted homemade. It was a terrific meal and I had to admit that even if the course proved to be a washout, the next two weeks promised to be a very satisfying gastronomic experience.

Note to self: if I'm going to eat like this every day I need to get out and start running again.

To drink there was local red and white wine. I tried them both – it was only polite, after all, or so I told myself – and found both good but decided to stick to the red. As the meal progressed, I could see that Jonah was consuming a considerable amount of wine and becoming ever more loquacious. From him we all learnt that the sparkling wine we had been drinking earlier wasn't Prosecco but a locally produced fizz made by a 'little man' just over the hill. In fact, it soon appeared that almost everything on the table had either been produced in their own garden or had been sourced within a very small radius of the villa. Tricia would definitely have approved – she's deeply into the whole sustainable food thing – although, as a vegan, she wouldn't have enjoyed the meats.

I chatted to Maria and to Rachel. Maria was a very charming and a most attentive hostess and she filled me in on the origins of the estate. Hearing that I was writing a book set in Renaissance times, she very kindly promised me a guided tour of the villa to show me some of the remaining medieval and post-medieval relics to be found here. Rachel the Canadian was a much quieter person but a glass of red helped to loosen her up and she was soon telling us about life in Vancouver where she and Will both lived and worked. Her day job was as a civil servant, working in some government office while her ambition was to make a name for herself as a writer. From the way she talked, she sounded as though she was looking forward to learning how to write erotica and I wished her luck.

At the end of the meal, Jonah rose to his feet – with the assistance of the edge of the table – and waved his half-empty glass of red benevolently in the direction of his guests. His hand wasn't any too steady and I hoped he wouldn't spill any on Maria or Agatha on either side of him.

'My friends, I want to thank you for coming and to wish you every success. I hope this course will help you all in your endeavours and that soon I'll be reading bestsellers written by you.' He stifled a burp. 'There's nothing like penning a bestseller, I can tell you. The rewards are considerable if you get it right. Winning prestigious awards like the Silver Dagger...' He waved his glass towards the mantelpiece and Agatha and Maria leant back in trepidation as the wineglass hovered ominously above them. Taking pride of place above the open fireplace was a ceremonial dagger on a wooden mount. 'Winning a global award can change your life. It changed mine.' The wine glass now waved vaguely around the room, as if to indicate that the villa had been his reward but, since talking to Agatha, I now knew better.

Returning the glass to his lips – mercifully without mishap – Jonah drained the last of his wine and set off on an unsteady tour of the table, bidding goodnight to his guests. This tour included overly affectionate touches to any bare skin visible on the younger women and when he returned to his wife, I saw her shrink back from him. As she did so, I intercepted a look on the butler's face that was far from what I would have expected to see on the face of an impassive servant. It looked as though I could add Antonio to the list of people here tonight for whom Jonah Moore wasn't flavour of the month. Apparently unaware of any disapproval around him, Jonah turned to his sister, who had been hovering nervously at his shoulder. 'And now, Millicent, I think I shall retire.'

He lurched off, leaving me reflecting that it was strange he should announce his intentions to his sister rather than his wife. The way she had almost cowered away from him made me wonder whether Jonah's excessive consumption of alcohol might be leading to physical abuse. I certainly hoped not. I'd seen enough battered brides in my day to have developed a deep and lasting loathing for any man who could do that. As family groups went, this one wasn't exactly as serene as it could have been – the word 'dysfunctional' came to mind. Any further reflection was interrupted by Millicent in full stentorian Duce mode. Raising herself to her full four foot eleven inches, she addressed us as if we were a bunch of naughty schoolchildren.

'Breakfast is from eight to nine. The course will take place in the seminar room just a bit further down the corridor. Course sessions begin at nine thirty – sharp! Goodnight.' She didn't add 'Dismissed' but she might as well have done.

We all rose to our feet and I joined a couple of others over at the fireplace to look at the 'prestigious award'. The handle was probably silver while the blade, almost a foot long, was made of gleaming steel and it was clearly an object that received regular polishing – quite probably by Jonah himself. A metal plaque on the wooden base indicated that it had been awarded to Jonah Moore by the International Confederation of Crime Writers fifteen years ago. I had never heard of the organisation and resolved to check them out, but Agatha saved me the trouble.

'Before you start getting ideas, this isn't what you think it is. This isn't one of the Crime Writers' Association daggers – they really *are* prestigious awards. This organisation's small beer in comparison.'

Somehow this didn't come as a surprise to me. The more I got to hear about Jonah, the more I began to think that the man's illustrious career was probably every bit as much of an invention as the plots of his books.

When the party broke up, I glanced at my watch and saw that it was just after ten – and that translated as only nine o'clock UK time – so I decided to go for a stroll in the garden before bed. I bade everybody goodnight and headed for the front door. As I got there, I hesitated, wondering whether I might find it locked on my return. I decided that it might be a good idea to check with Antonio first. It would be embarrassing to find myself locked out.

'Can I help you, sir?'

'Jesus!' I whirled around to find the cadaverous face of Antonio less than a foot from mine. 'Frightened the life out of me. I didn't hear a thing.'

'I'm sorry if I startled you, sir.'

I pulled myself together. 'It's fine, thanks, Antonio, and my name's Dan.'

'Yes, sir.'

I decided not to flog a dead horse. 'I was wondering if it would be all right if I go out for a stroll. You won't lock me out, will you?'

'Of course not, sir. We're still waiting for the last two course participants to arrive but if you ever need help, you can always call me.' He recited his phone number and I keyed it into my phone, trying not to smile. I couldn't help reflecting how bizarre it was to see Dracula with a mobile phone. A quick call to the crypt, saying, 'I'm sorry to disturb you, Count Dracula, but there's an angry mob brandishing pitchforks outside,' could have drastically changed many of the horror movies I'd seen.

Outside, night had fallen and the temperature had dropped by several degrees. A slight breeze had come up and it made the air feel fresher. I breathed deeply, enjoying being in the open I had only just walked down to the car park when I heard the crunch of gravel and a large black shape materialised beside me, tail wagging. I bent down and scratched the Labrador's ears, which were now bone dry again.

'Hello, Oscar. You out for a walk as well?'

I received a nudge from a cold, wet nose in return and the two of us set off through the trees and down the drive towards the olive grove. Although the moon hadn't yet risen, the sky was crystal clear and the glow from millions of stars reflected on the white gravel of the track sufficiently well for me to be able to make my way along it without difficulty. Down below us, the lights of the little town of Montevolpone twinkled and an orange glow in the far distance indicated the presence of the big city that I now knew to be Florence. It was a delightful night and I had a pleasant walk, enjoying the company of the dog, who seemed happy to trot ahead of me most of the time but came back now and then to nuzzle my hand. It was good to have affectionate company at my side for a change.

As we walked along, I digested not only the meal but also the first impressions I had picked up of my companions at the villa. Our illustrious leader appeared to be a less than perfect husband and a bit too full of himself – and red wine – for my taste. Not that there was anything new there: I'd come across Jonah's sort many times before, starting with O'Flaherty, my former superintendent at the Met. He, like our writing mentor, had an exaggerated sense of his own importance and deep disdain for those around him. And then there was Jonah's drinking. If Agatha was right about him being on the road to alcoholism, or maybe already close to the end of it, that didn't bode well for him or his marriage.

Otherwise, the rest of the bunch seemed nice enough and even the spooky butler had managed to muster a smile, although he clearly didn't approve of his master's behaviour towards his wife. Jonah's sister, Millicent, certainly wasn't exactly a bundle of laughs. Maria Moore was very nice, considering how hard it probably was to live with Jonah, and the others pleasant. Above all, I was feeling mightily relieved to find that my fellow students were turning out to be unexpectedly normal.

Agatha appeared to have already established herself as the leader of the pack and I was more than happy to let her get on with it. Red-haired Charlotte, in particular, had even managed to appeal to me on a physical level, which was going to take a bit of getting used to. Thoughts of her reminded me, yet again, of Helen and I found myself wondering where my wife was going for the next few days – and with whom. Since splitting up, I hadn't been near another woman, but I had no idea about her. Had she found herself another man? Tricia might well know, but I could hardly ask my daughter about her mother's love life, could I?

My reflections were interrupted by the sound of an engine and the sight of headlights coming up the gravel drive towards us. I hastily called Oscar, who came trotting back and the two of us stepped off the track onto a narrow path leading into the olive trees to let the car pass. It swept up the drive past us without slowing and probably without noticing us, and inevitably the dog and I were immediately swallowed up by the cloud of dust left in its wake. Keen to get away from the dust, Oscar and I jogged off along the path and I soon found myself back in the cypress trees around the villa once more. We were approaching the parking area when I heard a car door slam and instinctively caught hold of Oscar's collar in case the car was setting off again. Then I heard an American woman's voice.

'Mikey, I can't find my sunglasses.' She sounded a bit whiney.

'Just leave them, Jen. We can come look for them tomorrow.' He sounded tired and irritable.

'And for Christ's sake try to remember that over here I'm not Mikey, I'm Martin. Martin, got it?'

'Okay, Mi... Martin, I got it.'

'You better.'

Their feet crunched in the gravel as they headed up the path to the villa, but I waited with the dog until they reached the front door and disappeared inside before releasing my hold on Oscar's collar. Mikey? Martin? It sounded as though the latecomers were bringing some secrets with them. I released my hold on the dog's collar and glanced down at him.

'Looks like the next couple of weeks might turn out to be more interesting than I thought.'

In return I got a lick of the hand.

3

MONDAY

I slept like a log. It was a warm night and I slept under just a single sheet with the window open. I woke up on Monday morning relieved to have been untroubled by mosquitoes or other pesky insects. When I glanced at my watch, I saw that it was still early so I decided to go for a run before breakfast. I've always tried to keep myself in shape and since leaving the force I'd been hitting the gym quite regularly – as much for the companionship as anything else, if I'm honest.

Just as I emerged from the room, I heard the sound of a door closing a bit further along the corridor and glanced over to see Will, the Canadian.

From his clothing, it looked as though he'd had the same idea. He gave me a little wave of the hand.

'Hi, Dan. You thinking of a run as well? Want company?'

Will looked as though he was at least fifteen, maybe twenty, years younger than me so I decided to get my excuses in quick. 'Love to, but I'm more of a jogger these days so if you want to go charging off, don't let me stop you.'

'Jogging's good. I just need some fresh air after being cooped up in an aircraft for seven hours.'

'What about your sister? Isn't she coming?'

'I doubt it, but I don't know. If she's anything like me she's probably jetlagged to hell and needs all the sleep she can get.'

Downstairs, the hallway was empty but the front door was unlocked so we let ourselves out and set off. There was no sign of the Labrador this morning and I felt quite disappointed. Will said he was happy to go anywhere, so I led him back down the drive, but this time as we emerged from the trees, I turned left onto another track I had spotted last night and soon we were jogging along between two fine old drystone walls with olive trees on one side of us and a well-kept vineyard on the other. The track climbed steadily but not too steeply and I was pleased, and secretly relieved, to find I could keep up with Will and converse freely without panting.

Will queried what I did for a living and I just told him I was retired. Over the years I'd found that revealing I was a police officer could often lead to awkward conversations. Will was equally vague and just said he was a civil servant working for the Canadian government, and that was fine by me. By mutual agreement we were soon chatting about the weather, the villa, and what we expected to get out of the course. It rapidly emerged that Will didn't share his sister's interest in writing erotica and admitted that he had just come along to keep her company. I was quite relieved to hear it. The idea of siblings writing smut together had been bothering me.

It took us twenty minutes to get to the top of the hill, from where we were looking directly down over the villa and its gardens to the village of Montevolpone and the hills beyond. We paused here for a breather and admired the view. In the relative cool of the morning, the air was much clearer and Florence in the distance was a delight. The massive cupola of the duomo and Giotto's Campanile along-side it were unmistakable. Beyond it were the dark tree-covered slopes of the Apennines, while away to the left, stretching westwards towards the distant sea, were the muddy waters of the River Arno. As views went, this one took some beating.

I glanced across at Will, who was hardly per-spiring although I was streaming with sweat. The guy was fit, that was clear. Mind you, I reminded myself, he was also a youngster and I was getting old. The realisation that younger men could do some stuff better and faster than me was one of the reasons I had taken early retirement; that, and a de-sire to get away from Superintendent O'Flaherty. Although, to be totally honest, the main reason had been in the hope that this change in my life might make Helen rethink her decision to split up. I had gambled that maybe when she realised she would no longer be married to a policeman she might change her mind about us. But so far it hadn't worked and the way things were looking, the next step was likely to be divorce and I was dreading the finality of that. The first twenty years of our marriage had been so good, but slowly and inexorably she had changed, or maybe I had – all because of my job. Now it looked as though I had not only lost a job I loved but I was also losing the woman I had loved for thirty years. Shaking Helen's image from my head, I glanced across at the Canadian.

'Have you been to Tuscany before?'

Will shook his head. 'Nope, all new to me. That has to be Florence, right?'

'I haven't been here before either but, yes, that has to be Florence. Maria told me last night.' I rattled off the names of a few of the landmarks laid out before us, which I'd memorised in my research for my book. 'One of these days I intend to go down there and check the city out for myself.'

'Agatha told me there's an afternoon excursion to Florence later this week as a part of the course. Apparently Maria's an expert on Tuscan history and she gives a guided tour. I'll definitely hitch a ride on that one.'

That sounded good to me although I'd already decided to wander around on my own most of the time. In fact, as I had told Tricia, I thought I might even take a trip into the city by myself as early as tomorrow or the next day. That way I would be able to poke about in all the places on my research list, from big names like the Ponte Vecchio to far less well-known churches, museums, and other buildings that I needed for the book. So far I'd been writing with the aid of guide books and Google Earth, but of course there's no substitute for seeing it in the flesh.

By the time we got back to the villa it was well past eight, so I lost no time in heading for the shower. I stood under the stream of barely tepid water – my choice, not the fault of the plumbing – and let my mind consider a couple of things that were puzzling me. Firstly, although Will claimed to be Canadian, he didn't have a Canadian accent. I'd spent three months on secondment to the RCMP ten years ago and got used to the unusual way Canadians pronounce the letter *o*, decidedly differently from people living in the USA. And second, Will had talked about having just got off a seven-hour flight, although Vancouver to London is normally a twelve-hour flight.

As I pondered all this, I could almost hear

Helen's voice, bitterly critical: *You just can't take people at face value, can you? You're always questioning, questioning, questioning. And you do it to me too.*

She was probably right.

Will and I were the last to get down for breakfast and he just grabbed a cup of coffee before disappearing back upstairs again, leaving me on one side of the table with Maria Moore diagonally opposite. She was looking weary but, feeling my eyes on her, I saw her rally.

'Did you sleep well, Dan?'

'Like a log, thanks.'

I managed to restrain the impulse to ask her why she looked as if she hadn't slept a wink and concentrated on the excellent fresh fruit salad. Antonio appeared through the door from the kitchen carrying a plate of pancakes and demonstrated that he didn't miss much.

'Good morning, sir. Did you enjoy your run?'

'Will and I had an excellent run, thanks. Were you out yourself?' Although from his pasty complexion he would probably have spontaneously combusted in bright sunlight.

'No, sir, but I tend to keep one eye on the windows. Not much happens here that I don't see.'

At that moment we were interrupted by the arrival of Jonah, with bloodshot eyes and a face like thunder. He came storming in and I couldn't miss the way his wife instinctively flinched again, but it soon emerged that Jonah was annoyed at somebody else, or rather, something else.

'Do you know what that bloody dog's done now?' Without waiting for any of us to hazard a guess, he ploughed on. 'He's only gone and eaten the last of the bacon.'

Antonio looked aghast. 'But how did it happen, sir?'

'Cook put the plate with the freshly grilled bacon on the table and the damn dog stood up on his hind legs and scoffed the lot while her back was turned.' He gave an angry snort. 'I don't know what ever possessed me to get a dog in the first place.'

'He's a nice dog, Jonah.' I could hear how conciliatory Maria was trying to be. 'It's just that the smell of bacon must have been so tempting.'

'I should take him out and shoot him.'

This sounded excessive and I decided to weigh

in to try and pour some calming oil on troubled waters. 'That's maybe a bit extreme. He's still young, isn't he? He'll learn.'

Jonah raised his eyes toward me and I read the sort of openly hostile stare I've seen so many times in my life from criminals I've brought to justice. 'You think we haven't tried? Why don't you have a go if you're so bloody clever.'

'Jonah!'

Maria reached out and caught hold of his sleeve, trying to warn him to mind his manners. Feeling her touch, Jonah immediately transferred his hostility to her, jerked his arm violently away and in so doing managed to catch the plate of pancakes in Antonio's hands, sending them flying. One actually managed to wrap itself around Jonah's left ear and his already fiery complexion turned puce.

'For the love of God...!' And he swept off in high dudgeon, slamming the door behind him.

Maria turned towards me with an apologetic smile. 'You must excuse Jonah, Dan. He's been under a lot of pressure recently. I'm sure he'll calm down soon and come and apologise to you. We only got Oscar a few months ago and he's still learning.'

'Don't worry about me. I just feel sorry for the dog. Jonah wouldn't really do anything as drastic as shooting him, would he?'

'I'm sure he wouldn't.' In spite of her words, Maria didn't look convinced.

'Has he even got a gun? It might be wise to see that it's in a safe place if he has.'

'Of course. Now you enjoy your breakfast. I need to talk to Serena about this morning's course.'

I noticed that she hadn't answered my question about the gun. After she had left the room, I glanced at Antonio, who was still crouching down, picking up the scattered pancakes and pieces of broken china. 'He wouldn't shoot Oscar, would he, Antonio?'

'I sincerely hope not.'

'Has he got a gun?'

There was a moment's hesitation. 'I believe he has a pistol, sir, but I'm sure he wouldn't use it.'

'A pistol? Please tell me it's safely locked away.' I wondered if Jonah had a firearms certificate for a pistol. In the UK these are notoriously hard to obtain. The thought of an alcoholic with a gun was very uncomfortable and, for a moment, I seriously considered taking the matter further, but then I reminded myself – as I'm sure my wife would have done – that I was no longer a police officer.

Antonio was still looking deadpan. 'I really couldn't say, sir, but I expect so.'

'Well, just try to keep Oscar away from his master, will you? He's a good dog.'

'Even though he knocked you into the pool?' Antonio stood up and I spotted a ghost of a smile on his pale face.

'You really don't miss a thing, do you? Yes, I still think he's a good dog in spite of our little encounter yesterday. I certainly wouldn't want anything to happen to him.' I caught the butler's eye. 'And I wouldn't like anything to happen to Maria.'

The smile disappeared from his face in an instant.

* * *

The first session didn't start until a quarter to ten. Fortunately, Serena was in charge and Millicent (aka the headmistress) wasn't there to witness the late arrivals. She would probably have had them marched out and shot. Serena was wearing another exotic robe today and the bangles on her wrists jingled as she moved her arms. Gavin scraped in apologetically at nine thirty-five but Jennifer, the newly arrived American, only appeared ten minutes later. There was no sign of her companion, Martin or Mikey or whatever his name was, but it turned out that he, like Gavin's Emily, wasn't taking part in the course and had just come along to provide company. So, finally, we were all here and not a dirty raincoat in sight.

Serena welcomed us all and started by getting each of us in turn to introduce ourselves and to talk about our writing careers so far. In most cases, this was non-existent, although Agatha claimed to have published three books and Elaine was somewhat vague about her erotic offerings, although Agatha had been talking last night of her having published quite a few. Otherwise, they were all either in the middle of writing erotica like Diana the history professor, or writing some other genre like Gavin and me – or yet to start like Charlotte, Rachel the Canadian and her brother, and Jennifer. I was surprised to find that, in spite of my misgivings, I began to enjoy myself and the time passed remarkably quickly. I was genuinely surprised when the coffee break arrived, and we all wandered out through the French windows onto the terrace.

I was standing alongside Jennifer – 'Call me Jen' – when her companion joined the group. He was a big man, maybe in his early fifties, which would make him about twice her age. When I say big, I don't mean obese. From the breadth of his shoulders and his gorilla-sized hands, this was a strong, tough guy. He introduced himself as Martin and shook hands cordially with everybody before coming over to give Jen an affectionate hug and a kiss. For her part, she looked equally pleased to see him so my doubts about the disparity in their ages began to recede. Obviously it worked for them. Helen's only three years younger than me, although that didn't stop us from breaking up.

Over my coffee, I checked him out and got a feeling of familiarity; not that I knew the man, but somehow I felt sure I recognised the type. He was clearly on his best behaviour today but over my years in the force, I'd developed pretty sensitive antennae when it came to identifying what my colleagues and I commonly referred to as 'villains'. Something told me that Martin/Mikey probably wasn't as squeaky clean as he would like to appear.

Still, as long as the man kept his nose clean here, what business of mine was it anyway? As I had to keep reminding myself, I was no longer DCI Armstrong of the Met. Like it or not, I was retired and the task of maintaining law and order was someone else's problem. Not mine. That chapter of my life had finished and, however much I might secretly regret no longer being involved with the thrill of the chase and pitting my wits against the criminal fraternity, I knew I had to be realistic. What was done was done, and I was now an ex-detective and I should remember that.

The coffee break came to an end at eleven o'clock sharp, and we were summoned back inside. I was the last to follow and Maria caught hold of my arm and held me back for a few seconds. 'When we were talking yesterday, I promised to give you a tour of the villa. There are a few historic curiosities here that you might find useful for your writing.'

'That would be wonderful, thanks. Whenever it suits you.'

'Well, what about this afternoon? Shall we say three o'clock?'

* * *

Maria was waiting for me in the hall at three as arranged and she led me through to the kitchen, where I received a boisterous greeting from Oscar, who came rushing out from his wicker basket by the old fireplace although Maria with her allergy kept her distance. As we were alone in the kitchen, I decided to query why they had got the dog. Maria shook her head ruefully.

'I'm afraid Jonah can be a bit impulsive. A friend's Labrador had pups and he thought it would be a good idea to get a guard dog.'

'I didn't know Labradors were good guard dogs.'

Maria smiled. 'They aren't... or at least this one isn't. He's far too friendly towards most people to be any use as a guard dog, although he does have his likes and dislikes. Our postman's a lovely person but Oscar barks the place down every time he sees him. The same with the farmer next door and delivery drivers, but you can bet he'd lick a burglar to death and nothing more.'

'Why would you need a guard dog anyway? The walls of this place are about half a metre thick.'

The smile faded from her face and she glanced around almost furtively before replying. 'Jonah's been under a lot of strain lately and if I'm honest, he's maybe been getting a bit paranoid.' Her voice was little more than a whisper now. 'Anyway, I love him dearly, but I can't get near to him.'

I decided to lighten the mood. 'Is that Oscar or Jonah you're talking about?'

'The dog, of course, because of my allergy.' She hesitated. 'Jonah too, sometimes.'

She immediately changed the subject, but this indiscretion only served to reinforce the impression I'd already begun to form about their relationship. Clearly, all was not well in the Moore household.

Meanwhile, Maria led me across the big high-ceilinged room to the fireplace and pointed to the date carved into the lintel. '1564 – know what's significant about this date?'

I racked my brains for a moment or two before admitting defeat. 'Some battle, maybe?'

'It was the year Michelangelo died. Some say that marked the end of the Renaissance, although others have it lasting a bit longer.'

'So this villa dates back to the Renaissance?'

'Yes, but it was built on the foundations of an older medieval building. There's not much of that left now except the cellars. Come and see what you think, through there.' Maria pointed to a low, arched doorway in one corner of the room and took a long key from a nail set in the wall alongside it. She turned the key in the lock and pushed the door, which opened with an eerie creak. She wagged her finger at the dog. 'No, Oscar, you stay up here. No dogs down in the cellar. Dan, just mind your head. You're quite a lot taller than most people were way back then.'

Since medieval days somebody had thoughtfully put in electric lights and I followed Maria down a flight of narrow stone steps into a cellar with a low, vaulted ceiling. All around the walls of the first room were shelves filled with wine bottles while on the floor were half a dozen huge, bulbous, straw-covered glass containers holding even more wine. Clearly, if not only Jonah but all the inhabitants of the villa were to decide to drink themselves to death, there would be more than enough here to ensure the success of the endeavour.

'There are three more rooms along there.' Maria pointed towards another low archway. 'I'm not a big spider fan so I'll let you go and take a look for yourself.'

I'm not wildly keen on spiders either but my curiosity got the better of me. Fortunately, the electric lights continued into the next rooms and I was able to find my way around quite easily, give or take a spider's web or ten. I was wandering about when I heard Maria's voice from behind.

'See if you can spot the entrance to the secret passage.'

Intrigued, I cast a keen investigative eye over the walls but could see nothing but stonework and more spiders. One of them in particular was a sinister yellow and brown striped one the size of a plum, which eyed me malevolently through most of its eight eyes. I decided that if the secret passage was hidden behind this particular arachnid, it could stay hidden.

Finally returning to the first cellar, I asked for

more information. 'I couldn't see any sign of a secret passage. Where is it and where does it lead?'

Maria laughed. 'We haven't a clue. Legend has it
that there's at least one secret passage, but we've
never been able to find it – although to be totally
honest, we haven't tried too hard. It's clear that
these cellars pre-date the villa by several hundred
years so maybe there is some truth to it, but who
knows? Maybe these were dungeons once upon a
time.'

We climbed back up the steps and went out
with the dog through the back door into a brick-
paved courtyard with what looked like old stables
to one side. Against the far wall of the courtyard
was a spectacular piece of medieval art. It was
clearly a fountain, but it was far from simply func-
tional. The sculpted semi-circular marble trough
was fed through a copper pipe protruding from the
open mouth of a wonderfully realistic fox's face
while behind it was a carving of intricate, inter-
twined twigs and branches. It was spectacular. The
tinkling of running water echoed around the yard
and I looked on as Oscar trotted over, stood up on
his hind legs – no doubt the same way he had

stolen the bacon – and drank deeply. I returned my attention to Maria.

'The fox's head is presumably because the town's called Montevolpone, the mount of the fox, the big fox.'

'That's right, and it's never run dry. We've had the water analysed and it's excellent quality drinking water. They knew what they were doing when they built the villa here. There's no date on the fountain, but experts have provisionally dated it to the thirteenth century because it's very similar to the baptismal font in the church in the main piazza of Montevolpone. You might like to take a trip down there and see for yourself. There's also one that looks similar in a little church in Florence. Remind me when we're on the excursion the day after tomorrow and I'll point it out to you.'

'Thanks, that sounds great. I think I might walk down to Montevolpone right now. The exercise will do me good.' I glanced at the dog, who was sitting at our feet, idly scratching one ear with his hind paw. 'Does Oscar want to come with me?'

'I'm sure he'd love to. Hang on and I'll get you his lead.'

Oscar and I set off shortly after and were down at the town in less than half an hour. Once we emerged from the gravel drive onto the road, I clipped the lead onto his collar and there then ensued a brief struggle for supremacy until Oscar finally got the idea that he wasn't supposed to try to pull my arm out of its socket and choke himself in the process. It took a couple of hundred yards but we eventually came to a satisfactory compromise: as long as I let him stop and mark his territory from time to time, Oscar agreed to walk obediently at my side. Although all bets were off when he spotted one of the local cats and I almost ended up flat on my face.

It was only when we reached the central piazza that I realised my mistake: of course, I couldn't take the dog into the church and Oscar took a dim view of being tied up. I tried a couple of times but before I could get inside the church door the Labrador started howling pitifully and I had to give up on the idea of viewing the font for now. Instead, Oscar and I walked through the narrow streets of the *centro storico*. These had been constructed in a circular pattern around the church, almost like a snail's shell. Presumably this had been for defence back in turbulent medieval times when conflict was commonplace here in this part of Italy.

Finally, we emerged from the snail's shell into a busy street lined with charming old-fashioned shops like greengrocers', butchers' and ironmongers', without a single supermarket, charity shop, or fast-food outlet to be seen. It really was like stepping back in time and I took an instant liking to the place. Tricia would definitely have approved. A bit further along I was delighted to find a little piazza with a café with tables outside on the cobbles, where the dog and I sat down willingly in the shade of a faded parasol advertising Fanta.

A few seconds later, a waiter emerged to take my order and paused to chat. As far as I could see, I was the only customer so the man was probably bored. For my part, I was delighted to have the opportunity to practise my Italian. The conversation soon came round to the villa and the writing course. The barista, who was in fact the proprietor, didn't know about the writing course and I was definitely not going to tell him it was for erotic novelists, but it soon emerged that he knew all about the villa and its inhabitants.

'It's been in the Campese family for generations. Maria was an only child and she inherited the family fortune when her father died. He was a good man and she's a chip off the old block.'

'Do you know her husband?'

'Her second husband, the Englishman? Yes, I know him.' I couldn't miss the disdain in his voice.

'You don't like him?'

'I'm not one to talk out of turn but one thing's for sure: she could have done better.'

'Why's that?'

As if regretting his comment, the barista shook his head. 'Nothing, just gossip. Now let me go and get you your beer.' He glanced down. 'I daresay your dog could do with a drink as well.'

When he emerged from the bar, he was carrying a bowl of water for the dog and two bottles of beer. He set one down in front of me and then leant against the sun-warmed wall and took a mouthful of his while the dog slurped the water at our feet. It was certainly warm enough today. My curiosity prompted me to ask another question.

'You mentioned that the Englishman is Maria's second husband. Who was her first? I didn't know she'd been married twice.'

'He was Enrico Bianchi, the racing driver. He was killed in a horrific crash at Monza.'

I vaguely remembered hearing about that some years back. 'Was he a good man?'

The barista shook his head sadly. 'He was a good driver, but that's where it stopped. He treated her very poorly but she never complained.'

'It sounds as though she's fallen out of the frying pan into the fire with husband number two.' I was worried for Maria. She struck me as far too nice to be shackled to a narcissistic alcoholic and I sincerely hoped Jonah in private was a different man from the one I had seen. Otherwise, the future didn't look bright for Maria.

The barman shrugged and raised his eyes to heaven.

We continued to chat but neither of us brought up the subject of the inhabitants of the villa again. I learnt that his name was Tommaso and from him I discovered more about the history of the little township of Montevolpone and the surrounding area. He told me the best places to buy wine, oil, and cheese, as well as giving me a recommendation to try the trattoria on the far side of the church, Da Geppo, which apparently did the best grilled meat in Tuscany. Although all meals were provided at the villa, I decided to take Tommaso's advice and try the restaurant before I left. For a moment I wondered whether I might even invite Charlotte, the ravishing redhead, to dine with me but decided against it, although I wasn't totally sure why. Well, I suppose I did know really but I just didn't want to admit it to myself. Deep down I knew I was still clinging to the forlorn hope that Helen and I might get back together again.

By the time Oscar and I set off back to the villa again, I knew a whole lot more about the area and I'd picked up a number of useful bits of local colour to insert into the book. I'd also made a new friend and I promised Tommaso I'd be back to see him again before long.

When we got back at just before six, I delivered Oscar to the kitchen and returned to my room. I toyed with the idea of working on my book but as it was still very warm, I pulled on swimming shorts and a T-shirt and headed for the pool. Making sure I closed the wicker gate carefully behind me this time, I emerged through the rosemary bushes to a most unexpected scene.

There was nobody here apart from a couple over on the far side of the pool. They were stripped to their swimming things and were taking a shower together, and a very intimate one at that. The woman looked as though she was trying to choke the man with her tongue while his hands appeared to be kneading bread inside her bikini. I stopped dead and inched slowly back into the cover of the bushes. It wasn't what they were doing that struck me, as much as who they were. The amorous couple were none other than Will and Rachel, the Canadians.

And they were brother and sister.

I decided that retreat was the best option and moved quietly back until I could let myself out of the gate, closing it silently behind me. Unable to have a cooling swim, I headed along the path into the trees until I came to the bench where I had found Charlotte yesterday. Today it was empty. The branches overhead provided welcome shade; I sat down gratefully and fanned myself with my towel, turning over and over again in my head one of Dad's favourite expressions: *There's nowt so queer as folk.*

Maybe it was the long, dark winter nights in Canada, the cold, or some bizarre inbreeding but, as far as I was concerned, what I'd just seen was definitely not the sort of thing that siblings should be doing. Of course, it quickly occurred to me, the more likely explanation was that they weren't brother and sister after all. So, if they weren't brother and sister, what was their relationship and who were they? Were they even Rachel and Will Gordon? And if they weren't who they said they were, what were they doing here at an inoffensive – unless you counted the host – course for wannabe writers in the middle of the Tuscan countryside? No sooner did this thought cross my mind than I was reminded of the snippet of conversation with Mikey or Martin and his girlfriend I had overheard in the dark the previous night. It was looking very much as though *two* of the couples on this course were pretending to be somebody else.

And if so, why?

My internal debate was interrupted by my phone. I checked the caller ID and saw that it was Paul Wilson, formerly Sergeant Wilson, my most trusted lieutenant on the force and now Inspector Wilson. One of the last things I did – and I'm proud of it – before retiring was to push for Wilson to get the promotion he deserved. When addressing him now, I had to make a conscious effort to call him Paul. After years of 'Wilson', it was a stretch.

'Paul, hi, how's it going?'

'Fine thank you, sir.'

I couldn't help grinning. Clearly I wasn't the only one struggling to adapt to the new normal. 'We've been through this before: it's Dan and Paul now. So, what's the news from the sharp end?'

'The usual: gang members killing other gang members, wives cutting off bits of their husbands, and politicians behaving badly. Same old, same old. How about you? What's the writing course like?' I heard him stifle a chuckle. 'Learning any new tricks?'

'No, Paul, no new tricks. To be honest, it might turn out to be useful for my writing after all. And don't assume from that that I'm about to start writing dirty books.'

'That's good to hear. And your fellow students? Not too weird?'

Reflecting on the thoughts that had been going through my head only a few seconds ago, I answered cautiously. 'Not too weird, but definitely interesting... in fact I might say fascinating.'

'Does that mean they're all nymphomaniacs?'

I had a sudden image of Agatha and Elaine. 'I certainly hope not. No, they're all pretty ordinary people.'

'That's great. Listen, I called you because I've just come off the phone with my friend Virgilio. He says he'd love to meet you. Did you get a bottle of something at the duty-free like I asked?'

'A very expensive bottle of Arran single malt, no less. It's in my bag. When does he want to meet up?'

Before I left the UK, Wilson had given me the name of a good friend of his who worked in the murder squad in Florence. They had done a forensics course in the US together a couple of years ago and hit it off. When he heard where I was going, he gave me two twenty-pound notes and instructions to deliver a bottle of good booze to the Italian and say hello.

'Any time. Let me give you his number. He asked you to call him.' He dictated the number and after he rang off, I wasted no time before making the call. It was answered on the second ring.

'Pisano.'

I felt an immediate sense of kinship. On the job I, too, only ever answered the phone with my surname. It might only save a second or two each time but over the years I've probably saved days of my life. I explained who I was in my best Italian and the response was most welcoming.

'*Ciao*, Daniel. Paul told me you were coming over to Tuscany. It's good to hear from you and I'm relieved you speak such good Italian. My English is *crap*.' He used the English word for extra emphasis. 'Now, when can we meet?'

4

TUESDAY AFTERNOON

My little Fiat wasn't a happy car. On the way down from the hills towards Florence on Tuesday afternoon, it started coughing and spluttering and a cloud of blue smoke came pouring out of the exhaust every time I pressed the accelerator. After checking the location of the Florence branch of the car rental company on my phone, I decided to drive straight there so they could sort it out before it packed up on me. The office turned out to be in a narrow one-way street near the station and it was a real struggle to find a parking space. Finally, after squeezing it in between a German-registered Mercedes and a Dutch-registered Citroën, I dropped the keys off and told them I'd come back in a couple of hours once their mechanic had had a chance to look at it. The clerk behind the counter was very helpful and promised me a speedy repair or a replacement and I left them to it. A quick look at a map on the counter showed me that the *questura*, the police headquarters where Pisano worked, was less than five minutes' walk away, on the other side of the station.

I set off through the busy streets and found myself turning over in my head the events of the writing course this morning. Surprisingly, there had been little mention of erotica and a lot of time devoted to the practical nuts and bolts of the writing trade and I had to admit that I had found it both interesting and useful. As far as my fellow course participants were concerned, I noticed in the course of the morning that neither of the Canadians appeared particularly interested and this further reinforced my conviction that they might not be all they appeared to be. Although I emerged at the end of the morning feeling I had learnt a lot that would help me with my writing career, my investigative curiosity had been piqued and I resolved to keep a close eye all on my companions over the next two weeks.

I walked across Piazza della Stazione, pausing in the middle to admire the sheer size of the church of Santa Maria Novella on the right-hand side of the square with its cloisters and impressive bell tower. Above the roofs straight ahead of me I could just make out the top of Brunelleschi's magnificent cupola crowning the duomo. It's sobering to think that these wonderful buildings were already here, looking exactly the same, more than twenty years before Christopher Columbus set sail in search of a new world, and they're still mightily impressive more than five centuries on. For somebody with an interest in history such as me, Florence was really going to be a treasure trove. But first I had a bottle to deliver before I could start exploring.

When I got to the police headquarters, I checked in at the front desk and was escorted up to the third floor by a uniformed officer. Apart from the language, it could almost have been Scotland Yard, with the same background mix of voices, telephones, echoing footsteps, and slamming doors. The main difference between my office in London and the office belonging to Commissario Virgilio Pisano was the view from the window: out over a cobbled square towards the massive stone walls of the squat Fortezza da Basso, built in the fifteen hundreds by yet another member of the all-powerful Medici family.

I was shown in and the inspector jumped to his feet with a welcoming smile on his face. He came out from behind a desk that was absolutely laden down with piles of paperwork and this, too, was very familiar to me.

'Ciao, Daniel, come stai?'

I noted that Pisano was using the familiar *tu* form and this solved a linguistic problem. The Italians have formal and informal ways of addressing other people and I've always found it unnerving deciding which pronoun to use, for fear of offending somebody by being over-familiar or equally, by being too formal. We shook hands and as I passed over the bottle of whisky, still in its duty-free bag, I summoned my best Italian.

'*Ciao*, Virgilio. I've brought you a gift from Paul. He says hi.' I tipped my head towards the desk covered in paperwork. 'It's good of you to spare me a moment. I can see you're busy. The piles of paper look all too familiar.'

Virgilio shook his head in frustration and continued the conversation in Italian. 'Why is it that in an age of computers we still have to put so much down on paper? But there's nothing here that can't wait. Shall we go and have a coffee? Thanks for the whisky. I don't drink a lot, but when I do, I do enjoy the good stuff and I can see that this is definitely the good stuff.'

We went back downstairs and out into the sunshine. On the steps of the police station Virgilio stopped, stretched his arms above his head, breathed deeply, and grinned. 'First time out of my office since seven thirty this morning. It feels good.'

I knew exactly what he was talking about. One of the many problems with being a police officer is that the further up the pecking order you rise, the more you find yourself tied to a desk. Although at the time that I was still working this had often proved to be a pain, I couldn't help a little pang of nostalgia for my previous life. Surreptitiously, I checked out my Italian opposite number. Virgilio was probably five or six years younger than me –

maybe just hit fifty – and he looked fit. His head was completely shaved, but the dark designer stubble on his cheeks showed an attempt to compensate. He was dressed in a short-sleeved, white shirt and, unless he had a weapon tucked into his underpants or a back-up piece strapped to his ankle FBI-style, he was unarmed. I've never liked guns, although I did firearms training a few years back, and it came as a relief to find an officer not bristling with deadly weapons.

There was a café only a few hundred yards away – in my experience there's almost always a café near every police station – and I followed him into the air-conditioned interior, where we stood at the bar. Virgilio ordered a double espresso and a glass of water while I opted for a cold beer seeing as I was on holiday. The bar staff clearly knew Virgilio well and they addressed him as 'Dottore', the usual appellation for an Italian with a university degree or in a position of responsibility. I had no doubt that Commissario Virgilio Pisano qualified on both counts. We leant against the bar and chatted; I told him about the writing course I was doing, leaving out its true nature at least until I knew the guy better, and revealed the fact that it was a farewell present from my colleagues on the force. Virgilio said he knew Montevolpone, but was unfamiliar with the villa and he immediately picked up on my reference to retirement.

'How're you finding it, being retired? I've been wondering whether to take early retirement myself in a few years but I've a feeling I'd be bored stiff.'

I took a mouthful of beer before answering. 'It's certainly different, I can tell you that. For a start, I can have a cold beer on a weekday afternoon, and when the phone rings nowadays I'm almost pleased, it happens so rarely. Back when I was working, it never seemed to stop.'

Bang on cue, Virgilio's phone started ringing. He glanced at the caller ID and shot me an apologetic look. 'Sorry, Daniel, but I need to take this.'

I carried on sipping my beer while Virgilio listened intently to the caller, occasionally grunting or querying something. After a minute or so he concluded the conversation with the words, '*Vengo subito*.'

'I'm coming straight away' meant that our chat together was ending so I hastened to finish my beer while Virgilio dropped the phone back on the table and reached for the last of his coffee.

'Sorry, Daniel, I'm going to have to get back to work, but the weekend should be easier. How would you feel about coming round to my place for lunch on Sunday? I'll do a barbecue.'

'That sounds great, thanks, I'd love to, but only if I'm not putting you out.'

'Not in the slightest.' Virgilio pulled a paper napkin out of the dispenser on the bar and scribbled on it. 'Here's my address. It's in Scandicci, which is on the outskirts of Florence on the way to Montevolpone. You should find it easily and there's parking right in front of the house.' He drained his glass of water and checked his watch. 'Now I have to go. It seems that somebody's stuck a dagger into some guy's heart. You'd think they could have had the decency to wait until we'd had a chance to chat some more...' He dropped a five euro note on the bar, waved away my attempts to pay, and headed for the door.

After shaking hands with the friendly detective, I set off on foot on an initial tour of Florence but I had only got to Piazza del Duomo and was standing amid the crowds in front of the cathedral, admiring what has to be one of the most iconic buildings in the world, when my phone started ringing. To my surprise I saw that it was Virgilio, but I was even more surprised as I listened to what he had to say.

'*Ciao*, Daniel. Listen, the place where you're doing your writing course, it isn't called Villa Volpone by any chance? Belongs to a Signora Maria Campese.'

'Yes, it is. Why? What's up?'

'You know that guy I told you about who just got stabbed in the heart? Well, it turns out it's her husband.'

'Christ...!' The air whistled out of my lungs. Jonah Moore dead? Murdered? I'd never liked the guy, but I certainly hadn't expected this sort of development in the peace of the Tuscan countryside. Whether it was a conditioned reaction to hearing the word 'murder' or just a throwback to my recent past, I immediately felt my brain begin to whirl. Who could have done this and why? My thoughts were interrupted by Virgilio's voice.

'I was wondering... I'm on my way up there now and it would be a great help to me if you could come with me or follow me up there. My English isn't great and my sergeant who speaks good English is on leave this week. Have you got time? Could you help?'

I didn't hesitate. 'Of course, I'd be glad to. My rental car's in the garage so I'd better get a lift up with you. I won't get my car back or get a replacement until this evening.'

'No problem. Where are you?'

Less than five minutes later there was the unmistakable trumpeting sound of a police siren and a blue and white Alfa with *Polizia* emblazoned on the side screeched to a halt alongside Giotto's Campanile, where I was waiting. All heads turned as I jumped into the back seat alongside Virgilio, the driver stamped on the accelerator, and the car shot off again with a squeal of tyres. I looked around and the strangest feeling of familiarity came over me. I might be retired, and I might be in a different car belonging to a foreign police force, but this was what I knew and where I belonged, even if Helen had never been able to come to terms with it. I'd never dream of telling her, but it felt good.

On the way to Montevolpone, Virgilio filled me

in on what he knew so far, which wasn't a lot. 'The butler found the victim at just before four. He was slumped back in his chair in the dining room with some sort of ceremonial dagger lodged in his chest and his dog sleeping happily at his feet. The window was locked and the butler claims he would have noticed if anybody had tried to sneak into the villa.'

Although we were speaking Italian, the feeling of familiarity only increased. Virgilio was using the universal language of murder investigations any-where in the world and I did my best to help him. 'The butler's an observant sort of chap; I don't think much escapes him. So just Jonah and the dog in the room...?' I glanced across at Virgilio and shook my head in disbelief. 'Jonah, the victim, was threat-ening to kill the dog yesterday; that's irony for you. As for the murder weapon, I've a feeling I know ex-actly which dagger it might be. He was showing it off the other night.' I went on to tell him about Jon-ah's after dinner-speech while the car continued to speed through the streets of Florence, heading west, out of the city. We were away from the old his-toric centre and passing through the suburb of

Scandicci when Virgilio suddenly pointed to the left.

'My house is just down there. You can't miss it.' He then returned to the matter in hand. 'So if nobody could get in without being spotted by the butler, then it sounds as though the perpetrator either has to be one of the residents of the villa or one of the people on your writing course.' He gave me a little smile. 'At least you're in the clear. As alibis go, yours is pretty cast-iron.'

'Hang on until you get the pathologist's report.' I produced an answering grin. 'Maybe I stabbed him before I drove down here.' As for possible suspects, my brain was already churning. I realised that in spite of all my years in the force, I now found myself in a brand-new situation: I was almost certainly living in the same house as a murderer. The weird thing was that instead of feeling apprehensive, I found myself feeling intellectually drawn to this new challenge. Helen would never have understood.

Virgilio nodded. 'You're right, but I don't think I need to handcuff you just yet.'

The journey that had taken me forty minutes

was accomplished in barely half that time and five o'clock was just striking on the Montevolpone church clock as we sped through the town. We arrived in the car park in front of the villa less than an hour after the murder had been reported and I was impressed. That was pretty good going. There were two police cars and a motorbike already there and a uniformed officer stationed at the end of the path leading to the front door. When he recognised Virgilio, he drew himself up and saluted.

'*Buona sera, Commissario.*'

He gave me a curious glance but as I was with the detective inspector, he let me pass. Together with the uniformed driver, we walked up to the villa and went inside. Before doing so, Virgilio turned to his driver and issued an order for him to search the grounds in case any of the guests might still be out there, either blissfully ignorant of what had happened or seeking to distance themselves from the scene of a crime they had committed.

Inside, the first person we saw was Antonio, lurking in the hall. His normally bloodless complexion was now a ghostly white and I wished I'd thought to warn Virgilio in advance that Antonio looked like a character from a horror movie. I was impressed to see the inspector take the appearance of this spectral figure in his stride as he waved his ID in the butler's face and looked around.

'I'm Commissario Pisano. Where is everybody?'

'They're all in the seminar room, sir. Cook has just made them tea and coffee. This gentleman knows where that is.' The curiosity in Antonio's eyes was obvious as they flicked momentarily across to me before dropping. No doubt he wouldn't be the only one to be curious. A number of people were going to get a surprise when they discovered that I was now involved in the investigation, however peripherally.

'And the scene of the crime? Has anybody been in there?' Virgilio was still looking around, trying to get the feel of the place.

'Myself and the *signora*, and that's all until the first of the police officers arrived. As soon as we saw what had happened, I called the police and they said we should keep the door closed and the room sealed off.'

Virgilio nodded approvingly. 'That's good. Now, can we have a look at the body please?'

When he heard the word 'body', Antonio blanched even further and I genuinely wondered if he was about to faint, but he proved to be made of sterner stuff and pulled himself together. 'This way, sir.'

Another uniformed officer was guarding the dining room door and he saluted smartly and moved aside to let us in. Before opening the door, Virgilio gave instructions to Antonio for him and the cook to join the others in the seminar room to await questioning.

The scene that greeted us inside the dining room was unexpectedly peaceful. Jonah was still sitting at the end of the table, in the same seat where he usually sat. His body was sprawled back in the chair and behind him only a few paces away was the mantelpiece. The wooden stand on which the dagger had been displayed was now empty and there was no mistaking the silver handle protruding from the dead man's chest. There was no more than a drop or two of blood on the floor around the body and remarkably little on the victim's shirt. This was most unusual and had not gone unnoticed by the inspector.

'Whoever did this was either very lucky or knew his anatomy. Straight to the heart. No fuss, no thrashing about. Instant death.'

'Precisely.' I'd been thinking the very same thing. I glanced around the room. The table was bare except for a folder of papers, an empty glass, and a half-empty bottle of wine. I pulled out my pen and used it to lift the cover of the folder. This appeared to be full of fan letters addressed to Jonah Moore c/o a London publisher, and I informed Virgilio accordingly. Interestingly, the top letter in the pile was dated twelve years ago. Without gloves, I couldn't sift further through them but I had a suspicion they might all prove to be of a similar vintage. Maybe Jonah had been allowing himself a moment of nostalgia when the killer came in.

Virgilio's voice interrupted my thoughts. 'The victim's still sitting down and there's no sign of a struggle. That probably indicates that he knew the perpetrator.'

'I agree. And Antonio, the butler, said that the dog was stretched out on the floor, sleeping peacefully. That also points to the murderer being known to the victim and his dog.' I remembered what

Maria had said yesterday. 'Not that this particular dog is much good as a guard dog, although he does bark at some strangers. At least that means we can probably exclude the postman from our list of suspects.'

We wandered around the room, looking for anything anomalous, but we only came up with one possible clue. Making sure I touched nothing, I leant over to sniff the half-empty bottle and smelt nothing but wine, albeit a fairly rough vintage. However, in the empty glass, which had just a trace of dry red deposit remaining at the bottom, I thought I recognised the smell of something familiar. I beckoned to Virgilio.

'Come and take a sniff of this. What do you think? Wine doesn't normally smell like this.' I was pretty sure I knew what it was, but I thought I'd better wait until the local man confirmed it.

Virgilio came over and bent down with his nose close to the glass. He breathed in once or twice before straightening up. 'I think you're right.' He glanced across at me. 'Cyanide. Is that what you think?'

I nodded in agreement. *Cianuro*, that was a new

word for me and I filed it away in my memory banks. Essential vocabulary for a detective, but I hadn't expected to have to use it over here in Tuscany. 'Cyanide, definitely. I thought I caught a whiff of the bitter almond smell.'

'Maybe somebody drugged him before killing him or one person drugged him and another stabbed him. The pathologist should be here shortly and he should be able to confirm our suspicions. If not, the guys at the lab should be able to identify it. Of course, if the victim was unconscious when the killer came in that would explain why there was no struggle, but if he was already drugged, it also opens the door to the perpetrator not being somebody he knew after all.'

'Except that the dog didn't bark...' Even so, annoyingly, it was looking as though this possible clue might have just increased, rather than reduced, the cast of possible culprits. Virgilio headed for the door.

'Now, if you're ready to help out with the translating, I think it's time to speak to the inhabitants of the villa.'

5

TUESDAY EVENING

When we emerged into the corridor, Virgilio issued orders to the officer on guard. 'Get somebody to do a careful search of the villa, doors and windows, in case there's any sign of breaking and entering or anything left unlocked. We'll be in the seminar room. Can you ask the pathologist to call in with his preliminary report once he's had a look at the body? In the meantime, nobody to enter the dining room and nobody to leave the premises. Got that?'

I definitely approved. If I'd been in Virgilio's shoes, I would have issued the exact same orders. This guy knew what he was doing. I led the way down to the end of the corridor and opened the door to the seminar room. All eyes turned towards us as we walked in and Virgilio glanced across at me. 'Maybe you might like to explain what's happening and why I've asked you to help.'

I nodded and addressed the room. 'Good afternoon, everybody.' My eyes strayed to the lonely figure of Maria, sitting by herself in one corner. 'Maria, my condolences for your loss.' I spotted Millicent all on her own on the other side of the room and cast her a sympathetic glance that received no acknowledgement – not that this surprised me. 'I'm sure all of us are still shocked by what's happened. I'd better explain what I'm doing here. This is a friend of mine, Inspector Virgilio Pisano of the Florence murder squad. I just happened to be with him this afternoon and I offered to help with any language problems, although some of you are better qualified to translate than I am.' I caught Antonio's eye and gave him a hint of a smile before turning towards Virgilio for orders. 'What's next?'

Virgilio addressed the group in heavily accented but perfectly understandable English, and I couldn't help wondering whether his request for help might not have just been limited to linguistic assistance.

'Ladies and gentlemen, I'm sure we all want to reach a resolution to this tragedy so I would ask you to be patient while we take statements from each of you. We'll try not to keep you too long, but we need to establish where everybody was this afternoon and if you saw anything of interest, and it's best to get all the details down while everything's fresh in your minds.'

He glanced at me, lowered his voice and switched back to Italian. 'Would you mind waiting here with the others while I begin with the victim's widow, with whom there'll be no language difficulties? Ask whatever questions you like while I'm away. I'll stick an officer on the door. I'd like everybody to stay here for now.'

'Of course. Maria Campese is over there in the corner.'

Virgilio followed the direction of my eyes and walked across to Maria, who was sitting motionless, a tissue clenched tightly in one hand, her eyes red.

'Signora Campese, my condolences. I wonder if you could come with me. Is there somewhere we could sit down together while I ask you some questions?'

She stood up unsteadily, clearly still very shaken. 'We can go into the living room. It's just along the corridor.' Her voice was under control but the emotion made her sound husky.

After the door had closed behind them, I debated whether to explain to everybody that I used to be a detective but decided to keep my cards close to my chest for just a little bit longer. I went across to the side table where a tray of coffees and teas was standing, helped myself to a mug of tea, and took it with me to the table where I sat down between white-haired Elaine and red-haired Charlotte. No sooner had I done so than Agatha, our self-appointed leader, began to pump me for information from the other side of the table.

'Is it true Jonah was stabbed? How did it happen? Who can have done it? Do the police have any suspects?'

For now, I thought it best to plead ignorance. 'I gather that's what happened. As for suspects, you'd better ask the inspector, but I imagine it's still early days.'

'But why would anybody want to kill Jonah?' Agatha's brain was clearly working overtime. 'Of course, he wasn't a terribly nice man.' She cast an apologetic glance across at Millicent, whose face remained deadpan. 'I know one shouldn't speak ill of the dead, but he wasn't, was he? But, I mean, if all the not very nice people in the world were to be murdered, we'd probably lose half the population.'

'Indeed.' I took a sip of tea and wished it was an ice-cold beer. 'Let's hope the police can discover who did it as soon as possible.' I felt a tap on my arm and turned towards the sound of Charlotte's voice.

'Dan, why are they making us wait here? They don't think one of us did it, do they?'

Her freckled face was pink from the sun and she looked rather appealing and I felt that same sense of surprise that I could be attracted to another woman after all these years. I gave her a reassuring smile and continued to feign ignorance.

'I have no idea. I imagine it's just routine to question all possible witnesses. Like the inspector said, he needs to work out who was where and whether maybe one of you saw somebody or something that didn't seem right.' Aware that the attention of all of them was now directed towards me, I decided to throw the question out to the floor and see what happened. 'I was in Florence when it took place but for those of you who were here, did any of you see anything suspicious going on?'

There was a long silence before Gavin was the first to speak, the frustration and annoyance in his voice palpable. 'What the hell are we supposed to have seen? Antonio, didn't you say it happened in the dining room? None of us were near there in the middle of the afternoon, were we?'

His girlfriend was quick to echo his sentiments. 'We were down at the pool all afternoon. We didn't see a thing.' From the healthy tan on her face and arms, it was evident she had indeed been out in the sun.

'I think Charlotte might be right. The real reason they're keeping us here and questioning us is because they think one of us did it.' This time it was Professor Diana, sounding as puzzled as the others. All faces turned towards her and she dropped her eyes but continued speaking. 'After all, this is a pretty remote location. It's not very likely somebody could have sneaked in, killed Jonah, and then sneaked out again without being seen, is it?'

'Murder needs a motive.' Will Gordon's transatlantic voice cut across the table. 'Why the hell would any of us want to kill him? Apart from Maria, Millicent, the butler and the cook, the rest of us have only just met the guy.'

'Well, to be honest, this isn't my first course here so I have met him before, but I certainly didn't stab him.' Agatha was looking indignant. 'I hope they don't think *I'm* the murderer. Come to think of it, Serena, you knew him as well, didn't you?'

All eyes turned to Serena, who looked anything but serene. Although I'd got the impression that relations between her and Jonah had been strained, she looked as though she'd been crying. Clearly the murder had hit her hard, but violent death does that to most people. She took a deep breath before speaking. 'Yes, I've known him for a few years, but I didn't stick a dagger in him. Why should I do something like that?'

'Of course not, dear.' Agatha extended a hand and gave her a reassuring pat on the wrist. 'And the same applies to Antonio and Annarosa, doesn't it?

They wouldn't dream of doing any such thing, I'm sure.'

The attention of the room shifted to the butler and the elderly cook, who was looking positively distraught. Antonio cleared his throat before responding in exemplary English. 'Certainly not. Annarosa and I have known Signor Jonah for ten years. Why should one of us suddenly decide to kill him now? Besides, Annarosa went home at two o'clock and I was with Signora Maria all afternoon. Anyway, it's unthinkable that the *signora* might have done it. She's the sweetest person who wouldn't hurt a fly.'

Listening to the butler's words, I couldn't help thinking that I'd heard variations on this comment time and time again throughout my career, but all too often it was the 'sweetest' people that turned out to be capable of doing the most appalling things. While the others continued to express their bewilderment and disbelief, I took a good look around the table. Most of them appeared shell-shocked. The only ones to look relatively unfazed were Martin/Mikey and the Canadian couple of sibling lovers. From experience, this told me these three had maybe had something to do with it or were already familiar with violent death. I looked forward to sitting in on the interviews with them. Otherwise, there was Millicent, the victim's sister, whose features hadn't changed a jot since I came in, but it was impossible to tell what was going on underneath. She could have been carved from stone.

Ten minutes later, a uniformed officer appeared at the door and asked for Antonio to come with him. Five minutes later it was the turn of the cook and then, barely three minutes after that, Virgilio himself appeared and beckoned to me.

'Daniel, if you'd like to bring the first of the English-speaking witnesses with you, we can start on the initial interviews.' He went on to explain what he wanted me to say and all heads looked up as I translated.

'The inspector asks me to tell you that all he's trying to do for now is to build up a picture of where you all were and if you saw anything unusual at the time of the murder. He promises he'll do his best not to keep you waiting too long. He's asked Antonio to bring you some more refreshments in the meantime.'

Virgilio nodded gratefully. 'Thank you, Daniel. Let's start with the victim's sister.'

I glanced over at Millicent, who was sitting close to the door. 'Millicent, the inspector would like to talk to you first.'

As if waking from a dream, Millicent stood up, smoothing her long skirt with her hands before heading purposefully for the door. I followed on behind as she and Virgilio walked through to the sitting room and a uniformed officer took over from us in the seminar room. I hadn't been into the sitting room before and it was most impressive, even larger than the dining room and with an ornate marble fireplace on the end wall. This one didn't have a ceremonial dagger on the mantelpiece but then, of course, neither did the one in the dining room *now*.

Virgilio took a seat and indicated an armchair opposite him where Millicent sat down primly, hands clasped on her lap. Yet another police officer was sitting by a rather nice old writing desk over to one side with pen and paper at the ready. I perched on a stool next to Virgilio and prepared to translate, but to everybody's surprise, before Virgilio could say a word, it transpired that Millicent had something of her own to say.

'She did it, you know. It must have been her. She killed him.' I had a feeling I knew who Millicent was talking about and, knowing her as I now did, such a direct outburst didn't surprise me, but I left it to Virgilio to query her comment.

'Who killed him?' Virgilio had understood her English and sounded less surprised than I felt. He replied to her in English, 'Who do you mean, Signora Moore?'

'It's *Doctor* Moore, if you don't mind.' Her headmistress tone was back. 'Maria, of course. I could see it in her eyes. I've been afraid of something like this for weeks.'

'You're saying you think your brother was killed by his wife?' Virgilio's tone was still measured. 'And why would she want to do that?'

Millicent subjected the inspector to a withering glare. 'Why? Because Jonah was a brute, that's why. He was my brother, but he could be very difficult.' She hesitated for a moment while I checked to see whether Virgilio needed a translation, but he shook his head. His English was pretty good after all. I wondered if this pause meant that Millicent might be going to display some emotion but all she did was blow her nose before continuing in a stronger voice. 'He's been drinking far too much and I'm afraid he's been mistreating my sister-in-law. Have you ever heard of the straw that broke the camel's back? I think she just had enough and knew she couldn't bear the abuse any longer.'

'Abuse, *Dottoressa*? Do you mean verbal abuse or physical abuse?'

'Both, I'm afraid.' She was looking less confrontational now. 'I've never liked Maria much, but she didn't deserve the treatment he gave her.' She looked up. 'If you don't believe me, ask her to roll up her sleeve and show you her arm, her right arm. He squeezed her so tight last night, she's black and blue.'

'I see. Well, thank you, *Dottoressa*. Now, please can you tell me: when was the last time you saw your brother alive?'

'At lunch today.'

'Can you be more precise, please? Exactly what time did you leave his company and how did you spend the rest of the afternoon until the body was discovered?'

'Lunch was served at one and Jonah was still in the dining room when I left, maybe around a quarter to two. After that I sat in on an elective session run by Serena on self-publishing along with Elaine – you know, the white-haired lady – and Jennifer from America. We were still working when we heard what had happened. That would have been almost exactly four o'clock.'

'And this seminar session took place where?'

'In the seminar room.'

'And did you go straight in there from the dining room?'

For the first time Millicent showed signs of discomfort. 'I had to make a visit to my room first – a call of nature – but I was only there for a matter of minutes.'

Virgilio straightened up. 'Thank you, Dottoressa. That's all for now. We'll call you if we need a fuller statement.'

She stood up but remained facing the inspector. 'Are you going to arrest her? Maria, I mean.'

'We need to get all our facts straight before we

start arresting anybody but thank you for the information.' His tone was placatory.

Once the door had closed behind Millicent, I leant over towards Virgilio. 'Ever since I got here it's been clear to see that there's been tension between the victim and his wife and I've been wondering whether it went as far as physical violence. It's probably worth checking the bruising story.'

'Already done. Maria Moore herself told me the exact same thing a few minutes ago and showed me the marks. You can clearly see the imprint of all five fingers on her upper arm. Bastard!'

I shook my head in disgust. This didn't come as a surprise but it didn't make it any more palatable. 'So, do you think she might have killed Jonah, like her sister-in-law thinks?'

Virgilio didn't look convinced. 'Self-defence is a powerful motivator, but why do it in such an obvious way? Surely a wife could manage to kill her husband far more subtly.'

'I agree. A pillow over his face while he's lying there dead drunk would do the trick and leave little trace.' I managed a weak grin. 'In the last months of my marriage I made a point of never coming home drunk, just in case.'

'You're divorced? That's tough. I'm sorry.'

'Separated at present, but I imagine it'll lead to divorce. I'll tell you the whole sad story some other time if you're interested. But for now that gives us a suspect, doesn't it?'

'It actually gives us three suspects.' In response to my raised eyebrows, Virgilio expanded. 'Yes, there's Maria, but she says her husband was virtually no longer on speaking terms with his sister. He got Millicent and Serena to do all the work on these courses and he just lolled about drinking. Apparently, Jonah and Millicent had a screaming match only a few hours before you all arrived here the other day. According to Maria, Millicent actually picked up a carving knife and threatened him. Count Dracula was there, and he confirms it.'

I couldn't help grinning. 'I'm glad it's not just me that sees the resemblance. Anyway, do you think Millicent accusing her sister-in-law of the murder might be to cover her own tracks? Or Maria pointing the finger at Millicent might be her returning the favour. Interesting.'

'But the good news as far as Millicent's concerned is that she appears to have a very convincing alibi and at the same time she's provided alibis for Serena and two of the course participants who were all together in the seminar room.'

'And they're not the only ones. According to Antonio, he was with Maria all afternoon, so that neatly provides an alibi for both of them as well, unless they were in it together. It's frustrating. So who's the third suspect: Antonio, the butler, even though he claims to have been with his mistress all afternoon?'

'Of course. He was the last person who claims to have seen the victim alive, so he had the opportunity to do it. The thing is, he must have known he would have had little or no chance of getting away with it.' He paused for a few seconds. 'But maybe he's just a moron.'

'Criminal masterminds are very few and far between, I agree. I suppose it could have been Antonio but I'm struggling to find a motive and I don't believe him to be stupid. In fact, I think of him as a bright sort of guy who knows pretty much everything that happens around here. From what I've seen, he would appear to have a soft spot for Maria but I can't see how that could have developed into murderous tendencies. Besides, if that's what he wanted to do, surely he must have had a multitude of far less obvious opportunities to kill his employer. Why in such an outrageous manner with a houseful of potential witnesses and why would she give him an alibi?'

Virgilio just shrugged helplessly and I knew how he felt.

Next, Virgilio questioned Serena, Elaine, and Jennifer, who confirmed that they had been in the seminar room all afternoon, although Serena admitted to having taken a quick trip to the loo partway through. After them we spoke to Charlotte, Gavin, and his girlfriend, Emily, who all confirmed that they had spent the afternoon at the pool and could vouch for each other's presence there. Professor Diana told us she had spent an hour snoozing in her room before meeting up with Agatha, and together they had then gone down to the pool where they found the others. This left us with Mikey/Martin and the two Canadians. Before getting them in, I revealed to Virgilio what I had overheard in the car park the first night where the big American had clearly been doing his best to conceal his identity. I also mentioned the scene of passion between the Canadians by the pool the previous day and saw Virgilio's eyes open wide in disbelief. He started with them, and we were both looking forward to hearing what Will, the first to be called in, might have to say for himself.

Will came in and sat down and Virgilio started. 'Your name is William Gordon and you are Canadian?'

'No and no.' We both looked up in surprise as he continued, 'Before I explain, Inspector, can I ask Dan a question?' He turned his head and looked over at me. 'Can I ask just who you are, Dan? How come you're sitting in on a murder investigation? This is more than just idle curiosity. It's important.'

I exchanged glances with Virgilio, who shrugged his shoulders, so I told Will the truth. 'It's a fair question. Until I retired six months ago, I was a chief inspector in the Metropolitan Police murder squad in London. Otherwise, it's like I said to the others: I'm just helping a friend.'

Will nodded a couple of times as if he'd been

expecting something of the sort. 'I had a feeling you were a cop. Don't ask me why. The thing is, what I have to tell you is highly confidential. Can I be sure it'll stay that way as far as both of you are concerned?' He glanced across at the uniformed officer by the desk. 'And that applies to that guy too.'

Virgilio answered for all of us. 'Unless what you're about to give us is a confession to murder, you can be sure this will remain between us.' He grinned. 'Besides, Officer Draghi over there can't speak a word of English. He's just here for effect.' Hearing his name, the officer looked up, but Virgilio just gave him a reassuring wave. '*Niente, Draghi, niente. Ritorna a dormire.* Go back to sleep.'

Will gave a little smile in return then reached into his pocket, pulled out his wallet, and brandished an ID card. 'Okay, so I'm not Canadian. My first name really is William, but it's William Cook. I'm a US federal agent with the DEA. My "sister"...' He did that thing people do with their fingers to indicate quotation marks. '...Rachel is Rachel O'Neill and she's my partner at the DEA. I apologise for the deception, but we're here on an undercover surveillance mission.'

Suddenly everything became clear. The US Drug Enforcement Administration are major players in the intelligence world and I realised what must be going on. 'And the person you're keeping tabs on is the man who calls himself Martin, or should I say Mikey?'

Now it was the DEA man's turn to look surprised. 'You know who he is?' He sounded impressed. 'But how? Are you guys on his tail as well?'

I shook my head and revealed how I had overheard the snippet of conversation the other night. 'All I know is that his real name is Mikey. I don't even know his last name.'

Will looked relieved. 'That's good. The fewer people know who he is, the better. His name is Michael Martin Cornish and he's a big noise in the drug world in New York. He's also either very clever or very lucky, probably both. We've been on his tail for almost a year now and we still can't even stick him with a parking ticket. He posts accounts for a respectable import business – would you believe cuddly toys? – and he pays his taxes. He appears to be Mr Squeaky Clean but we're sure he's behind drugs coming into the US worth many millions of dollars. Rachel and I are here keeping an eye on him just in case he lets his guard down.' He shook his head ruefully. 'But we're not holding our breath.'

Virgilio responded. 'Thank you for filling us in. Now, as far as this murder investigation is concerned, my first question is simply: do you think Michael Martin Cornish could somehow be involved?'

Will looked doubtful. 'Rachel and I've been asking ourselves the same thing ever since we heard what happened. I suppose it's just possible that Jonah Moore saw or heard something compromising and had to be eliminated but, knowing Cornish as we do, I seriously doubt it. Like I said, he keeps his hands scrupulously clean, and murder in broad daylight is definitely not his style. And, besides, for almost all the afternoon *we* are his alibi.'

'You are?'

'This afternoon at just before two, Cornish left his fiancée in the seminar room while he drove down to the local town. We followed him on his walkabout through the streets. He went in and out of the church, into a few shops, and Rach even "accidentally" bumped into him and they sat down and drank coffee together. From two until we all got back here just after four and walked straight into all the uproar, he never left our sight.' He opened his palms helplessly. 'Sorry, guys.'

Rachel O'Neill was duly called and she confirmed everything her partner had said. Finally, Virgilio summoned Martin (aka Mikey aka Michael Martin Cornish), and the American described his movements that afternoon precisely as the two DEA agents had recounted. He was polite, cordial even, and gave the impression of being totally open and frank. I'd come across this sort before and I knew that they're the most dangerous. A desperate druggie with *HATE* tattooed on his forehead and a rusty blade in his hand, or a sixteen-year-old gang member from a deprived housing complex brandishing a World War Two pistol, are small beer in comparison to the death and destruction this sort of plausible character could leave in his wake. But for now, Martin/Mikey looked as though butter wouldn't melt in his mouth. He even produced a little box from his pocket with touching sincerity and exhibited the ring he'd just bought for Jennifer.

Maybe this was true, but there was no way of telling.

Moments after Martin/Mikey left the room there was a knock at the door. It was the pathologist with some interesting news that further muddied the waters of this increasingly puzzling case.

'I have a feeling the victim wasn't a popular man, Virgilio.' He and Pisano obviously went way back and he gave the inspector a knowing wink. 'It appears that person or persons unknown had two different goes at trying to kill him.'

'You think it really is poison in the glass?'

'It smells like cyanide to me. I'm pretty sure, but my people at the lab should be able to analyse the residue in the glass and the remaining wine in the bottle and confirm it. I'll do the autopsy tomorrow but from what I can see, he was poisoned and then stabbed.'

Virgilio shook his head slowly. 'The murderer was certainly trying to make sure.'

'Or the *murderers*, plural.' The pathologist was quick to add the proviso, 'I'm not sure the two actions happened simultaneously.'

'Are you telling me you think he was poisoned

and then somebody went to the trouble of sticking a dagger in him some time later on, just for good measure, even though he was already dead?'

'Maybe they couldn't tell if he was dead or alive. I'm not totally sure what poison it was yet but some toxins can put the victim into a coma-like state but they still have a pulse. The killer wanted to be sure he was dead.'

'Can you at least give me a time of death?'

'The best I can do is somewhere between one and three. I might get a better idea after I've done the autopsy, but don't get your hopes up.'

Virgilio sighed in frustration. 'Let me have your report as soon as you can, will you, Gianni? I tell you, you don't make my life any easier, you know.'

'Just doing my job, Virgilio, just doing my job.'

After he left, Virgilio turned to the uniformed officer. 'Go and collect all the passports or ID cards. The fingerprint team should be here by now. I want prints of everybody. Tell them it's merely for exclusion, but nobody is to leave the area until I say so. Okay?'

The finger of suspicion appeared to be pointing ever more inexorably in one direction even though, in my bones, I just couldn't see Antonio as the murderer. I caught Virgilio's eye. 'This suddenly propels the butler up the list of suspects, doesn't it? He presumably brought the bottle of wine and the glass. We only have his word for it that he didn't put poison in one or both although, like you said before, he must have known he'd be caught.'

'I agree. Unless he's a complete idiot, he had to know he'd be caught and, anyway, why on earth should a faithful servant of ten years suddenly decide to kill his master? It doesn't make sense.'

'Unless he felt he was protecting his mistress. Like I said, I think he has a soft spot for Maria.'

By the time the body had been removed to the morgue, the crime scene closed off and sealed, the passports collected and the local police dismissed, it was almost half past seven and I decided to leave it until the next day to pick up the car in Florence. Antonio informed me that there was a regular bus service from Montevolpone but Virgilio said he would be happy to send a squad car to collect me in the afternoon. I walked outside with him and we stood there in silence, looking back at the beautiful villa, its façade turned an ethereal pink by the setting sun, both of us lost in our thoughts.

Finally, I had a go at summing up the situation as I saw it. 'One victim, murdered in broad daylight by at least one, maybe two different perpetrators and a cast of characters who all appear to have alibis. Along with this we have at least three people living here, maybe four if we include the American drug boss, with a possible motive.' I glanced across at Virgilio and grinned. 'Somehow I get the feeling you're going to have your work cut out.'

'Of course, not all of the alibis are watertight.' The inspector had been flicking through his notebook. 'There's a brief hiatus between the end of lunch and the start of the writing seminar. And the black lady and the tall mouthy one, Agatha Something, both claim to have been asleep in their rooms from two to three but nobody can confirm that.' He looked up from his notebook. 'If I was a betting man, my money would be on the butler, but it's tenuous in the extreme. What is pretty clear is that he was the last person to see the victim alive and he says he left him still sitting there with a bottle of wine at ten to two.'

'There's an old saying in English that the butler usually did it, but I have my doubts in this case.'

'I know what you mean, but if we ignore the butler as a suspect for a moment and ignore the ladies having a siesta, there's still a ten-minute window of opportunity between the butler leaving the victim alone at ten to two and the seminar starting at two. Ten minutes is enough time for almost any of them to have done it, but it's a hell of a tight one.' He snapped the notebook shut and opened the car door. 'Thanks a lot for your help, Daniel. I look forward to seeing you for lunch on Sunday.'

I held out my hand. 'See you then, Virgilio.' I hesitated before coming to a decision. I was supposed to be retired now and on holiday, but I'd always liked a challenge and I'd enjoyed these last few hours more than my wife would have been able to comprehend. 'Listen, I'd like to help, if you think I can be useful to you, but the last thing I want is to get in your way. I can keep sniffing about if you like and I'll let you know if I come up with any clues. Maria mentioned to me yesterday that Jonah had been stressed – so stressed, apparently, he even bought himself a pistol and a guard dog. I'll see if I can get to the bottom of what that's all about.'

'What you're telling me is that if he felt he had to defend himself there may be yet another possible suspect...' Virgilio gave a theatrical sigh. 'I have a feeling Paul's bottle of whisky is going to get opened tonight. *Ciao*, Daniel, and any help you can provide will be very welcome. Thank you for offering. I'm going to need all the help I can get with this case.'

* * *

Dinner at the villa was excellent as usual but the atmosphere around the table was decidedly subdued. The dining room was now out of bounds with adhesive seals and police *Crime Scene – Do Not Enter* tape stretched across the doorway so we were eating in the seminar room. There were two main topics of conversation, the first of which was the immediate future. Inevitably, it was Agatha who brought it up.

'What happens to us? My flight home's booked for twelve days' time and I can't change it. Is the course going to carry on? What happens if we all have to leave here? Where will we go?'

Diana and Elaine hastened to add their voices to the chorus of concern but they were all silenced by Millicent, still dressed like an Edwardian grande dame. Understandably, Maria had opted to dine alone this evening, but Millicent had stepped into her shoes and positioned herself at the head of the table.

'The course will go on. Be in no doubt about that. We will fulfil our obligations.' Her tone was as uncompromising as ever. 'As Agatha will remember from last year, my brother had little to do with the course and his absence will make minimal difference. Serena and I will soldier on. Antonio and Annarosa will continue to look after you and the maid will continue to come in every morning to make up your rooms. Don't worry. The show will go on.'

I joined everybody in nodding appreciatively and even Agatha settled down. I realised that I was actually enjoying the course and at least some of the stuff we were doing was going to be really useful. After all, the sessions on writing technique could be applied to any genre, not just erotica.

A moment later, Millicent brought up the second burning question of the night: me.

'And now, Dan, perhaps you'll be good enough to explain to us how you come to be involved in the police investigation.' I could imagine her using the same ominous tones to query why one of her students might have committed the cardinal sin of not handing in an assignment on time. My background had been bound to come out sooner or later, so I decided it was time to reveal all.

'I recently retired from the Metropolitan Police, where I was a detective chief inspector.' I saw a few eyebrows raise. In particular I thought I caught a glint in Mikey/Martin's eyes. 'I only met Inspector Pisano today for the first time. He's a friend of one of my former colleagues and it was sheer chance that I happened to be visiting him when everything happened today.'

'And will you be involved in the investigation?' From the expressions on the faces around the table, Agatha was voicing what they all had in mind. 'Are you going to be investigating us?' There was just enough outrage in her voice to arouse a low mumble of support from some of the others. I tried to give her my most disarming smile.

'Perish the thought, Agatha. Like I told you, I'm retired and I was just lending a hand with interpreting, which as it turned out wasn't really necessary after all. I have absolutely no intention of getting involved with somebody else's murder investigation.' I let my smile embrace the room. 'Particularly without getting paid. No, I'm retired and I'm here on this course and, like you, I'm delighted it's going to continue. Just so long as nobody tries to murder me, I'm staying right out of it.'

Dinner proceeded and the atmosphere gradually mellowed, to some extent. Charlotte proved to be more communicative than before and she quizzed me on my time in the police, interestingly focusing more on its effect on my personal life than on my duties. In the end I found myself telling her how my job and a few other things had led to the break-up of my marriage. She expressed sympathy while Agatha, whose hearing was more like that of a lynx than a septuagenarian, seized on this as validation of her decision to ensure that the marriage of a police officer in her latest novel ended in divorce.

After a final espresso, I escaped into the night air. It was barely half past nine but so much had happened that I felt quite weary, although that might have been the red wine. I sat down on the stone steps above the croquet lawn and almost wished I hadn't given up smoking thirty years ago. Night had fallen and as before, the starlight illuminated the surroundings remarkably clearly. It felt comfortable and increasingly familiar. It was hard to believe that only a matter of hours earlier it had been the scene of violent death. The other thought that I couldn't shift was that even though I was on holiday and no longer on the force, I now found myself plunged back into my old life and I was loving it. There was no getting away from the fact that this return to my old familiar turf was welcome, even though my wife would have thrown up her hands in horror. But still, I reminded myself, the way things had been going I no longer needed to worry about what my wife might think. I was a free agent and, as such, could involve myself as much or as little as I liked in this investigation.

I had only been there for a minute or two when I heard the soft patter of paws on the stones behind me and a cold, wet nose started nuzzling my ear. I fended him off gently and turned to see his eyes glowing green in the starlight.

'*Ciao*, Oscar. It's good to see you.'

The dog did his best to climb onto my lap before finally settling down beside me and resting his big, hairy head on my knee. As I stroked him, I looked at his face.

'Who did it, Oscar? You were there. You must have seen what happened?'

All I got in response was a lick of the fingers and I lapsed into silence once more, my brain trying to sift through all the stories I'd heard and make sense of the events here at Villa Volpone this afternoon. I wished I had my whiteboard. Back in my office at the Met, I had a big board and marker pens in a selection of colours that I used to build up a picture of each case: laying out the crime scene, the main suspects and their back stories, as well as maps and photos. All I had here was an A4 pad I had brought with me and a black biro. Still, I had told Virgilio I wanted to be involved so I resolved to use the limited resources at my disposal to try to sort it all out.

Jonah Moore had been an objectionable character but, as Agatha had so rightly said, there are an awful lot of objectionable people in the world, but unpleasantness alone is no justification for murdering them. So who could it have been? The battered wife after years of domestic abuse? The sister who felt used and exploited? The butler of ten years suddenly gone doolally or rushing to the aid of his mistress? A ruthless drug lord who had acted to snuff out a potential witness to some shady deal? And what had Maria meant when she had talked of her husband being stressed and paranoid? Had he made enemies? Had he been threatened? If so, by whom? One thing was for sure: a lot of investigation needed to be done into the background of Jonah Moore and those around him.

After a while, I got to my feet and my four-legged friend and I went for a stroll through the grounds of the villa. It was another delightful night and the air was filled with a heady mix of aromas ranging from honeysuckle to wisteria, rosemary to lavender. The shadows under the trees sparkled with the minute yellow flashes of fireflies and an owl was hooting from high up in one of the cypress trees. I breathed deeply and decided I rather liked Tuscany. It occurred to me that Helen would have loved this place as well but, alas, it looked as though she was never going to experience it – at least not with me. In spite of the idyllic surroundings, my spirits fell, and I could feel myself once more descending into melancholy.

I didn't have much time to wallow in self-pity. Just as the dog and I reached the far end of the vegetable garden, I spotted a dark shape coming along the path towards me. As it drew nearer, it separated into one large lump and one smaller one. It was Mikey/Martin and his young companion, Jennifer. The dog trotted amiably across to say hello so I slowed and stopped.

'You two trying to clear your heads as well after the drama of the day?'

'Hey, Dan. For once, my head's completely clear.' Mikey/Martin sounded relaxed. 'In fact, you can be the first to hear what's just happened.' He turned his head towards Jen, who was petting the dog with one hand while clinging on to

Mikey/Martin with her other. 'You wanna tell him, sweetie?'

She straightened up. 'Martin's just asked me to marry him and I said yes.' She sounded thrilled and reached up to kiss her new fiancé on the cheek. 'I'm so excited.'

'Congratulations to you both.' I realised that this either confirmed what Mikey/Martin had told us earlier or signified that Jen was now complicit in helping him establish his cover story. 'I wish you a lifetime of happiness together.' Crook or not, I hoped he managed to achieve it.

Inevitably, this got me thinking of Helen again but it came as a considerable surprise to me to find that Mikey/Martin was also thinking of her.

'I couldn't help overhearing that your marriage broke up, Dan. I'm sorry about that. I'm afraid it's not the first time I've heard of it happening to cops. Was it the unsocial hours?' He sounded genuinely concerned and I had to remind myself that this guy was in all probability on America's most wanted list.

'Thanks, Martin. It was a lot of things, but

funny hours and my being out of the house so much didn't help.'

'Too bad.' A big hand stretched out and patted me on the shoulder. 'Still, you're a smart guy; you'll find yourself another lady.'

After the happy couple had headed back in the direction of the villa, Oscar and I carried on through the trees to our familiar bench where I pulled out my phone and came close to calling Helen just to hear her voice before chickening out and calling my daughter instead.

'Hi, sweetie, how's things?' It struck me as I spoke that I had just used the same term of endearment I'd copied from a man who was quite likely a vicious criminal.

'Hi, Dad. I'm fine thanks. Tell me how your course is going. Booker Prize next year?'

I told her about the course and the other students but decided against telling her what had happened to Jonah. That could wait. After a while, I finally asked the question that had been burning away in the back of my mind.

'Have you spoken to your mum? She sent me a text saying she was going away for a few days. Any idea where?' I managed to stop myself from asking with whom.

'Somewhere near Bournemouth. It's a golf course... I mean it's a course for people learning to play golf and naturally it takes place on a golf course. You know what I mean. She's there with a friend, I think. I'm not too sure.'

'Ah, right... well, if she calls you, say hi from me, won't you?'

'Oh, Dad...' I heard her falter and then recover. 'Of course I'll tell her. You look after yourself, you hear. And enjoy the course.'

'I'll do my best. To be honest, they're not a bad bunch.'

Apart from a murderer or two.

6
WEDNESDAY / THURSDAY

Next day, after a morning devoted to the difficulties and pitfalls of writing convincing dialogue followed by a fascinating but excruciating discussion of acceptable synonyms to describe male and female genitalia and the act of coitus, I had lunch with the others and then retired to my room with my A4 pad. I was up there working on my attempt to produce a timeline showing where everybody claimed to have been between one and three the previous day when my phone started ringing. It was Virgilio.

'*Ciao*, Daniel. How's your course? Is it carrying on?'

'*Ciao*, Virgilio. Yes, it's business as usual, so long

as I manage to concentrate. To tell the truth, I'm more interested in the murder. I've just been sitting here trying to put down on paper everything that happened yesterday. Any developments on that score?'

'Yes, but it doesn't make my job any easier. I've just been handed the toxicology report. You said you were sitting down? Good. That's just as well, because it now turns out there were no fewer than *three* attempts on Jonah Moore's life yesterday.'

'Three? I've never come across a case like this before. Maybe they were all in on the act.'

'Three's what the report says and I'm beginning to wonder the same thing. There's the dagger to the heart – dead centre as I thought – and there's the residue in his glass, which is definitely potassium cyanide, but get this: analysis of the wine in the bottle reveals the presence of an extract of oleandrin, which can cause seizures and even death. The report said the concentration of the toxins in the bottle wouldn't have been fatal, although it would have made the victim as sick as a dog for a few days.'

'Oleandrin? I've never heard of it. What is it?'

'Believe it or not it's fairly easily produced from oleander plants. Every bit of their leaves, stems and flowers is toxic and I couldn't help noticing that the gardens around the villa are filled with them – you know, the bushes lining the drive covered in lovely pink and red flowers.'

I'm no gardener but I knew exactly which plants he meant and had to agree that the flowers were beautiful, although the news that they could be so toxic came as a shock. Meanwhile, the full ramifications of what I'd just been told were starting to sink in. 'So let's get this straight: there was a dagger in Jonah's heart, traces of cyanide in his empty glass, and a dose of this flowery stuff in the wine bottle, although not necessarily a lethal dose. Bloody hell, the pathologist was right, some people really didn't like him at all. So, what actually killed him? The cyanide, presumably?'

'Yes. It was highly concentrated and would have paralysed him in a matter of seconds and killed him in no more than a minute, max.'

'And the dagger...?'

'Because of the lack of blood, he must have been stabbed after the heart had stopped beating but Gianni, the pathologist, can't say yet whether it was done immediately after, or it could even have been up to an hour later. He's doing the autopsy later on and that might shed a bit more light.'

'So we could be looking for two perpetrators: one who administered the cyanide that killed him and one who came along later, saw him comatose and stabbed him, unaware that he was already dead, or just for the hell of it.' I needed to pause to take it all in. 'Or even three different people if the oleander stuff was put there by yet another would-be killer. God almighty...'

'I couldn't agree more; a bit of divine intervention would be very welcome. Anyway, look, I was wondering... I promised I'd send a driver to pick you up so you can collect your rental car. I don't suppose you feel like coming here first for half an hour so I can talk you through the investigation so far, do you? A British perspective on it might be what we need. I feel as though I'm in quicksand at the moment.'

'I'd be pleased to help any way I can.'

'So if I send the car at, say, five?'

I was collected by the same officer who had

driven Virgilio and me up to the villa the previous day and from him I learnt that requests had been sent to London for background information on the dead man and on all of the current residents of the villa. Results were expected by Friday at the latest. Investigations here in Italy into the Italian nationals had already taken place and produced nothing untoward. Maria and Annarosa the cook had apparently led blameless lives and Antonio had only had a caution twenty-five years ago for his involvement in a fight after a football match and that was all. There appeared to be no skeletons in any of their pasts. Checks had also been done on the Romanian chambermaid, who only worked in the mornings, and on the gardener, who was currently on holiday in Sardinia with his wife. Nothing there either.

At Virgilio's office in the *questura*, I was gratified to find a fine-looking whiteboard, now covered with the names of all the players, both real and their aliases. The inspector was on the phone and while I waited, I checked through what I could see on the board. It didn't take me long to work out that Virgilio, too, operated a traffic light system for suspects. Antonio, Maria, Millicent and Mikey/Martin were in red, I was in green along with the two Cana-dians, and all the others were in orange. There was only one glaring omission. When Virgilio came off the phone and walked across to shake hands, I felt I had to point it out to him.

'You've forgotten Oscar.' As usual I addressed him in Italian.

'Oscar?'

'The dog. After all, he's our only witness.'

'The way things are going, he's probably our best hope.' We shook hands and he filled me in on developments – of which there were precious few. 'That was Gianni, the pathologist. He's pretty sure the stab wound was inflicted some time – up to an hour – after the poison had already killed the victim.'

'So it's looking more and more likely that we have a choice of murderers on our hands: one who did the job with poison and then a second one who stabbed a dead body, presumably thinking he was still alive. And don't let's forget a third party who either hoped to kill him with the oleander poison or at least make him very ill.'

Virgilio nodded. 'Exactly. Doesn't help us much,

does it? Until we hear back from the UK, we know next to nothing about the course participants, or indeed about the victim himself before he settled over here. Assuming they all come back lily-white, where do we go from here? There's no way I can put any kind of case together against any of the main suspects without hard evidence. Surprise, surprise, the handle of the knife had been wiped clean and the only fingerprints on the glass and the bottle belonged to the victim, with a couple of partials belonging to the butler, but he's already told us he brought in the bottle and the glass. There's not enough there to charge him, although to my mind he's still the number one suspect.'

'I suppose I have to agree, but without a motive we're still in the dark. Don't forget he claims to have a fairly solid alibi as well. My gut feeling is that he didn't do it but he needs to be seen again. What're you going to do? Pull him into the station for questioning?'

'I thought I'd come up to the villa tomorrow and put him through the wringer.' I smiled at the thought. He used the Italian word *torchiare*, which I had only learnt recently. It was the word used by farmers to describe the process of squeezing every last bit of juice out of grapes to make wine or out of olives to produce oil. There was no doubt about it, all this conversation with Virgilio in Italian was doing wonders for expanding my vocabulary. Virgilio gave me a shrug of the shoulders. 'Who knows? If he's stupid enough to do it, maybe he's stupid enough to confess.'

'What do you think about the two female suspects – Maria and her sister-in-law, Millicent – and what about the big American? I honestly can't see any of them being the murderer but I don't really see Antonio either. Maybe it was somebody from outside after all.'

'I don't know either. After seeing and talking to Maria yesterday I find it hard to believe she could have done it – but stranger things have happened. As for the dead man's sister, I could believe her capable of anything but, again, without proof, we're just wasting our time.' He gave a sigh of resignation. 'There's no getting away from it, though, they both need to be spoken to again. I'll start with the butler tomorrow and then move on to the two women.'

'If you need a hand with interpreting for Millicent, just shout. One thing about her: she does speak loud and clear. You probably won't need me.'

'Thanks. If I run into trouble, I'll call you. You have lessons all morning, right?'

'Yes, I'll be there. And what about Michael Martin Cornish? Personally, I don't think he's involved but still...'

'There's been a development on that score. I took a call from God himself, the *questore*, an hour ago. He's had his ear bent by the powers-that-be at the ministry in Rome, no less. Apparently, the American Embassy have been in touch at the highest diplomatic levels. They would "greatly appreciate" it if we were to lay off Cornish unless we have something definite on him. And by definite they mean a smoking gun. They want him to believe he's still free to move about and that nobody's onto him. The death of a random Englishman is apparently far less important than the chance of nailing a major drug dealer.'

'Now why doesn't that come as a surprise? Politics, drugs and, of course, the reputations of the rich and famous do you have a habit of taking precedence over more mundane issues. It's happened before and we both know it'll happen again.' This had been another of the reasons that had contributed to my decision to leave the force. Maybe I'm just old-fashioned but I subscribe to the belief that justice should be the same for everybody.

* * *

Next morning, I went for another run with Will, and this time Rachel came with us. We had made the arrangement the previous evening after another very good, but far from relaxed, meal. Once again Maria was absent and Millicent sat at the head of the table. Nobody had been surprised to hear her announce that the scheduled excursion to Florence had been postponed. Since Maria was supposed to have been the guide, this was understandable to everybody. I didn't mind. I'd already made up my mind to drive back down to Florence in my replacement – upgraded – rental car and wander about on my own for my research, although I was finding it hard to concentrate on my novel when my brain was still fully occupied trying to make sense of Tuesday afternoon's events.

I set off on the run with the two DEA agents and once we were clear of the villa and away from any possible prying ears, the three of us discussed the case as we jogged along. Will and Rachel had already been informed by their embassy that Mikey/Martin would be left out of the investigation and they sounded relieved, still hoping to nail him for something big. They both repeated what they had told Virgilio – that cold-blooded murder wasn't part of Michael Martin Cornish's playbook and they genuinely didn't believe he could be involved. I told them about the engagement announcement in the garden and Rachel confirmed that his new fiancée, Jennifer, had been showing off the remarkably classy ring to all the ladies. Crook he might well be, but Mikey/Martin clearly had good taste.

We followed the same route as we had done on Monday morning and stopped at the top to admire the view. Up here we could speak freely, so I decided I should pass on a word of advice.

'Um... there's something I feel I'd better say to you guys.' Will and Rachel were standing side by side, looking down over the olive groves and vineyards towards Florence, and they turned their heads towards me. 'Seeing as your cover story is brother and sister, you might do well to be a little less affectionate in public.' I went on to tell them about the shower scene at the pool and both of them blushed. Rachel was the first to react.

'You're dead right, Dan. Thanks for the warning. The thing is...' She glanced back at Will. 'Relations between work colleagues are frowned on in our business but we've been getting closer and closer. Being over here probably made us go a bit crazy. We'll rein it in, I promise, even though it's not easy.' The loving look she then gave Will awakened poignant memories for me. 'At least in public.'

Will added his thanks. 'We'll definitely take more care. The fact is that things are getting serious between us now. When we get back to the US, we're going to have to do something about it.'

By now I had managed to banish memories of the early days with Helen and I gave them both a grin. 'Maybe follow in the footsteps of Michael Martin Cornish and young Jen? That way this trip to Tuscany won't be a complete failure, even if you fail to catch him doing something he shouldn't be doing.'

On the way back in the direction of the villa, I reflected on the irony of the hunters and the hunted following a similar trajectory in their private lives. I hoped it would work out for both couples.

Better than it had done for me.

When all the course participants emerged from the seminar room for a welcome mid-morning break after wrestling with the Oxford comma, the semicolon, and the degree of anatomical detail necessary when describing the act of coitus, there were three police cars in the car park. We were drinking our teas and coffees when an officer came to ask us all not to return to our rooms as a full search of the villa was taking place. Apart from a few predictable protests about infringement of rights by Agatha, we all accepted the inevitable and I wondered if the search would come up with any results. Presumably they were looking for evidence of toxic substances, discarded gloves, or empty containers, but after almost forty-eight hours I had little doubt that all but the stupidest of murderers would have disposed of any incriminating evidence by now.

Still, it had to be done and I was glad there was nothing embarrassing in my room apart from a photo of me with Helen in Ibiza in happier times. The close-cropped hairstyle I had in those days had never suited me but I had stuck obstinately to it for several years before she managed to talk me out of it.

The second half of the morning turned into a debate about something I had always considered to be a very ordinary, everyday garment: underpants. I listened with ever-increasing amazement to the interest this generated. The first to start it off, innocently enough, was Charlotte, who suggested that the correct nomenclature for female underpants was simply 'pants'. Diana disagreed.

'In the UK, yes, but not in America. Pants are what we call trousers.' She looked across at Jennifer for confirmation.

'Yeah, that's right.'

'So what do you call what we call pants?' Charlotte was looking puzzled.

'Panties.' Jen looked around the table. 'You have panties in England, right?'

Agatha stepped in firmly. 'We most certainly do not. "Panties" is a *horrible* word.' She added extra emphasis to the word so there could be no misunderstanding. 'I never use it.'

'Then what do you say?'

'Pants.'

'Yes, but...'

I was beginning to enjoy it by now so I offered a humble suggestion. 'What about "knickers"?'

This drew universal disdain from my fellow students. Kindly, Elaine tried to explain.

'"Knickers" is such an old-fashioned word. It's almost as bad as "bloomers" or "drawers".'

Charlotte had another try. 'Would a suggestion be to make all characters wear thongs? That way we could avoid the pants confusion?'

Alas, this suggestion was quickly shot down in flames, this time by Serena. 'In Australia, thongs are what we call flip-flops in the UK. The Aussies wear them on their feet.'

'So what do they call what we call thongs? God... it's complicated.'

The debate continued until Elaine asked me what I was wearing. For the record, I have always worn Marks & Spencer white boxers and Helen had been buying these for me for the last thirty years, but for some reason I was feeling a bit flippant by this time so I told them I wasn't wearing any, expecting outrage. Instead, there was a low murmur around the table and I got an approving look from Elaine, who muttered, 'Ah, commando.'

I was still trying to convince them – without dropping my trousers – that I had just been joking when lunchtime came around and the session concluded with the two sides agreeing to differ. I was beginning to realise that there's more to writing an erotic novel than meets the eye.

To everybody's surprise, Maria appeared at the lunch table and slipped into the chair previously occupied by her husband, with Millicent at her side. The food was served by Antonio so it was pretty obvious that the interviews carried out this morning couldn't have produced any confessions or conclusive proof of guilt and the room-to-room searches hadn't revealed any secrets. If anything, Maria looked relieved, although the red rings around her eyes attested to her continued grief. Considering the way Jonah had treated her, this was unexpected, but I'd come across many cases of far more brutal domestic abuse in my time where the injured parties still somehow remained emotionally drawn to their aggressors. What was that thing Dad used to say about folk...?

The suspicious detective in me did throw up another possible scenario: could it be that Maria had for some reason invented the story of domestic violence and Jonah was not the monster we thought? No sooner had I posited it than I discarded the notion. Apart from anything else, it struck me that it would have been extremely difficult for somebody with small hands like hers to bruise herself in such a way as to make it look as if her arm had been squeezed. Besides, what possible motive could she have had for such a charade?

Maria apologised for the postponement of today's Florence trip and announced that it would take place tomorrow. Almost everybody, myself included, indicated that we intended joining in and so I decided to put off my planned drive down to Florence this afternoon and resolved to stick around the Montevolpone area and maybe do a bit more digging of my own. At the end of lunch, I went over to ask Maria if she minded if I took Oscar for a walk and she readily agreed.

'He'd love that. With all the police milling about this morning, he's been shut up in the kitchen. Come and collect him whenever you like.'

The others had almost all got up and left by now, so I leant closer and lowered my voice. 'How're you holding up?'

She gave a little nod and reached into her sleeve for a tissue to blow her nose before replying. 'I'm okay, thanks, Dan. I had a long session with the police this morning but I don't know if they're any closer to discovering what happened. I couldn't really help very much.'

'From what I've seen, Inspector Pisano's a good man and a smart detective. I'm sure he'll get to the bottom of it.' I slid into Millicent's now empty seat. 'Did you tell him what you told me about Jonah being stressed? What was all that about?'

'I told him what I could.' I saw Maria glance around but the room was now empty apart from the two of us. 'Jonah started getting letters – you know, anonymous poison pen letters.'

'Since when?'

'Since the beginning of the year, roughly one a month.'

'And what did they say?'

'He never showed me any of them, but one evening he let slip that at least one of them had been a death threat.'

'And were they in English or Italian?'

'English, I think...' I saw her rack her brains. 'I'm almost certain they must have been. I saw one of the envelopes before he took it away to open in private and I'm sure it had a British stamp.'

'And where are the letters now?'

'I have no idea. I've been looking everywhere but there's no sign of them. I can only assume he must have destroyed them. Inspector Pisano told his men to search for them this morning but I haven't heard if they found them.'

I had been watching her closely as she relayed this information to me, checking to see if her body language revealed any signs of guilt, but I could see nothing but bemused frustration. If she was acting, it was one hell of a performance.

I suppressed an annoyed grunt when I heard that the letters hadn't turned up. They would have been a vital clue and would have gone a long way towards supporting Maria's innocence. Even so, my gut feeling was that she was telling the truth and if so, the arrival of poison pen letters from the UK suddenly opened the door to the possibility that at least one of the perpetrators might be a Brit – and that, of course, included half a dozen of the current residents of the villa. Maybe the killer or killers weren't from Jonah's close circle here in Italy after all. But what could he have done to cause somebody to threaten him with death – or indeed kill him? I was also mildly surprised that these threats had been delivered by snail mail. In this day and age I would have expected them to have come by electronic means. Did this maybe point towards somebody older and less computer-savvy?

I went down to the kitchen to collect my walking companion and was greeted enthusiastically by the Labrador. Antonio was also in there, sitting at the table poring over what looked like a stamp album, and I took advantage of the fact that we were alone to ask a few questions of my own. I started by trying to put him at his ease. Somehow it didn't come as a surprise to see that his hobby was stamp collecting. It rather suited his somewhat reticent personality.

'Have you been collecting stamps for a long time? My dad was a great stamp collector.'

This elicited a hint of a nervous smile from him. 'All my life. I find it a very peaceful and relaxing pastime.'

'How did it go with the inspector this morning?'

The butler's gaunt features looked even more doleful this afternoon and the reason for his unhappiness immediately became obvious.

'I'm sure the inspector thinks I killed Signor Jonah; he almost said as much.' He looked beseechingly at me and actually started wringing his hands, not something you see every day. 'I didn't do it, sir, I didn't. I told the inspector but I'm sure he didn't believe me. What if they arrest me and send me to prison? My mother would die of shame and my father would probably kill himself.'

'From what the inspector told me, I don't think

he's made up his mind yet. Your problem is that you were the last person to be with Jonah but that doesn't make you a killer.' I paused, wondering how much Virgilio had revealed, before deciding to feel my way cautiously 'Did he tell you how Jonah died?'

'I *know* how he died. I was the person who found him with that awful dagger stuck in his chest.'

So it would appear that the poisoning still remained a secret. I nodded approvingly to myself. This was a smart move by Virgilio. Only the murderer would know the full truth of how Jonah had died and he or she might be lulled into making a mistake. I made another attempt to get Antonio to open up.

'So you were the last to see him alive and the first to find him dead. I agree that looks suspicious but, like I say, it doesn't prove you're a murderer. Tell me, how long is it since Jonah started drinking heavily? Ever since you first met him, what, ten years ago?'

'I first met him six months or so before he married the *signora*, so that would be just over ten years ago. I've worked here for almost thirty years now. I was first engaged by the *signora's* father, long before she married her first husband, Signor Enrico.'

'That's Enrico Bianchi, the racing driver?'

'Yes, sir.'

'And what can you tell me about Jonah?'

'He always drank quite a lot – but you English often do, don't you? But he never started drinking to excess until quite recently.' He paused for thought. 'I suppose it's only been since the start of the year that he's been getting drunk most nights.'

That, of course, tied in with Maria's story of the poison pen letters.

'And how long had he been violent towards Maria?'

Antonio's expression changed from despondency to something very different: anger, maybe? 'That was also quite recent. There were times when I almost stepped in, but she always told me to stay out of it. She told me she could handle him.'

'You and Maria go way back, don't you? If you started here thirty years ago, she must have been, what, twenty?'

'She was nineteen and I was twenty-three.'

A thought occurred to me. 'Tell me, were you two ever... intimate?'

For the very first time I saw a wave of colour sweep across the butler's pallid features. 'No, sir, never.' I then had the bizarre sight of this Count Dracula look-alike crossing himself superstitiously. 'Dear God, no. There was never anything like that between us.'

'But you are very close all the same.'

'Yes, sir, but only in a pure and decent way. *Dio buono... Maremma cane...*'

His voice tailed off into another handful of increasingly colourful Tuscan expletives, which I couldn't follow – although the general gist was clear. Antonio had never laid a finger on Maria.

But he had maybe wanted to.

Jealousy and lust, as detectives all over the world know all too well, are powerful motives for murder and the butler's problem was that he now had not only the opportunity and the means, but a possible motive for committing murder. Things weren't looking good for him and that was a fact. I liked the guy and knew I would be sorry if it turned out he really was the killer. His expression was so miserable I patted him on the shoulder and told him to take it easy. Leaving him to his stamps, I went across to the back door where the dog was still sitting patiently, eyes glued to the handle.

'Come on then, Oscar. Let's go for a walk.' Collecting the lead from the hook, I opened the door and we went out into the warm afternoon sunshine.

We headed down to Montevolpone once more but this time by a different route, following a narrow track between two vineyards. The earth underfoot was compacted hard and bone dry. In fact, the ground had started cracking into miniature canyons and every step I took raised a tiny cloud of dust. I glanced up at the sky and for the first time saw grey clouds on the horizon to the north. Might they be bringing much-needed rain? There was little doubt that the farmers around here must be praying for it.

Our walk took us through the streets of the town and I stopped off at a shoe shop to buy replacements for my old ones, which had never fully recovered from their sortie into the swimming pool. The lady in the shop very kindly allowed me to bring Oscar in with me and he behaved impeccably, sitting alongside me so primly that the lady even went off and brought him a biscuit as a reward. I was not in the least surprised to see it disappear down the dog's throat in a nanosecond.

Picking up the bag with the new shoes, I returned to the street, and we walked around to Tommaso's bar in the little piazza, where we both received a friendly welcome. It very quickly emerged that news of Jonah's death had become the talk of the town. This time Tommaso not only came out to chat, he pulled up a chair and sat down right opposite me.

'Is it true he was stabbed in the heart?'

There seemed little point in denying it so I nodded. 'I'm afraid so.'

'There were police swarming all over town this morning, asking around. Have they found the killer yet?'

I decided to stay out of it as much as I could. 'Not as far as I know, but I'm just a visitor, I'm afraid.'

'But you're still living up at the villa?' Seeing me nod, he continued in hushed tones. 'But aren't you worried it could be you next?'

'Why me? Nobody knows me around here.'

'So they think it was somebody who knew him, do they? But couldn't it have been a burglary gone wrong, maybe?'

'I really don't know. Next time you see the police, ask them. As for me, I'm pretty confident the same thing isn't going to happen to me.'

'So if they think it's somebody who knew him...' Tommaso was evidently thinking out loud. 'Who could it be?' Another pause before he leant towards me and lowered his voice to a whisper. 'He wasn't a popular man, you know.'

'I've already gathered that, but that's hardly a reason for sticking a dagger in him.'

He nodded in agreement. 'Of course, but if I were the police, I'd check out Puppo and Antonio. They both hated him.'

My ears pricked up, but I did my best not to show too much interest. 'Oh? You mean Antonio the butler?'

'Yes. You know what I think?' Tommaso leant forward on his elbows and lowered his voice. 'I think Antonio's been in love with Signora Maria for years. He hated her first husband – he told me so –

and he hated this one, and I bet it's because he was jealous. I wonder if he did it. Mind you, he's a peaceable sort of man... at least these days.'

'These days?'

'He used to have a bit of a name in the town for getting into fights, but he's calmed right down now.' He caught my eye and smiled. 'We all calm down as we get older, don't we?'

'Most of us do.' I took a big slug of cold beer and reflected on what sounded very much like confirmation of my suspicion that Antonio might well have been jealously protective of his beloved Maria. But enough to kill? And with two different types of poison and a dagger? 'And who was that other guy you mentioned – Puppo, wasn't it?'

He nodded. 'Puppo Marinetti; he runs the local garage.'

'And what reason might he have had to kill Jonah?' It was hard to avoid sounding like a detective but Tommaso didn't appear to notice anything too intrusive in my questioning.

'Money.'

'Did Jonah owe him money? Didn't pay his bills maybe?'

'Much worse than that. You know that Rico, Signora Maria's first husband, was a racing driver, don't you?'

'Enrico Bianchi, yes, you told me that.'

'Rico was a local boy and he went to school here like the rest of us and everybody knew him. In particular, his best friend was Puppo. They started out racing go-karts together and when Rico was killed in that awful crash, we were all upset and Puppo in particular was inconsolable.'

'But he could hardly blame Jonah for the car crash, could he? Besides, didn't you say it was a question of money?'

'Yes, money, or to be more precise, a car. Rico knew he was in a dangerous profession and he always said that if ever anything happened to him he wanted Puppo to get his beloved Lamborghini in memory of him. The car was barely a year old when Rico was killed so you can imagine how much it was worth. If Puppo had got it and sold it on he could have revamped his garage from head to toe and it would have changed his life.'

'But Jonah hung on to the car. He was still driving around in it a few days ago. Wasn't it mentioned in the will?'

'That's the thing, it wasn't. Apparently, it was a simple two-line will leaving everything to his wife. But Maria knew all about the bequest, as did most of us here because Rico often spoke about it and we all envied Puppo for his good luck. But, like you say, when it came to it, Jonah refused to give the car up.'

'But surely it was up to Maria what to do with her money.'

'That Jonah man was a what's-it-called... a control freak. You know, he insisted on taking all the decisions and she wasn't able to stand up to him. When Rico's estate was finally wound up a year or more after his death, Jonah had already moved in on Maria and he stopped her from giving the car to its rightful owner.'

'I can see why Puppo might be angry with him, but why wait ten years to get revenge?' As a motive for murder, it was tenuous in the extreme.

Any further conjecture was interrupted by the appearance of two familiar faces. Coming along the road towards me were Agatha and Elaine, out for an afternoon stroll. It was too late to run because they'd already spotted me and were making a bee-line for my table.

'Hello, Dan. Have you and Oscar come for a walk before the storm hits?' As usual, Agatha was the spokesperson.

'Storm? I saw some clouds. Are they predicting a big storm?'

'Unusually wet and windy for July, or so Milli-cent said. It's going to be a very rough night but clearing through by morning.'

'I see.' I was wondering whether politeness de-creed that I should invite the two ladies to join me but Agatha had already made up her mind. Without ceremony, she pulled out a chair and plonked herself down alongside me and beckoned to Elaine. 'Here, let's sit down with the detective chief inspector.'

Elaine obeyed her companion's instructions and Tommaso got to his feet and asked them in halting English what they would like to drink. Unexpect-edly, the answer wasn't tea, but two gin and tonics. I was impressed: G&Ts at four o'clock in the after-noon was starting early by any standards. Maybe the drinks would loosen the ladies' tongues. While

I had no reason to suspect either of them, I had no doubt that very little escaped Agatha. Maybe she had some useful piece of evidence to pass on. It came as no surprise to find that she wasted no time beating about the bush.

'So who do you think did it, Dan?'

I answered honestly. 'I really don't know.'

'Any suspects?'

'I suppose you're all suspects.'

This elicited a response from the usually taciturn Elaine. 'Surely the police don't think *we* could do something like that?'

'As we used to say in the trade, I imagine the police are keeping an open mind for now and not discounting anything.' I threw Agatha's question back at the two of them. 'Do *you* have any ideas who our killer might be?' I almost added 'or killers' but stopped myself in time. For now, the dagger story remained the official cause of death.

Agatha had clearly already been turning this over in her head. 'Well, if you want to know what I think, and I know it sounds corny, but I think the butler might have done it. After all, he was still in the dining room after we'd all left. Elaine and I know that because we were the last of the guests to leave the table and Antonio was still there, opening yet another bottle of wine for Jonah.' She shook her head sadly. 'Poor Jonah. Whatever we might have thought of him, he didn't deserve to be murdered.'

'No, I suppose not, but he wasn't a nice man, was he?' Elaine didn't sound particularly saddened by the demise of Jonah.

'Nobody's denying that, Elaine, but surely murder's a bit extreme?'

I did a bit more prodding. 'So your money's on Antonio, Agatha. What about you, Elaine? Do you think the butler did it as well?'

'I'm not as sure as Agatha. I don't know the people here as well as she does but even I could see that Millicent, and Serena for that matter, had a fractious relationship with Jonah. There was always tension in the air when they were talking to him.'

Agatha agreed. 'That's true enough. Serena told me he didn't pay them very much for teaching on this course and he made them do all the work. Needless to say, he made sure he took any credit that was going. Still, it's not exactly a motive for murder, is it?'

Elaine nodded slowly. 'Of course you're right, so I agree the most likely suspect has to be the butler, but the most likely suspect doesn't necessarily always turn out to be the real culprit, does he? Besides, Antonio's such a kind, helpful man and I'm sure I heard that he was with Maria all afternoon so he couldn't have done it.'

'Oh yes he could. He could have done it in the few minutes between serving Jonah his wine and going off to meet Maria. It doesn't take long to stick a knife in somebody.' Agatha was right, of course, but, by the same token, Millicent had also been unaccounted for before going into the lecture at two o'clock and Serena had admitted to going for a comfort break in the course of the afternoon. Any one of them could have done it but I still wasn't convinced.

I decided there wasn't much point asking for any more theories on the identity of the murderer and I was searching for a change of subject when Tommaso returned and provided a welcome interruption. He was carrying a tray with a bottle of Gordon's and two glasses loaded with ice, into which he proceeded to tip eye-watering quantities of gin. I could only look on in awe. There was enough alcohol here to sedate a horse and I found myself wondering how Agatha and Elaine were going to manage to walk back up the hill to the villa afterwards. After depositing two little bottles of tonic, Tommaso shot me a wink and withdrew. I thought about getting up and leaving as well but part of me was curious to see what effect the gin might have on these English ladies of mature years, so I stayed a bit longer.

Agatha and Elaine added tonic and then clinked their glasses together before taking big mouthfuls. Agatha sat back and wiped her lips and then her brow with a paper napkin from the dispenser on the table.

'I needed that. It's so hot and humid today, isn't it?'

After a minute or two more on the subject of the predicted storm, I turned the conversation around to the reason we had come to Tuscany – the writing.

'Have either of you ladies managed to get any writing done since getting here? I haven't written a word.' Unless you counted the numerous sheets of

A4 paper covered in my scribbles about this murder case, but I wasn't going to mention that.

Agatha shook her head but Elaine nodded. 'I've written a fresh chapter for my new book. I finished it at midnight last night.'

Agatha looked surprised. 'Really? I was in bed by ten.'

I was also mildly surprised. I had assumed the two were sharing a room but clearly they had opted for two singles. Maybe they weren't quite as friendly as I had first thought. 'And what was the new chapter about?' The answer surprised me considerably more.

'It was a really steamy lesbian scene involving my heroine, Simone, and two members of a female neo-Nazi group. They tie her up and do all sorts of things to her.' The funny thing was that while I found myself feeling increasingly uncomfortable, mousy little Elaine was able to go into graphic detail without batting an eyelid, talking about acts that even a hardened veteran of the police force found fairly gut-wrenching. To my further amazement, Agatha also looked completely unruffled. After Elaine had come to the end of her exposé and swallowed another mouthful of gin, Agatha added a few words of clarification.

'You can see why Elaine and I write under pseudonyms, can't you? She'd be thrown out of the Littlehampton bridge club if they knew what she did for a living.'

I took a swig of beer to clear my throat before replying. 'For a living? So does this mean you've published lots of books, Elaine?'

'This'll be my thirty-third. I've been writing erotica since I was fifty-five – that's almost twenty years now.'

'Thirty-three books? That's amazing, I haven't even finished my first one. And all... um... pornographic?'

She wrinkled up her nose in distaste. 'I don't like that adjective. I prefer "erotic". It sounds so much nicer.'

The scene in the neo-Nazi dungeon had sounded anything but 'nice' to me but I decided not to comment. I still couldn't get my head around the fact that this prim and proper little lady wrote such raunchy books, but each to his, or her, own. 'So what's your nom de plume, then? I didn't realise I was in the presence of such a prolific author.'

For the first time, Elaine looked a tad embarrassed. 'You won't go telling everybody, now, will you? You see, it was my very first publisher who dreamt up my penname and it's a bit vulgar so I try not to advertise the fact too much.' She actually stopped talking and glanced around apprehensively before lowering her voice and confessing, 'I write under the name Fanny Lovesit.'

It took a heroic effort on my part not to start giggling but with the help of another big mouthful of beer, I managed it. Miraculously, I was even able to keep the conversation going. 'All erotic, or are any of your books whodunits?'

Agatha chimed in before Elaine could answer. 'Who done *who* is more like it.' And she erupted into a fit of giggles.

The gin was no doubt helping, but clearly these two ladies were considerably less starched than they appeared at first sight. Elaine gave her friend a tolerant smile and answered my question.

'There's a lot of sex in all of them but I did write

one with a murder mystery element as well: *Dying of Love*, it was called. It sold rather well.'

'What about you, Agatha? What's your penname?'

Agatha appeared to have recovered from her moment of ribaldry by now. 'Mine's quite ordinary. I write under the name Felicity Farnborough.' She smiled. 'All three of mine are available online, as are Elaine's. Why don't you read some of our work and tell us what you think?'

'I might well do that.'

Although whether I would ever be able to look either of these ladies in the eye again afterwards was another matter.

7

FRIDAY

The minibus to Florence on Friday afternoon was packed and I made a point of taking a seat at the back, as far from Elaine as I could get after the steamy prose I had read last night. The rain had started in earnest just after midnight, accompanied by an apocalyptic thunderstorm that made any chance of getting back to sleep a forlorn hope, so I had paid the princely sum of ninety-nine pence and downloaded *Dying of Love* by Fanny Lovesit. By the time the storm finally passed through in the small hours, I had learnt more about weird sex than in thirty years in the police force. One thing was clear: either Elaine had a very, very fertile imagination or her experiences made Christian Grey from the *Fifty Shades* books look like a boy scout.

I ended up squashed into the back seat between Serena and Diana for the excursion to Florence. Serena was clearly still in shock after Jonah's murder and barely said a word all trip but Diana was soon talking animatedly about her work and prattled on about raunchy romps in ancient Rome almost without a break. I listened with half an ear and threw in a few monosyllabic responses from time to time, but I suddenly woke up with a start when Diana started talking about the emperor Nero.

'He used to poison his enemies all the time.' She spoke of it as if she was describing a hobby like darts or knitting. 'He used the services of a lethal trio of women: Canidia, Martina, and Locusta, who were specialists in the field. There's a long list of people he poisoned, including his half-brother.'

I tried to sound as casual as I could. 'What was his poison of choice: arsenic?'

'Vegetable poisons, mainly; you know, things you could find growing in the fields and gardens around Rome. Deadly nightshade, hemlock, yew, and a whole host of others. It's amazing how many of the plants we still see around us on a daily basis are highly toxic.'

'And have you included a poisoning or two in your book?'

'Of course. One of my characters, Octavia, has a wonderful body – and she knows how to use it – but she's a very nasty woman and she kills several people with hemlock mixed with honey to disguise the taste.' She chuckled happily. 'But she's going to get her comeuppance at the end when she inadvertently eats a bowl of soup containing poisonous mushrooms.'

'Amazing.' Still trying to sound as casual as possible, I pressed her a little more. 'How do you know all this stuff? Are you a scientist? A botanist? I thought you were a historian.'

She chuckled again. 'It's called research, Dan. Just look on the internet and you can easily find out how to produce all sorts of poisons.' Suddenly looking more serious, she lowered her voice. 'I can't understand why somebody chose to stab poor Jonah to death when it's so easy to make and administer a lethal dose of poison and there's no mess.'

Further conversation was interrupted by Maria's voice from the front. 'We'll be coming up to Piazzale Michelangelo in just a minute. I can't stop for long so I'll drop you off and go and park. Wait for me up there. I should be back in five minutes or so. The views down over Florence are delightful. It'll be crowded, so keep your hands on your valuables.'

When the minibus came to a halt, we filed off and threaded our way through the mass of souvenir sellers and tourists to the edge of the wide piazza on the hill to the south of Florence, but I was barely conscious of the vista of red roofs, spires, towers and domes that opened up below us. I couldn't shift the thought of Nero's lethal trio and their home-made poisons. If they could produce poisons from common ingredients, so could almost anybody – now as well as then. The fact that Diana had brought up the subject and spoken to me about it so freely, knowing that I was involved in the investigation, made it unlikely that she was involved in poisoning Jonah but, of course, it might be a double bluff.

I was standing there, ostensibly admiring the view, which after the rain was crystal clear all the way across to the Apennines in the far distance, but in fact I barely registered the spectacular panorama. Somehow, I thought it unlikely that Diana could have been involved with the murder but she, unlike most of the others, had no alibi for that afternoon, having claimed she had been lying down in her room alone. I was still wondering whether she might in fact be involved when my phone started ringing. It was Virgilio. I glanced around to check I wasn't being overheard before answering.

'*Ciao*, Virgilio, how's it going?'

'*Ciao*, Dan, things are going okay but I was wondering if I could ask for a bit of help. The background reports have come in from the UK and there are a few points I'd like to discuss with you if you could find time. Can I send a car to pick you up?'

'No problem, I'll walk. I'm actually here in Florence now. I can be with you in half an hour or so.'

I went to Serena and asked her to tell Maria that I was going off on my own. She was still looking miles away but she nodded and told me they would text me the time and place to meet up for the return journey. From studying Google Maps I knew I needed to go past the duomo to reach the *questura*, so I set off down a long flight of steps that turned into a narrow lane leading in the direction of the *centro storico*.

I was so deep in thoughts of poison and murder that it was only when I found myself on the Ponte Vecchio that my mind came back to the present and I stopped dead. Here I was, standing on one of the most famous landmarks in Florence, if not the world. Below me, the River Arno was reduced to a muddy stream and it was hard to imagine the devastating floods of 1966, which had engulfed the centre of this world-heritage city, destroying so many priceless things.

On either side of the humpback bridge were tiny jewellery shops with people stopping to gaze at the jewels on display. This made it hard for the crowds on the bridge to get by and I could well imagine Helen spending ages – and lots of money – on jewellery here. As I thought of her, for a moment or two I even considered buying her a little present, but the thought quickly passed. Even back in the days when I thought she loved me, she had never been too keen on my taste as far as presents were concerned. I would never forget the fate of the only item of clothing I ever dared to buy her: a little black dress as recommended by the lady in the women's fashion section of John Lewis. I spotted it some years later lining the cats' bed, which they rarely used anyway as they almost always seemed to be asleep on ours.

Fighting my way through the mass of humanity, taking avoiding action from time to time to avoid losing an eye to a selfie stick, I walked past the Uffizi Gallery and emerged onto the Piazza della Signoria. Another crowd of people – this time composed mostly of women – were ogling the huge statue of David. This is justifiably reputed to be one of the greatest works of art in the world but all I can say is that it was probably a very cold day when Michelangelo sculpted the part of the statue's anatomy that was attracting most of the attention.

I gradually worked my way across town and by the time I reached police headquarters my mind was firmly back on the case once more. Virgilio welcomed me with a handshake and waved me into a seat across the desk from him. As before, the desk was heaped with files. From one of these, the inspector produced a sheaf of papers and brandished them. As ever, we spoke in Italian.

'These came in this morning. I know you're on holiday but I thought you might be interested.'

'Definitely. I'm still trying to find our murderer but it's tricky. I presume your questioning of Antonio, Maria, and Millicent yesterday morning drew a blank.'

'Nothing new. They all sounded credible. The butler, in particular, was very emotional about his innocence.'

'I noticed that as well, but if it wasn't him, who? The only other possible candidate I have for you is the local mechanic.'

I went on to give him a brief summary of what Tommaso at the bar had said about the Lamborghini and Virgilio promised to get one of his men to question Puppo Marinetti, but he shared my scepticism that the mechanic would have waited ten years to get revenge. I also recounted my conversations with Antonio and Maria, as well as Agatha and Elaine and told him what Diana had just said about poisons. Virgilio made a few notes on a pad and then flicked through the pages in his hands.

'Thanks for all that, Daniel. Anyway, let's start with the victim: Jonah Christopher Moore, fifty-six. Lecturer in English literature at the University of Exeter for ten years until he left in 1999. Presumably he thought he'd hit the big time with his books and gave up teaching. He can't have made much money or he was living beyond his means, because he was declared bankrupt in the UK fifteen years ago, after which he moved to Tuscany. Part-time teacher of English here in Florence until he met and married Maria Campese ten years ago. Things suddenly looked up for him then, at least financially.'

'Any mention of any enemies he might have made? Maybe somebody who lost out big time when he went bankrupt?'

'Nothing registered. There's a note here saying most of his debts were to the UK tax authorities. Evidently, he couldn't pay his taxes. Otherwise, nothing that sheds any light on why he should have been targeted.'

'I'm sure the Inland Revenue don't like people who don't pay their taxes, but they're hardly likely to have sent a hitman to kill him. What about the others?'

'Elaine Daphne Brown, age seventy-four, lives just outside Littlehampton, Hampshire. Unmarried. Worked as a librarian before becoming a full-time author. No criminal record.'

'Either the library where she worked was unlike any library I've ever been to, or she really has one hell of an imagination. I'm reading one of her erotic books at the moment and it would make your hair curl.' Considering his shaved head this probably wasn't the ideal expression to use, but he got the message. 'What about her friend, Agatha, with the blue hair?'

'Agatha Rosemary Kirby, age seventy-six, widowed eleven years ago, also lives in Littlehampton. Worked for thirty-five years in admin at Hampshire Constabulary. A glowing reference from the chief constable, no less, when she retired. Not a stain on her character either.'

This made me wonder whether there might even be budding erotic novelists lurking among my old staff at the Met. I couldn't immediately think of any, although Paul Wilson did have a rather fine turn of phrase. And then there was Sergeant Harris in victim support, and she had a bit of a reputation as a man-eater...

Meanwhile, Virgilio was still checking through the printouts. 'Professor Diana Forsythe, forty-seven, divorced eight years ago, lives in Bristol and teaches history at the university. Another one with no criminal record.'

'No surprises so far. What else have you got for me?'

'There's Mr Gavin Mackenzie-Pearce, age twenty-nine. Dropped out of university and doesn't seem to have done very much since. His address is given as Mayfair, London and even I know that places there don't come cheap. His father, Sir Lionel Mackenzie-Pearce, appears to own half of England.'

'So no shortage of money for young Gavin.'

'Definitely not, as long as Papa's happy to keep subbing him. Since leaving university Gavin has bummed around, spent a number of years in

Southeast Asia on the hippy trail, and while he was over there he must have bumped into Emily Gardner, age twenty-seven. She finished university a few years back and has also been drifting since.'

'Sounds like they're made for each other. What about the rest of the suspects?'

'Now it begins to get more exciting. First, there's the course tutor, Serena Kempton, age thirty-nine. She's an interesting one. She worked as British Airways cabin crew for twelve years before serving eighteen months in Welikada Prison in Sri Lanka for drug smuggling. Needless to say she lost her job with BA and as far as I can see, she's been working in a pub in Manchester since she came back to the UK early last year.'

'Well, well.' Thinking about it, with her hippy looks an involvement with drugs wasn't that surprising, although I hadn't expected somebody as meek and mild as her to have a criminal record. Something told me Serena would warrant closer investigation. 'Come to think of it, on the first night there was talk of her former girlfriend – they've since broken up – and her name sounded Indian. I wonder if they met over there, maybe even in the jail.' My memory banks suddenly belched out the information. 'Lihini, I think she said. That just leaves us with Charlotte. Don't tell me she has a criminal record.'

'No, Charlotte Thompson, forty-nine years old, widowed last year. Works for a big printing company in Bridgwater, Somerset. Not even a late library book, but there is one other person, and this is where it gets really interesting.'

The name I'd overlooked came to me while he was still speaking: 'Of course, Millicent.'

'Indeed. Millicent Hermione Moore, sister of the victim, age sixty-two, teaches at the University of Warwick. She's unmarried, but twenty years ago she was engaged to be married, but he died.' He raised his eyes from the sheet of paper and looked me straight in the eye. 'Ask me how he died.'

'A dagger to the heart?'

'Good try but wrong. The coroner's report records his death as accidental. He died after mistaking an *Amanita phalloides* for an ordinary field mushroom, even though he was an experienced forager. I've just looked up *Amanita phalloides*. Its common name in Italian is *angelo della morte* and in

English it's death cap. You may be interested to hear that it kills numerous people throughout the world every year and it might even have been used to kill Emperor Claudius two thousand years ago. Millicent and her fiancé ate together that night but apparently she doesn't like mushrooms. Lucky, really...'

'Wow, that's quite a coincidence. You interviewed her yesterday, didn't you? How did she come across?'

'She won't win any prizes for personal charm, but she answered all my questions without any obvious hesitation. I wouldn't want to sit next to her at a dinner party, but I came out of the interview feeling pretty sure she had nothing to do with her brother's death. This report might make me change my mind. That's what I wanted to see you about: how would you feel about trying to sit down with her and getting her to talk?' He waved a calming hand as he saw my expression. 'It's all right; I'm not asking you to take her out on a date, but I just thought if the opportunity arises, you might like to have a go.'

'I'll try, but she's about as approachable as a

rabid dog. I'll also see if I can get Serena talking. Sounds like she must have a few tales to tell. Prison in Sri Lanka can't have been a lot of fun. That sort of thing can seriously affect a person.' Another thought occurred to me. 'By the way, did you mention that Jonah had been poisoned to any of them?'

He shook his head. 'No, but after receiving this report about her fiancé and the mushrooms, I think it's time we queried it with Millicent. If you can manage to question her about it, please do.'

'Okay, I'll see how it goes. You never know, I might be able to shock a reaction out of her.'

Virgilio dropped the sheaf of papers onto his cluttered desk and leant back in his chair. 'It's not an easy case to crack, this one.'

'You can say that again. Apart from anything else, there's the small matter of *three* attempts being made on Jonah's life at the same time. Does that mean it was one person hedging his or her bets or three different perpetrators? Who's your money on?'

'It strikes me we've got a number of people with a motive but few have the opportunity. The oleandrin poison in the bottle wouldn't have had an immediate effect and so could have been put in at an earlier stage, but the cyanide in the glass must have been shortly after the butler left – assuming he didn't put it in there himself – and the dagger to the heart not long after that. There's a brief window of opportunity between the end of lunch – when the others claim to have seen the victim still alive and alone with the butler – and the start of the seminar for some, while others went down to the pool. Agatha and Professor Diana claim to have been in their rooms for the next hour or so without witnesses but I don't honestly see either of them as the murderer. Assuming the four Americans are out of the equation, that only leaves us with the widow or the butler, or maybe the mechanic from the village although I wouldn't hold my breath as far as he's concerned. I suppose there's also just an outside chance of person or persons unknown getting in and out unseen but, again, it isn't very likely, particularly as it seems nothing has been stolen.'

'And our only witness is the dog, who saw the whole thing.'

'Ah, yes, the dog. Pity he can't tell us who did it.'

At that moment there was beep from my phone. It was from Maria and it said simply:

Outside Palazzo Pitti 5.30

'That's my ride home, but it's not until five thirty. I came down in the minibus with the rest of them – all but our drug lord and his new fiancée. You got time for a coffee before I go and see the sights?'

Virgilio waved weakly in the direction of the accumulation of paperwork on his desk. 'You go and have fun. I'm probably going to be stuck here for the next twenty-four hours. I'll see you lunchtime on Sunday. Twelve thirty okay?'

I spent the next two hours walking through the streets of Florence, doing my best to concentrate on what I could see around me today rather than what had happened to Jonah Moore. I took a load of photos and visited two different churches, as well as the Medici Riccardi Palace, which would hopefully figure heavily in my book. Inside the imposing stone exterior was a delightful series of high-ceilinged rooms with frescoes and marble floors as well as the famous Chapel of the Magi, its walls completely covered in medieval scenes. By the time I emerged, I had successfully banished the mysterious death of Jonah Moore from my mind, but not for long. A newsagent's in a side street had an impressive array of foreign newspapers on display and among these was yesterday's copy of *The Times*. As my eyes ran over the front page, I was struck by a small article near the bottom on the right.

British Author Murdered

British author Jonah Moore (56) has been found stabbed to death in his luxury villa in Tuscany. See page six.

Intrigued, I went in and bought the paper. It was almost five by now so I made my way back along Via Tornabuoni with its eye-wateringly expensive designer shops until I reached the river. On the other side of the Ponte Santa Trinità, I came across a gelateria with tables outside in the shade where I ordered a big glass of sparkling water and a bowl of strawberry, banana, and kiwi ice cream. I read the short article on page six of the newspaper while I had my very refreshing afternoon snack. There was a grainy photo of Jonah receiving his dagger award along with a brief biography, mentioning his one bestselling book. As far as the murder itself was concerned, the article merely said that the Italian police were still investigating. And that was that.

A glance at my watch told me I needed to make a move. After hastily shovelling down the last of the ice cream, I picked up the paper and headed for the rendezvous point, reflecting that Jonah would probably have been proud to have made it to the front page of *The Times*, even if the newspaper had devoted barely a few lines to his life and death.

The opportunity to sit down and talk to Serena came sooner than I'd hoped. At six thirty that evening, I came out of my room and found she had just come up the stairs and was grasping the handle of the little door leading up to the tower in the middle of the roof. I seized my opportunity.

'Hi, Serena, are you going up to the tower? I don't suppose I'd be allowed to come and take a look by any chance?' She didn't need to know that I'd already been up there.

She looked as though she was just emerging from a dream.

'Hi, Dan, um, yes, of course. Come on up.'

I followed her up the narrow staircase into the dovecote and made a show of admiring the room and the views as if for the first time.

'Did this used to be a dovecote?'

She nodded. 'A lot of the houses around here had them. Maria says it was to provide people with a constant supply of fresh eggs and meat well out of the way of foxes and poachers down at ground level.'

She had tied her hair in a ponytail and changed into yoga pants and a tight top but she was still looking shell-shocked. I tried to engineer the conversation – such as it was – around to Tuesday's events. I started by trying to get her talking about where we were currently standing.

'If I had the great good fortune to own a villa like this, with a tower room like this, I'd spend all my time up here. The views are amazing.' And they were.

A hint of a smile appeared on her face, and this was just about the first time that I'd seen her look even vaguely happy. 'I completely agree. I come up here when I can. It's so quiet and peaceful. It's the perfect place for yoga.'

For the first time I realised the significance of the rubber roll in the corner.

'Do you do a lot of yoga?'

'Every day if I can. Apart from being such good exercise, I find it wonderfully calming and sooth-ing.' She caught my eye. 'And we all need calming and soothing this week, don't we?'

'Too true.' A glimmer of an idea came to me. 'Where did you learn yoga? Over here or while you were in Welikada?'

An expression of almost panic spread across her face to be replaced almost as quickly by one of res-ignation. She slumped down on the arm of a fine old sofa facing out in the direction of Florence. 'You know about that, do you?'

'Eighteen months in jail in there can't have been much fun.' She didn't look up and she didn't reply.

'Listen, Serena, that's all in the past. It came up when the police did a background check on all the villa's guests. It's standard procedure. Nobody's accusing you of anything.'

I had to wait a long time for a reply. When it came, it was delivered in a monotone voice. 'It was my own stupid fault. A friend asked me to take a package back to the UK, and the Sri Lankan customs opened it at the airport and found it contained drugs. I should have known better... I did know better, but I still did it.'

'And was your time in prison bad?'

For the first time she looked up. 'My time in Welikada was awful, truly awful. I can't begin to describe it to you. It was only yoga and a dear friend that got me through it.'

The thought that had occurred to me in Virgilio's office raised its head once more. 'And might that friend have been Lihini, who was here with you last year, by any chance?'

There was a flash of something in her eyes – surprise, anger maybe, but also deep sadness. 'Yes.'

'But I gather from what you said that the two of you broke up?'

Now there was just sadness in her eyes. 'We didn't break up. She died last August.'

'I'm sorry to hear that.' I felt sorry for adding to her sadness but I had to ask. 'What happened?'

There was an inevitability about her answer. 'Overdose.'

'I'm sorry. Did she at least enjoy her stay in Tuscany with you in the summer?'

The expression on her face said it all. 'It was a disaster.'

I would have liked to ask what had happened but I could see that she was barely holding herself together so I let her off the hook for now. 'That's such a pity. Listen, Serena, these things happen but life goes on. You'll maybe never get over it fully, but time is a great healer and these things do take time.' I pointed at her yoga mat. 'I'm sorry, I interrupted your yoga session. I'll leave you in peace.' I was heading for the door when I heard my name and glanced back.

'Dan... thanks.'

She looked very vulnerable and I could suddenly see the naïve young woman whose momentary indiscretion had so screwed up her life. Thank God she wasn't my daughter.

Seeing as there was still time before dinner, I went out into the garden and headed for the now familiar bench in the shade and was delighted to meet my four-legged friend amid the trees, snuffling about among the dead leaves. The moment he saw me, he came bounding over and almost knocked me on my back under the impact of his enthusiastic greeting. I sat on the bench and he gradually settled down beside me while I stroked him. One thing was for sure: if things really were over between me and Helen, I was going to get myself a dog.

Once he had subsided onto the ground at my feet, I took out my phone and called Tricia. If Jonah's murder had made it into the British press, it was only fair she heard about it from me.

'Hi, Dad, how's it going?'

'Hi, sweetheart, the course is fine but something's happened.' I went on to relate the events of the past few days and her reaction was not unexpected.

'So you're back to being a policeman again. I

might have known.' She sounded exasperated but sort of in a good way, like me trying to tell Oscar off when he almost managed to knock me over. It was just the way the dog and I were made and my daughter understands that about me, even if her mother never really did. 'Just tell me you aren't going to give up on the course so you can play detective again.'

'No, I promise. The course is actually turning out to be pretty useful and I spent all this afternoon walking around Florence taking photos and collecting details for my book.' I decided to leave out the fact that I had also spent half an hour at the *questura*.

'So what about the murder of this chap? Is everybody terribly upset?'

'Some more than others.' I also thought it wiser not to tell her that my fellow residents were all possible murder suspects and I repeated what I'd just said to Serena. 'But life goes on. To be honest, he was no great loss to humanity.'

We chatted and she told me about work – she had just finished her articles to qualify as a solicitor – and about Shaun, her regular boyfriend of several years now. I asked her if she'd heard from her mother, and I definitely caught hesitation before she answered. 'She called last night. It's going well. She's enjoying herself.'

'Oh, good.' What else could I say? 'Say hi from me next time you talk to her.'

She just said, 'Of course,' and we left it at that.

After ringing off, I left Oscar to his stroll and went inside for a beer. There was a fridge in the seminar room for course participants and an honesty box for payment. Two euros per beer or per glass of cold white wine seemed pretty fair to me so I was only too happy to drop in a couple of coins and help myself to the coldest bottle of Peroni in there. I swallowed half of it in one go and heard a voice at the open French windows.

'You look as if you needed that.'

It was Charlotte and she was looking as alluring as ever. I wandered across. 'You can say that again. After an afternoon tramping about in the hot sun, it certainly hits the spot. What's that thing about mad dogs and Englishmen? Can I get you a drink?'

She shook her head. 'No, thanks. I'm saving myself for dinner. I've developed a taste for the local white, but if I start drinking before I eat, you'll have to carry me up to bed afterwards.'

The way she said it I got the feeling, probably unwarranted, that she might like that to happen. I immediately changed the subject. Once again, I pretended to myself that I didn't know why I was refusing to flirt. But I did know, really.

'What did you think of Florence?' I thought it best to stick to prosaic stuff.

'It's gorgeous but oh so many people. I'd like to go back again, but not in mid-summer. I'll make sure it's out of season next time. What about you, did you find some stuff for your book?' If she was disappointed that I didn't react to the carrying-to-bed comment, she didn't show it. Maybe I was just imagining things.

We chatted about my book and her plans for an erotic novel – which sounded as flimsy as the pants, panties, knickers, or bloomers or whatever they were called in Fanny Lovesit's books – until we were joined by, of all people, Millicent. She rarely mixed with us and I wondered what might have brought her here. I was on my second bottle of beer by this time so I asked her if I could get her a drink. To my surprise she accepted a glass of white wine. I made the same offer to Charlotte once more but she shook her head and said she was going up to her room to change. This very conveniently left me alone with Millicent but, after I'd poured her a glass of wine and was just about to start quizzing her, Antonio arrived and started bustling about, setting the table for dinner. I was already rueing the missed opportunity when Millicent pointed to the French windows.

'Shall we go outside and give Antonio some space to work?'

I wouldn't say she sounded friendly by any means, but it did sound as if she wanted to talk and that was a first. I wondered if she had something on her mind and followed her out onto the terrace, where the bulk of the villa now provided welcome shade from the sun even though this was low in the western sky. We walked to the far end of the terrace, where she stopped and set her glass down on the balustrade before turning towards me.

'Do you mind if I ask you a question, Dan?'

'Not if I can ask you one afterwards.'

'All right.' She hesitated, searching for the right

words before finally giving it a go. 'Do you really think that one of us is the murderer?'

'Yes, I do.' The answer came automatically. I didn't even need to think about it. 'The odds on somebody sneaking in from outside, killing your brother, and then sneaking out again without being seen are a thousand to one. I see no alternative: it has to be somebody currently staying here.'

She just nodded, reached for her glass and took a mouthful of wine. Then there was a long silence. I deliberately didn't interrupt. She was the one who had initiated this conversation so it was up to her to carry it on. Finally, she looked up from her glass.

'You said you had a question for me. What is it?'

'Assuming that I'm right and the perpetrator is among us, who do you think it is? Still Maria? That was your first reaction, after all.'

'Technically that's two questions, but I'll answer anyway. To be completely honest, the answer is no. I'm not so sure now that she did it. I'm afraid I'm beginning to believe that it has to be Antonio. It pains me greatly. I've always got on well with him, but I can't see how it could have been anybody else.'

'So you're telling me you think the butler did it?'

'I'm telling you I think the butler *might* have done it. I'm not at all sure.'

'There's a story going around that you threatened your brother with a knife just before we all arrived here at the villa. Is that right?'

She straightened up and I saw her take a deep breath. 'Yes, but like I told the inspector it was just a moment of frustration. I would never have stabbed him in a million years. Like it or lump it, he is... he was my brother.'

I found myself coming around to Virgilio's opinion. She might not be a laugh a minute, but she didn't sound like a murderer. So did this mean it really had been Antonio, (aka Count Dracula)? I still couldn't see it, but if not him then who else was there? As a last resort, I brought up the subject of poison.

'Do you know anything about poison?' I watched her face very closely as she registered the question.

'Poison? No, of course not. Why poison? Are you trying to tell me he was poisoned? I didn't see him – Antonio and Maria said it was too gruesome and they wouldn't let me into the dining room after they found him – but everybody says he was stabbed.'

She looked confused, amazed, indignant even, but not suspicious and not guilty. I wondered whether to mention what had happened to her fiancé with the toxic mushrooms, but there seemed to be little need. If she was our poisoner – or *one* of our poisoners – she was a masterful actor and would surely be able to convince any jury of her innocence.

8

SATURDAY

When I woke up on Saturday morning, I still had poison on my mind, but not in connection with Millicent now. I had gone up to bed quite early and, as I wasn't feeling particularly tired, I downloaded a book, *Fluttering Hearts* by Felicity Farnborough, (aka Agatha). This, like Elaine's books, was an erotic novel, although far less hardcore than her shy little companion's offerings, and with a generous shot of whodunit thrown in for good measure.

To be honest, it wasn't a bad book and there were clear similarities – not physical ones – between her nymphomaniac detective inspector and Agatha herself: always asking questions, although how her detective found the energy after bonking almost every man – and several women – she met, I found it hard to comprehend. I read it quite willingly and rather liked the surprise ending where the villain fell to his death from a hot-air balloon. Her thirty-five years with Hampshire Constabulary showed through in much of the detail and she was clearly familiar with the jargon. But I suddenly sat up and took notice in particular when the fitness instructor/drug dealer with the rock-hard abs (her words, not mine) was killed off by Cressida, the delightful nymph (sic) using none other than a poison made from a distillate of the flowers and leaves of the humble foxglove. Clearly Agatha, like Diana, knew her stuff when it came to poisons. As Diana had said: it was just a question of research.

If you Google *poisons* as I did that night, you'll find a wealth of information about deadly and not so deadly poisons that exist all around us in plants and animals, ranging from highly poisonous frogs in the Amazon to our friend the oleander just outside the front door of the villa. The process of turning this and other naturally poisonous plants into a deadly concentrate is remarkably simple and

I couldn't help wondering why whoever spiked Jonah's bottle of wine hadn't used a lethal dose. Either they didn't follow the instructions – which are far from complicated – or they only intended to make him very sick, but not actually kill him. So this might well mean we should be looking for person or persons intent on killing him with cyanide and a dagger plus somebody else whose intention was merely temporary bodily discomfort rather than murder.

Could this person even be Agatha, seeing as she clearly had knowledge of such things? Considering that this was her third visit to the villa, this scenario seemed unlikely. Why wait until her third visit to poison Jonah? And why do so anyway? Apart from being a fairly obnoxious human being, what could Jonah have done to a woman twenty years his senior to incite her to wreak such radical revenge? Nothing came readily to mind. He had lived here in Tuscany for fifteen years and before that he had worked at the University of Exeter. From what Virgilio had told me yesterday, Agatha had spent her life in Hampshire and it was extremely unlikely that the two of them would have come into contact with each other anywhere but here. Of course, just because it was unlikely didn't mean it was impossible, but if I were in Virgilio's shoes, I wouldn't be locking her up just yet.

And the same applied to Professor Diana. She, too, had made it clear yesterday that she also knew about poisons but how could Jonah have so aggravated a middle-aged university lecturer that she had come all the way to Tuscany with the intention of trying to kill him, or at least make him very sick? Of course, there was the possibility that she and Jonah might have crossed swords professionally at some time in the past but academic jealousies rarely escalated to more than fisticuffs in the quadrangle or, these days, a bit of bad-mouthing on social media. But if it wasn't Agatha and it wasn't Diana, who was it?

This conundrum was still going around in my head when I got down for breakfast. The room was empty apart from Antonio, and I assumed this might be because it was Saturday and there weren't any classes so people had opted for a long lie-in. Poor old Antonio looked dreadful, and considering he usually looked like one of the undead, today he really was a grim sight. If anything, he was even thinner than ever and his pale features were blood-less and drawn. The dark waistcoat he always wore was literally hanging from his bony shoulders. Al-though I had a sinking feeling there was a very good chance that he would be charged with murder some time soon, I took pity on him and went over to do my best to cheer him up.

'Hi, Antonio. It's another beautiful morning. Do you get a day off today as well?'

He nodded morosely. Clearly, the idea of time off meant little or nothing to him at the moment. 'Good morning, sir. Today's my free day but I won't be doing anything special.' He caught my eye. 'How can I watch a match or go fishing when the sword of Damocles is hanging over me?'

The classical reference was impressive, as was his obvious wretchedness. Like Millicent, if he was acting, he was doing it really well. 'Try not to worry, Antonio. As far as I know, the inspector hasn't found any conclusive proof of guilt by anybody yet. If you are innocent like you told me, you should have nothing to worry about, so try to cheer up.' I was aware as I said it that it was probably like telling a zombie not to eat human brains but I genuinely felt sorry for the guy. The more I saw him and got to know him, the less credible it was that he could be our murderer. But if it wasn't Antonio, then who?

'Your usual cappuccino, sir?' In spite of his worries, he was still a red-hot waiter.

'Yes, please, and some fresh orange juice please.'

He went off to get my drinks and I helped myself to a couple of warm croissants and took a seat, looking out of the French windows into the garden. I spotted Emily, up remarkably early. From her wet hair I assumed she'd been for an early morning swim. I didn't feel like a run this morning but decided that a swim later on might be a good idea. I'd used the pool a couple of times now and the water temperature was perfect. Mind you, there were lots of places on my must-see list that I hadn't visited yet: San Gimignano, Siena, Volterra...

'Morning, Dan, can I join you?' It was Charlotte. From the state of her hair she, too, had just been for a swim.

'Yes, of course. I've just been thinking about

where I want to go today. You know, for research for my book.'

'Not back to Florence, I hope. On a sunny Saturday it'll be packed out.' She helped herself to a bowl of fresh fruit salad and took a seat opposite me. She was wearing a light top that clung to her slightly damp body and she looked good. With her fair skin and freckles, she had pretty obviously been avoiding the sun but she looked fit and healthy all the same. And, if I was honest with myself, very desirable.

'Definitely not Florence.' I made a decision. 'I think I'll try Lucca. It's supposed to be a very historic city.'

'Want company?'

The honest answer was no. If I was on my own I could poke around unhindered, stopping where I wanted and doing what I wanted, but I don't like to be rude. Besides, company – particularly female company – was something I'd missed over the past months.

'Yes, of course, if you don't mind traipsing around the back streets and in and out of old churches.'

'Sounds lovely. What time are you thinking of setting off?'

We left at ten o'clock. My upgraded rental car was a Volkswagen Golf and it was brand new. Most importantly, the aircon worked really effectively, which was just as well since the digital thermometer outside the chemist in Montevolpone indicated a temperature of twenty-nine degrees as we drove past. It was going to be a hot one. Beside me, Charlotte had clearly anticipated the high temperature as she had changed into a short skirt. Having a pair of bare legs beside me was something else I'd missed over the past months.

I'd been studying the map and had decided to avoid the *autostrada* or the *superstrada* (I think the difference is that you pay for one but not the other, but I might be wrong) and stuck to the ordinary roads. We followed the meandering River Arno for a while, heading west, and along the side of the road we passed potteries producing immense terracotta urns, pots, and statues. I wondered idly how much EasyJet would charge me in excess baggage if I bought a replica statue of David. Probably several times more than the total fare. Thought of air tickets reminded me that I had paid extra so as to be able to change my return flight, currently booked for a week's time. The idea was that I might want to stay on for a holiday at the end of my course and I was still trying to make up my mind what to do. I definitely liked this area but would I enjoy a week or two completely on my own? Mind you, if I went back to the flat in Bromley, it wasn't as if there was anybody waiting for me there, was there?

We chatted as we drove along and Charlotte told me the sad story of how her husband of over twenty years had been killed by a truck while out on his bike one day the previous summer. From the way she talked about him, it was clear she had loved him dearly and I found myself comparing the heartache of losing a loved one in an accident to the pain of separation and divorce. Unwillingly, I found myself telling her more about why it hadn't worked out for Helen and me. She asked almost the exact same question that Mikey/Martin, the big American, had asked me the other night.

'Was it your job? Did you work unsocial hours?'

'Partly, but I suppose if I'm honest, we just

drifted apart after our daughter left home. Helen, my wife, probably needed me more, but I was too caught up with my work to realise it until it was too late.'

'So did she leave you?'

'Indirectly. I moved out, but she's the one who wanted us to split up.'

'And do you wish you were still together?'

I took my time before replying. It wasn't an easy question to answer. I saw a sign off to the left for San Miniato and turned onto a narrower road that started to wind slowly uphill. I'd read about San Miniato. By all accounts it was a historical little town with a whole host of medieval and Renaissance buildings, starting with its very own duomo.

'Sorry, I shouldn't have asked.' She sounded apologetic.

'No, it's a fair question. The answer's probably a qualified yes. Yes, I miss her. Yes, I wish we were back together and things were like they used to be but, deep down, I feel things will never be like they used to be again.'

'I'm sorry.'

She briefly laid a soothing hand on my bare

knee, but the sensation was anything but soothing. The feel of a woman's hand on my skin was something else I'd been missing out on for a while now. It was a relief when we reached San Miniato and climbed out into the sunshine. I was wearing my old shoes today in a final attempt to see if they would regain some sort of shape after their immersion in the pool. For some reason, since drying, the toes were stubbornly pointing upwards like clown shoes and as we set off into town I could feel them chafing not only my toes but my heels as well. I had a feeling this might have been a big mistake.

We spent a most enjoyable morning wandering around the little town, which was buzzing with life on a Saturday morning but many of the people we met looked as if they were locals, not tourists, and the atmosphere was quintessentially Italian, rather than cosmopolitan, and I liked that. I even stopped at a house agent's window and checked out the properties to rent. There were quite a few and they cost a fraction of what I was paying back home. I even glanced at a few of the properties for sale and saw that they, too, were loads cheaper than London. Now there was an idea; maybe I should give up the flat in Bromley and move here. My pension would go a whole lot further if I did. Of course, this would separate me from Helen all the more. Appealing as it sounded, it was maybe a step too far – at least for now.

San Miniato was an exceptional little place. Despite being a third of the size of Bromley, it boasted a twelfth-century cathedral, the remnants of a medieval castle, and an eleventh-century bishop's palace. The town was built on a series of hills and there were very few flat roads. We walked through the *centro storico*, where the narrow streets were paved with flagstones and flanked by fine historic buildings mainly painted in a multitude of tints of ochre, varying from cream, through beige and brown to orange: the natural colours of the earth of Tuscany. The views back down towards the valley of the River Arno were far-reaching, and the views behind the town into the Tuscan hills were charming.

We had lunch sitting outside under a parasol in a little square and I surreptitiously slipped off my shoes under the table and let the slight breeze soothe my blisters. There was a family of Germans at a table just along from us but everybody else sounded as if they were Italian. I've always thought that it's best to go to the places the locals frequent rather than risk being ripped off in a tourist trap. My only visit to Italy before this had been to Venice with Helen a few years back. Although we finally found a restaurant with good food at vaguely acceptable prices, we had got royally screwed quite a few times before that. From what I could see of the prices here in San Miniato, it was a whole lot cheaper than Venice, or London for that matter.

The restaurant specialised in fish and seafood so we let the waiter convince us to try a fritto misto. This turned out to be an inspired choice. I loved the mixture of whitebait, prawns, octopus, and squid, just dipped in flour and lightly fried. We each got a heaped plateful accompanied by a refreshing salad of lettuce, tomato, and cucumber, laced with wonderful extra-virgin olive oil and old-fashioned red wine vinegar. We shared a bottle of sparkling mineral water and a half-litre carafe of cold red wine. I could almost hear my old super, who was a real wine snob, scoffing but in a temperature of thirty degrees plus, from the fridge was definitely the way to go. We rounded the meal off with panna cotta splashed with syrupy blackberry puree and followed it with two little espresso coffees and I was already wondering how I could engineer another visit to San Miniato before I left Tuscany. A meal this good had to be repeated.

'That was one of the best meals I've ever had.' Charlotte insisted on paying half and sounded as though she had enjoyed it as much as I had. I made a quick decision.

'Completely agree. Why don't I bring you back here one evening next week for the same again – my treat this time?'

She caught my eye and grinned. 'Are you asking me out on a date?'

'I suppose I am... if you like.' A shot of excitement, tempered almost immediately by a liberal helping of guilt, ran through me. It had been a long time since I had done anything like this before. But what about Helen?'

She gave my leg a little squeeze. 'That sounds wonderful. I can't wait.'

The drive across country to Lucca took almost an hour on minor roads and we passed through a series of pretty little villages en route. The road ran along the broad, flat base of the valley of the Arno where the surrounding scenery was no longer the undulating hills of Tuscany. Down here it was featureless and fairly boring; however, the plethora of ancient stone buildings in villages along the way and the bulk of the Apennines to our right made it scenic in its own way. I couldn't help noticing that oleanders grew wild around here in huge pink, red and white clumps. Evidently there was no shortage of raw materials for any would-be poisoner.

As we drove along, I glanced across at my passenger from time to time. She looked happy, but maybe not totally at ease. Whether this was simply because she was uncomfortable at finding herself with a man again, considering that the death of her husband had only been a year ago, or because of the investigation, was hard to call. Of course, theoretically she was still a murder suspect, although with no motive and with a rock-hard alibi I had decided it was probably pretty safe to discount her from any further investigation. For a moment I even started wondering if this might be the beginning of something between us but, of course, nothing could begin until things between me and Helen reached some sort of conclusion.

Lucca lived up to its billing. We parked outside the massive red-brick walls of the *centro storico* and walked – or, in my case, limped as my blisters multiplied – in through an imposing gateway to get to the old town. It was a wonderful mix of buildings, some probably going back a thousand years, and I almost managed to forget my sore feet for a while as I tried to take it all in. The white marble-faced duomo, begun in 1063, with the two-tone pink and white bell tower alongside, were a delight, as were numerous other churches and historic buildings along the way. A sign told us it was possible to walk around the city walls, but the way my feet were feeling, that would have to be for another day and another pair of shoes, if not feet. By the time we sat down for a well-earned cold drink in the stunning oval Piazza dell'Anfiteatro, surrounded by cream-coloured buildings dating back to medieval times, I had taken a load of photos and had made copious notes. Lucca was definitely going into my book. And my shoes into the bin.

Charlotte ordered an iced tea while I tried a

non-alcoholic beer, which turned out to be a lot better than I had expected. She asked me about my job and I asked about hers. I felt remarkably relaxed in her company and we got on very well. She told me about working in a printing firm that produced a lot of paperbacks but she said she couldn't remember seeing anything by any of the course participants. I told her I'd read one by Elaine and one by Agatha but admitted that erotica wasn't really my genre of choice. At one point she even brought up the subject of the murder, which we had both been avoiding so far, and asked if the police had got a suspect. I played down my involvement.

'I have no idea. I might know better tomorrow. I've been invited for lunch with Inspector Pisano.' I went on to explain that I only knew him because he was a friend of my former sergeant. 'But he seems very clued up. Maybe he's got his eye on somebody. Of course, he may prefer not to talk about it. After all, I'm staying at the villa myself and might even be involved somehow.'

She scoffed. 'You? Never!'

'It wouldn't be the first time a police officer has

gone rogue. Why, I might be planning on beating you to death with my beer bottle right now.' I assumed a threatening expression and she shrank back in mock fear.

'But you wouldn't hurt me, would you?' For emphasis, she took hold of my hand on the tabletop and gave it a little squeeze. 'We're friends, aren't we?'

She was right. We were friends, and maybe we might become more than friends.

9

SUNDAY

On Sunday morning I didn't feel like going for a run or even a walk. Antonio had managed to find me some sticking plasters last night, but even in my trainers it was still painful to walk. My old shoes had now been consigned to the waste bin and I knew I definitely wouldn't be sorry if I never touched them again. Downstairs in my flip-flops, I found myself all alone at the breakfast table once more and this gave me time to think.

Yesterday evening when we got back from Lucca, I had left Charlotte downstairs and retreated to my room with the excuse that my feet were killing me. Although this was absolutely true – I swear I had blisters on my blisters by this stage – I knew it was also an attempt to slow things down with her as I was still a married man. Whether my wife was behaving the same way remained the great unknown.

After soaking my feet in cold water in the bidet – yes, I know that's not really what it's supposed to be for but needs must – for ten blissful minutes, I had retired to my bed and downloaded the most recent book by Sabrina Butterfly, (aka Serena). It turned out to be a fascinating tale with a poignant, other-worldly feel to it. Yes, there was some sex, but, to my increasingly expert eye as far as erotic writing was concerned – this was my third, after all – I found this one a genuinely good read. It related the inexorable downward spiral towards self-destruction of a young woman just looking for friendship and I found myself transposing the careworn face of Serena herself onto my image of the main protagonist. It was a disturbingly good fit. Clearly there was a lot of Serena in this book and I emerged from it feeling deeply saddened for the main character but also for the author. Somebody who could write that well shouldn't be so unhappy and I resolved to tell her the first chance I got.

After breakfast, I wandered down to the pool for a bit of exercise and managed to do thirty lengths before calling it a day and coming back out again. I lay there feeling content, staring up at the branches of the massive fig tree overhanging one end of the pool, and all I could hear was the incessant buzzing of wasps, gorging themselves on the ripening fruit. It was another beautiful Tuscan morning and, apart from the minor matter of an unsolved murder, I felt at one with the world and at peace.

It didn't last.

My phone pinged and I stretched down to pick it up. It was an email from Helen. Over the past few months, she normally only communicated with me by staccato text messages about bills mainly, so an email was an exception. It wasn't long, but its impact was hefty.

Dan, I've found somebody else. His name is Timothy and things have been going really well between us. I think the time has come for you and me to divorce. I've spoken to a solicitor and he thinks we should put the house on the market. I suggest you speak to David. Helen.

Short and not so sweet. David was my friendly local solicitor. I'd known him for years and we often played tennis together. I copied and pasted Helen's email into a message to him and just added:

Divorce it is. Please tell me what I need to do next. Thanks.

After pressing *Send*, I lay back and contemplated what had just happened: I was getting a divorce. Of course, it had been pretty clear for months that things had been heading in that direction but I now realised that all along I'd been hoping it wouldn't happen. But it had. What did this mean for me, for the rest of my life? Well, I told myself, in an attempt to look on the bright side, it meant that if things were to progress between me and Charlotte, I wouldn't need to feel guilty. It also meant that if I were to decide to rent a little place over here and move out of London, there was now nothing to stop me. The downside, of course, was that there would be no more Helen in my life and, after thirty years, that felt strange.

I was still holding the phone so I gave Tricia a call.

'Hi sweetheart, it's me.'

'Hi, Dad. You okay?' From her subdued tone it was obvious she already knew. I tried to soften the blow.

'I'm okay, thanks. She's told you, I'm sure. If it's what's going to make her happy then that's fine with me.'

'Oh, Dad...' She sounded close to tears.

'Don't let it get to you, sweetie.' For a moment I almost let it get to me as well but managed to carry on. 'We both know that your mother and I've been heading in this direction for months now, even if I maybe haven't been prepared to admit it to myself. At least we all now have some clarity.' I searched desperately for something a bit more up-beat before hitting on Tuscany. 'How would you feel about knowing there's a holiday home for you over here in Italy any time you want to come and stay?'

'Are you thinking of buying a holiday home?' At least she sounded a bit more animated.

'Buying or renting. For me it would just be a home. How would you feel if I moved over here? I mean permanently. I've been looking at flights and I can fly from here to Birmingham faster and cheaper than taking the train up from Bromley. Living here would be far less expensive than the UK and I really like it over here.' I hesitated, waiting for a response, and hastened to add, 'But I'd only do it if you don't mind. You know you're the most important thing in my life.'

'Oh, Dad...' I heard her sniffle a bit but then she pulled herself together. 'I think that sounds a great idea. So does this mean you're enjoying yourself over there?'

'Yes, I am.' I went on to describe my day out yesterday but omitted to mention my companion. There would be time for that if ever things developed between me and Charlotte. Thought of partners, of course, made me think of Helen again and I couldn't resist asking: 'Do you know this guy, Timothy? Have you met him?'

'He and Mum came up to Birmingham for

lunch yesterday and I met him for the first time. He's something high up in a big finance company and they turned up in a flashy new Jaguar – you'd have hated it. He's a nice enough bloke but he isn't you, Dad.'

'That's probably just as well, as patently I'm not suited to your mum. I'm glad they did that. That was the grown-up thing to do. I hope you gave them your blessing.'

'What else could I do? It's like you say, if it makes her happy, I'll support her.' Her voice was a bit stronger now. 'And I'll support you, too, Dad. I promise the first thing I'll do if you get a place over there will be to come and help you move in. What sort of place did you have in mind? A penthouse flat overlooking the Ponte Vecchio, maybe?'

'Apart from the fact that places like that no doubt cost the earth, I rather fancy somewhere in the country.' My original idea came to me and as I voiced it, it grew in attraction. 'And the first thing I'm going to do is get a dog.' I went on to tell her about my budding friendship with Oscar and by the end of our conversation she was sounding almost cheerful again.

* * *

At half past twelve, I drove down to Virgilio's place in Scandicci. He lived in the end house of a modern terrace overlooking a murky river. Although it was in a fairly charmless suburb of Florence, there was a pleasantly rural feel to the place among the reeds and lollipop-shaped pines, and the smell of the barbecue was very welcoming. I'm sure my newfound Labrador friend would have agreed. I followed my nose and found Virgilio in the back garden. He was wearing an apron with the torso of the Incredible Hulk printed on it and every time I looked at him all I saw was a green mass of bulging pecs and abs. He followed the direction of my eyes and shrugged apologetically.

'My son's sense of humour. *Ciao*, Daniel, welcome.' The house had one of those sliding folding French windows that effectively opened the whole wall and he turned and shouted through it. 'Lina, he's here. Come and see what an English author looks like.'

A friendly-looking, dark-haired lady appeared, wiping her hands on a cloth, and came out to greet me with a handshake. 'Good afternoon, I'm Lina. It's lovely to meet you.' She waved towards a seat under the awning. 'Do take a seat.'

After shaking hands, I gave her the bunch of flowers I had bought on my way home from Lucca yesterday and put a bottle of Montevolpone red down on the wall alongside the barbecue. 'This is a lovely place.'

Virgilio handed me a cold beer from a cool box and we drank a toast. Predictably, it concerned work. 'Cheers, Daniel. Here's to a rapid resolution of our murder.'

I glanced across at Lina and saw her long-suffering expression. Needless to say, this made me think, yet again, about Helen and something must have shown on my face as Virgilio revealed that he was an observant sort of chap.

'What's the matter, my friend? You're looking a bit down. Something happened?'

All the way here in the car I'd been telling myself to keep this morning's bombshell to myself. This was one of Virgilio's few days off and he didn't need it to be darkened by my news but, before I could stop myself, I was telling them all about the separation and today's email. Their reaction was one of immense sympathy and I found it really touching. Lina came over and squeezed my arm.

'It's probably for the best, Daniel. This way you can make a new life for yourself.'

Her husband joined in. 'Lina's right; think of it as a new beginning.'

I did my best to sound positive. 'To be honest, that's what I have been doing. I'm even thinking of looking for a little place in the country around here and maybe putting down roots in Tuscany.'

Lina looked up with interest. 'What, you mean move over here to live?'

'That's right. I really love it here.'

Virgilio tore himself away from the massive steak he was grilling and clapped me warmly on the back before looking across at his wife. 'I told you he was a bright boy, didn't I? He understands that Tuscany's the best place in the whole world. Good for you, Daniel.'

'Thanks, Virgilio. By the way, I've been meaning to say: call me Dan. Everybody does.'

'Dan, I look forward to having you as a neighbour.' He turned back to the barbecue and as his wife returned to the kitchen, he talked to me over his shoulder. 'Anything new as far as Mr Jonah Moore's concerned?'

I recounted my conversations with Serena and Millicent and repeated my gut feeling that the butler – in spite of everything pointing to the contrary – wasn't our perpetrator. It appeared that Virgilio shared my feeling.

'My boss is on at me to arrest him. He thinks if we bring him in, lock him up, and make him sweat, he'll crack and admit the whole thing.'

'Sounds like my old super. He was a firm believer in locking people up, guilty or not. The fact is, though, I really don't think Antonio did it. I know what you're going to say: if not him then who? Maybe it was somebody outside the family group, maybe from the UK...' A sudden thought came to me. 'When your guys were searching the villa, in particular the murder scene itself, did anybody go through the file of letters on the table in front of the victim?'

He didn't answer immediately as he was obviously tracking back, trying to remember. Finally he replied. 'To be honest, I don't know. I certainly didn't. My sergeant who speaks good English is on vacation and I'm not sure to what extent the others can read and understand English. Why...?' He answered the question before he had finished asking it. 'Of course, the poison pen letters! Maybe there's a clue in there.' He turned towards me. 'Is the dining room still closed off?'

'Yes, the tape was still up when I looked this morning and the seals were unbroken.'

'Great, well in that case I'll come up tomorrow morning and we can take a look together if you can spare the time. No, you have lessons in the morning, so let's make it later on. Why don't I come at the end of the afternoon? Say about five? It can wait a few hours more. Maria reckoned the letters came from the UK, didn't she? If we could match the handwriting with one of your fellow students, that would be a major breakthrough. More to the point, this gives me a perfectly reasonable excuse for not arresting the butler yet.'

'By the way, any joy with Puppo the garage owner?'

'Nothing concrete. My man who interviewed him said it was clear he hated the victim but he claims to have a witness who can testify that he was in his garage all day on the day of the murder, although he didn't come across as totally convincing. We'll check, of course, but he appears to be in the clear.'

'Oh well, worth a shot.'

I watched as he flipped the meat over with a practised hand. I'd never seen such an enormous T-bone steak before – the size and thickness of a King James Bible. A moment later he looked up and grinned at me. 'Paul was dead right.'

'Paul? About what?'

'He told me you were one of the best detectives he'd ever met. I can see why.'

I had no idea how to respond to something like that so I just gave him a smile in return and took a big mouthful of beer.

Lunch was exceptional. It started with slices of the lovely unsalted Tuscan bread to which I was rapidly becoming addicted. Virgilio grilled the bread and then rubbed the slices with raw garlic and soused them in olive oil from an unmarked bottle. The oil itself was thick and green and looked like the kind of stuff you would normally expect to see being drained out of an old engine, but the taste was wonderful: so tangy it tickled the throat. He spooned chopped tomatoes smothered in oil onto other pieces of the toasted bread and we helped ourselves to thin slices of cured ham, freshly carved from a leg sitting in its own special metal holder. Lina told me it would keep for ages like this without needing to go in the fridge, just taking a few slices every now and then, and I immediately told them that if I really did settle down here, the first thing I was going to buy myself would be my very own ham holder. You don't see many of them in Bromley.

Before the meat we had plates of *pappardelle alla lepre*, and it transpired that Lina had been responsible for making not only the rich, gamey sauce but also the broad strips of fresh pasta. By the time the meat arrived, accompanied by grilled skewers of mixed vegetables including slices of aubergine, red peppers, courgettes, onions, and cherry tomatoes, I was seriously worried I was going to have to undo my belt, but it was all too good to refuse. Virgilio sliced the steak vertically and served it sprinkled with a handful of fresh rocket leaves, shavings of

Parmesan cheese, and more of that wonderful oil. This *bistecca alla fiorentina* was without a shadow of a doubt the best meat I had ever tasted and I told him so. Accompanied by yet another unlabelled bottle, this time containing excellent red wine made by a 'little man up the hill', it was a meal fit for a king.

After creamy vanilla ice cream mixed with crushed meringue pieces, accompanied by a fresh fruit salad of white-flesh nectarines and peaches, I had a feeling I wouldn't want to eat again for a week. It had been another unforgettable Tuscan meal. As we sat in the shade and sipped our coffees, I realised I'd almost forgotten about Helen for now. I wondered how long that would last. Virgilio offered me a glass of grappa from, yes, you've guessed it, yet another unmarked bottle, but I thought it prudent to refuse. I was driving after all and although I'd been taking it slow with the wine, it would have been embarrassing to say the least if a former police inspector who had just dined with another police inspector were to be done for driving under the influence.

We spent a lazy afternoon chatting about life in

general and I discovered that we had a shared inter-est: tennis. He told me he'd invite me to his club for a game during the week if he could get away but I told him to make it the end of the week as my blis-ters were still painful, and I recounted the scene at the pool on the first day when the dog had pushed me in. When she had finished laughing, Lina rushed off and brought me a tube of cream, which she assured me would sort me out. As a couple they couldn't have been more hospitable and it was with real regret that I finally bade them farewell and made my way back to the villa.

The first thing I did when I got home was to pull off my shoes and slap ointment all over my sore feet. The mystery cream worked remarkably well and within a few minutes the pain had almost gone. After staying up late last night reading Sere-na's book and after today's massive meal, I lay down on the bed – with my bare feet sticking out over the end – and was asleep within minutes. When I woke up, my watch told me it was past six. I'd been asleep for well over an hour. I was just heading for the bathroom for a much-needed pee when there was a knock at the door. It was Charlotte.

'You've been having a siesta, haven't you?' Her tone was accusing but there was a smile on her face. 'You smell of garlic, but I don't mind. Did somebody have a big lunch?'

'Somebody had an enormous lunch, and an excellent one.'

'Can I come in?'

I stepped back and she walked in. I noticed that she was wearing that same short skirt again and when she perched on the edge of the bed it suddenly became a very short skirt. I did my best to sound nonchalant although the need to pee was becoming more urgent. All that beer and wine and mineral water at lunchtime was surely to blame. I did my best to make conversation.

'I hope you've had a good afternoon.'

'It was fine, thanks. I didn't do much. I was getting bored so I thought I'd come and see you.' She leant back and surveyed the room, a gentle smile on her face. For a second or two I thought I maybe even recognised that expression. If I hadn't been in the middle of a murder investigation, I might even have wondered if it signified interest on her part, although why she might be interested in a middle-aged ex-copper with greying hair was beyond me. However, any further conjecture on my part was extinguished as my body reminded me even more forcibly that I really, really, needed a trip to the loo. I stood there and tried to avoid squirming.

'Erm, was there something you wanted?' It was a struggle just to get the words out.

She just smiled and leant back a bit more. 'Nothing special. Is there anything you want?' That little half smile was still on her face.

Yes, there was as a matter of fact, I wanted to pee, but I could hardly tell her that. Instead, I took refuge in a little obfuscation. 'A bit of time to think, if I'm honest. I had an email from my wife today and my head's all over the place.' Not to mention my bladder.

An expression of understanding plus what might have been regret crossed her face and she stood up, smoothing her skirt against her thighs as she did so. 'I'm sorry. I picked a bad time.' She headed for the door but turned back as she got there. 'What did the inspector say? Is he any closer to solving the mystery?'

'Maybe. It sounds as though he might have

found a new lead. In fact, he's coming back up here tomorrow.'

She looked interested. 'Really? What sort of lead or aren't you allowed to tell me?'

No, I was not allowed to tell her, but there was no point making it sound as though I didn't trust the woman who might even have come here to throw herself at me for all I knew. Once again, I resorted to a little white lie. 'He didn't say. Let's just hope it works.'

She looked disappointed but then gave a resigned shrug. 'Let's hope so indeed. It's creepy living in a house where there's almost certainly a killer.' Her expression brightened. 'If I get scared in the night, I know where to come now, don't I?'

I didn't answer and just smiled gormlessly back at her as she turned and exited. The moment the door closed behind her, I made a run for the bathroom, telling myself that was the only reason I had sent her away, but knowing that it wasn't. Yes, I needed to go to the toilet, but there was more to it than that. Helen might have got over me, but had I got over her?

* * *

When dinner time came, I was amazed to find that I actually felt hungry again, in spite of the huge lunch I had consumed just a few hours previously. I took a seat at the table and was joined by Mikey/Martin on one side of me with Rachel and Will from the DEA on the opposite side. The conversation turned to hockey and both Will and Mikey became animated. It took me a few minutes to work out that what they called hockey was what I would call ice hockey and, by the sound of it, their game seemed to involve lots of big men with no teeth punching each other. Tricia played hockey, the grass version, at school and to the best of my knowledge she'd never punched anybody and still had all her teeth. I was mulling over this fundamental difference between the behaviour of people on opposite sides of the Atlantic when Professor Diana slipped into the free seat to my right.

'Hello, Dan, had a good weekend?' She sounded cheerful and the Caribbean lilt was stronger than ever tonight.

'I've had a great weekend, thanks. Couldn't have

been better.' Apart from that email... for a second or two I caught Charlotte's eye just a bit further along on the other side of the table and she winked, but I hastily returned my attention to Diana. 'What about you? Have you been a tourist or a student?'

'A bit of both. I went into Florence again with Gavin and Emily yesterday, but today I've been writing.' She then went on to describe to the table at large the orgy scene she had been crafting and I realised that I was now able to listen to her graphic description of sexual acts almost without noticing, although I did sit up and take note when she started talking about the emperor and the sheep. Fortunately, by then Agatha and Elaine had joined in and I was able to return my attention to the Americans. Hockey had now been replaced by Italian history as a topic of conversation and I was better prepared to participate.

Antonio and Annarosa appeared with trays of antipasti but I limited myself to a couple of slices of aromatic orange-fleshed melon. I followed this with a very small helping of risotto with porcini mush-rooms, allegedly found in the nearby woods, which was excellent. I only took a couple of small spoonfuls of the chicken casserole that came next but, by the time I'd found it impossible to refuse a serving of tiramisu, I knew I needed to get out for a walk before I exploded. Bidding my fellow students goodnight, I headed for the kitchen in search of my four-legged walking companion. I was wearing my trainers and Lina's magic ointment had done a marvellous job; all I could feel was the slightest hint of sensitivity from my feet so hopefully a short walk wasn't likely to hurt too much.

I found Antonio in the kitchen looking glum while he and Annarosa washed the dishes. It was plain to see that his weekend had been anything but enjoyable, but all I could do for now was to smile and say '*Buona sera*'. If the poison pen letters turned up and we could identify a UK connection, this should take the heat off the butler but I couldn't say anything about that yet.

I got a boisterous welcome from the dog and we set off into the cool of the evening. The sky was cloudy tonight and I wondered if this meant we were in for more rain. The rain that had fallen during the storm the other night had already disappeared into the ground as if it never happened and the bone-dry leaves under my feet were making a crunching noise again. We followed my morning jogging route uphill between the vines and olive trees and although there was no starlight, the pale gravel of the track made it easy for me to find my way up towards the observation point at the top. Oscar trotted alongside me and this reminded me of what I had told Tricia this morning: I needed to get myself a dog. It was so good to have a companion, not least a companion who only needed food, a roof over its head, and frequent walks to make it love you. No fear of divorce with a dog.

Needless to say, thought of divorce brought me back to reality with a bump. I was still thinking about it as we crested the rise and a panorama of shadowy hills loomed into sight. The hills were dotted with tiny pinpricks of light indicating other villas and farms, with the orange glow of Florence in the distance. I sat down on the remains of a collapsed dry-stone wall and surveyed the view. Along with the view, I surveyed my future. The dog wandered over, sat down beside me with a thud and rested his head on my knee. I ruffled his ears and let my mind roam.

I was getting a divorce. The reality of the situation had finally sunk in.

David was a good lawyer and a good friend so I knew I could rely on him to do things right. Selling the house should raise a good bit of capital – we had finished paying off the mortgage just last year – and I assumed half would go to Helen. No doubt a share of my pension would also go to her and that would leave me with limited income. On that basis, and remembering the house prices I had seen in San Miniato yesterday, a move to Tuscany would probably make solid financial sense. Of course, this would mean opening a bank account and probably obtaining some sort of residence permit but even after Brexit that shouldn't be impossible, particularly as I now had a good friend who was a big noise in the local police. Everybody had been telling me that personal recommendation still counted for a lot over here, so hopefully Virgilio would be able to put in a word for me if need be.

The next question was whether to rent or buy. Probably renting in the first instance would be the best idea. That way if I got fed up with it, it would be easier to pack up and leave. Virgilio had told me that this part of Italy could get cold and wet in the winter months and I had never lived out in the countryside anywhere for any length of time before. There was always the chance that I might find it less attractive when the nights started to draw in and the weather turned nasty so it made sense not to get myself anything too permanent until I'd spent a winter here. No sooner had this thought passed through my head than a raindrop landed on me. This was followed by another, then another and soon it was pouring down, so I jumped up and hurried back. At least, I consoled myself, I now knew that my phone was waterproof and I was wearing my trainers, not my new shoes.

By the time we got back to the villa, Oscar and I were both drenched. It was also a lot cooler now but I was far from cold. In fact, it was exhilarating and I decided not to go inside just yet. I headed for the steps above the croquet lawn and sat there, enjoying the feel of the rain streaming down my face and the sound of running water all around me as impromptu little rivulets formed and created puddles. The dog appeared to feel the same way as I did and he was soon rolling about on his back in a puddle, snuffling to himself and growling happily, all four big paws waving in the air and his tail making waves in the water.

I reflected that if Helen could see me now she would be appalled, but not surprised. This, in her eyes, would be just another example of how I've failed to grow up. She often accused me of behaving like a child – so I like skimming stones across lakes, kicking a football about, and laughing at silly sitcoms, who doesn't? – and this would have proved her right. But, so what? For just about the first time, I found myself really taking in what had just happened to me. As Virgilio and Lina had said, I'd been handed the chance to make a fresh start, living my life on my own terms, and that's what I now intended to do. I glanced down at the dog, who had given up on the puddle and was now sitting beside me, leaning against my leg.

'A new start, Oscar, how good does that feel?'

He looked up at the sound of his name and licked my hand. I took that as agreement.

Note to self: must get a dog.

10

WEEK TWO – MONDAY

Monday morning's first session was on the major decisions an author has to make before embarking on a new novel. Things like whether to write in the first person – *I see, I think, I hope* – or through the eyes of a single character – *she ate, she drank, she left* – or as a 'God-like' author who sees what goes on behind doors and reads the characters' minds. I had already decided to go with the latter, but listening to the others, I began to question whether this was in fact the right approach. There was no doubt about it: stripping away the erotica, there was still a lot of interesting stuff in this course and, grudgingly, I had to agree that my former colleagues had got it right. I resolved to send them a postcard to say thank you. Tricia would have been proud of me.

After the mid-morning coffee break, Millicent announced she was going to lead a discussion on how best to write about 'stimulating the most sensuous parts of the body' and I opted out. If it had been *sensitive* parts, I would probably have had to mention my feet, although they were a lot better today, but as far as anything more intimate was concerned, the idea of sitting in a room with a bunch of ladies discussing sexual stimulation had me backpedalling furiously. The others traipsed back inside and I was left with just Mikey/Martin outside on the terrace. He came over and rested against the balustrade beside me.

'I'm glad I got you on your own, Dan. I need to talk to you. I like you. You're a good guy and I wouldn't want anything to happen to you.'

I took a closer look at him. Was this some sort of veiled threat? 'That's good to hear, Martin. For what it's worth, I like you, too, but what sort of something don't you want to happen to me?'

He glanced around to check that we weren't

being overheard. 'It's like this: half an hour ago I
was out here, waiting for Jen to come out of class,
and I was watching Antonio, the butler. He was
laying out the coffees and teas and I couldn't help
noticing something. When he came close to where
I was standing, I couldn't miss the fact that either
he was very pleased to see me or he had a gun in
his pocket.' He caught my eye and raised his palms
to emphasise his innocence of such matters. 'I
mean, who knows? He might have a funny-shaped
cell phone or a couple of rolls of quarters in his
pocket but to an untrained eye I thought it looked
like the shape of a gun. Not that I have any great experience of that sort of thing.'

From what the two DEA agents had told me,
Mikey had quite possibly written the book on concealed offensive weapons, but his words got me
thinking. Both Antonio and Maria had indicated
that Jonah almost certainly had a handgun. Might
the butler have got his hands on it? And if so, why?
Was he planning on killing somebody? If so, who?
Maybe he'd heard that the inspector was coming
back here this afternoon and he was afraid this
would mean his arrest. Was he intending to shoot

his way out? From what I knew of Antonio, that hardly seemed likely. No, the more I thought about it, the more I came around to thinking that the only person he might want to kill might be himself, either to avoid being convicted of a crime of which he was guilty or to spare himself the anguish of being imprisoned for a crime he didn't commit. Either way, I needed to find out what he had in his pocket and, if it was indeed a weapon, to get it off him.

'That's good of you to tell me, Martin. Thank you. I think I'll go and have a little chat to Antonio. As you say, it may be nothing but there's no harm in checking.'

'You take care now.'

He gave me an encouraging punch on the shoulder that sent me reeling backwards. One thing was definite: I wouldn't want to be on the receiving end of a real punch from this guy.

I found Antonio in the kitchen, sipping a cup of coffee at the table. As I came in, he and the Labrador both leapt to their feet but I waved him back into his seat and sat down myself, doing my best to discourage the dog from climbing onto my lap. Antonio looked enquiringly at me.

'Another coffee, maybe? Or some tea?'

I shook my head and paused for thought. I needed to decide how I was going to handle this. Discretion was definitely the better part of valour in these cases. Only once in my career had I had to talk down a man with a gun and the sight of the two huge barrels of the shotgun, like the entrance to the Underground, pointing straight at me still returned to haunt me on occasions. Although I thought it very unlikely in this case, I wasn't too keen on being shot so I decided the best course of action was to tackle the matter obliquely.

'How're you holding up, Antonio? I thought I'd come and see how you are.'

He set his cup down on its saucer and started the familiar hand-wringing again.

'If you really want to know, I think I'm in danger of losing my mind.'

This wasn't the sort of thing you want to hear from a man potentially carrying a lethal weapon, so I set about trying to calm him down. 'There's no need to feel like that. I was talking to the inspector yesterday and neither of us believe you did it.'

He looked up with real interest. 'Is that true? If

so, does that mean you have a suspect?' He had started looking and sounding far brighter and I decided the time was almost right to bring up the subject of the gun.

'I'm not sure about other suspects, but that's what he said about you.' I glanced down at his coffee cup. 'Come to think of it, I could use an espresso if you don't mind.'

'Of course, it'll just take a minute.' He jumped to his feet and as he did so, something heavy made contact with the table, producing a metallic clunk. He was now standing side-on to me at the coffee machine and I realised that Mikey was right. There was definitely something in Antonio's pocket and from here, I had to agree that it looked like a gun. I reached across the table and picked up his heavy stamp album. It wouldn't be much protection against a bullet but if I slung it at him hard enough it might give me time to get out of the door if he decided to use the weapon. The coffee machine suddenly lapsed into silence and he turned towards me with the little cup in his right hand, steaming gently. Hopefully this would further hinder him if he decided to make a lunge for the gun. I took a long, calming breath before speaking.

'Don't you think you should maybe give me the gun, Antonio?'

The silence was suddenly total. He stopped dead and stared down at me with wild eyes. I leant forward onto the balls of my feet, elbows on the tabletop, ready to spring up and make a run for it if he flipped, but then he just sighed.

'It's not what you think, sir.' He sounded deflated, but the gun was still in his pocket.

'I think I know what it's for, Antonio, and we both know that would be crazy. Trust me: the inspector's following a new lead. He's coming here this afternoon specially to check something out. And it's not you. You don't need to be afraid.' I held out my hand, palm upwards. 'Give me the gun, please.'

He bent slightly at the waist and set my coffee down gently in front of me, even turning the saucer formally so that the handle was facing towards me. Then, very slowly, he reached into his trouser pocket with his right hand and pulled out the weapon. My muscles tensed even more but he then just laid it down alongside the coffee and returned to his seat. I started breathing again and he murmured a few words of explanation.

'I couldn't have lived with the shame. I know I'm innocent, but innocent men have been convicted before and I know the effect it would have on me and my family. Signor Jonah kept this thing.' He cast a disparaging glance at the weapon, which was still lying there. 'He kept it in the bedside table, only a metre or two from the *signora*. It's loaded, you know, and there isn't a safety.' He looked up at me. 'Just think: the *signora* might have reached into the drawer for something and shot herself by accident. It's crazy. Take it, please. Just looking at the thing sends shivers up and down my spine.'

I put down the stamp album and picked up the weapon. I hate guns and I knew exactly how he felt as I touched the smooth black metal. I immediately recognised it as a Glock 19 – we trained on these weapons – and it looked brand new. I wondered if it had ever been fired. I located the release button on the side and ejected the magazine. It was full. Fifteen rounds if I remember right. Jonah must have been absolutely terrified of something or someone to keep something like this beside his bed. I slipped the magazine into one pocket and the gun into another and reached for my espresso, reflecting that a glass of brandy or grappa would have had distinct appeal at the moment. I sipped the hot coffee and felt my heart rate drop back from coronary imminent to just crazy fast and then begin to slow down even more. I was very glad I didn't have to do something like this every day of the week.

We sat there and chatted for some time as we both calmed down. I could see that Antonio was relieved both by what I had told him and to have got rid of the weapon. I got him talking about his stamp collection and discovered that the Italian word for his hobby is *filatelia*. This sounded uncomfortably close to some of the acts I'd been reading about over the past few nights but I chose not to tell him. I asked him where he lived and he expressed surprise that I didn't already know.

'Out there.' He pointed towards the back door. 'My apartment's above the old stables.'

'And Annarosa, the cook?'

'She lives in the town with her husband.'

'And has she worked here for as long as you?'

'Longer. Almost forty years, I think.' He looked up with a concerned expression on his face. 'Why do you ask? You don't think Annarosa killed Signor Jonah, do you? She would never...'

I hastened to calm him down. 'No, I was just curious and don't worry, I'm sure neither of you had anything to do with it.' I drank the last of my coffee and looked down at the dog, who had subsided onto the floor at my feet by now. 'I wonder what'll happen to Oscar now that his master's dead. Maria told me she's allergic to dog hair.'

'It's such a pity. I imagine she'll see if she can find a good home for him. I'd take him myself but seeing as I spend most of my time in here I'd either have to leave him on his own or he'd be with me and she'd find herself excluded from her own kitchen.'

'A good home?' A thought occurred to me. 'I'm seriously thinking of settling down over here. If I find somewhere suitable to rent, I might ask Maria if I could take him. He's a lovely dog.'

'I'm sure she would love that and I know he would. He's really taken to you, sir.'

'It's Dan, Antonio, not sir. Okay.'

'Yes, sir... Signor Dan.'

I was about to correct him but decided to leave that for another day. We'd both had enough drama this morning. Instead, I stood up. 'And now, if it's all right with you, I'll take Oscar for a little walk.'

Antonio jumped up and extended his hand towards me. 'Thank you, Signor Dan. I'm really grateful.'

'Don't mention it. I'll just get rid of this thing and then I'll be right back.'

Leaving the Labrador there for a few minutes, I ran upstairs to my room, went into the bathroom and splashed several handfuls of cold water onto my face while I gradually settled down. If Helen had known what I had just done, she would have been horrified. For a moment I spared her a sympathetic thought. It can't have been much fun being married to somebody with a job like mine. Although nothing like as dangerous as being a cop in the US, where so many people have weapons, there was no getting away from the fact that police work anywhere carried with it an unavoidable element of risk. My heart went out to her yet again but, alas, it was now too late for regrets.

I hid the pistol in among my dirty clothes and dropped the magazine into the cistern behind the toilet before retrieving my trainers from the window ledge where they'd been drying in the sun. Although they were still a bit damp inside, they were just about okay so I put them on and hurried back to the kitchen to collect the dog, who was predictably delighted to go for a walk.

On the way around the side of the house, Oscar and I passed the terrace and I saw that Mikey/Martin was still there. I called to attract his attention and gave him a thumbs up.

'Thanks again, Martin. I owe you.'

'You're welcome. Just wanted to help. Enjoy your walk.'

Considering his reputation, he couldn't have been friendlier and there was no doubt he had helped avoid a potentially lethal situation. I couldn't help wondering if the Kray twins would have been equally obliging.

* * *

After an enjoyable walk with the dog, I returned him to the kitchen and found Maria in there, talking to Annarosa. There was a wonderful smell of food coming from the oven – something rich and spicy – and I realised sadly that in spite of all the food I had consumed yesterday, I was hungry again. Amazing thing, the human body.

'*Ciao*, Dan. Did you have a good walk?' Maria was doing her best to sound cheerful but I could see the effort it was costing her. Assuming she was innocent – and I was increasingly convinced of this – it had to be unbearable living in a house where she knew that one of the other residents had killed her husband.

'Oscar and I had a lovely walk, thanks. I wanted to ask you something. I'm seriously thinking about looking for somewhere to rent or buy around here with a view to settling down in Tuscany. I've been talking to Antonio and I was wondering if by any chance you might be looking for a good home for Oscar. I'd be delighted to take him off your hands. I'll pay you, of course...'

An expression of relief spread across her face. 'That's a wonderful idea, but there's no need to pay me anything. I've been wondering what to do with Oscar. He's such a sweet dog and the idea of him ending up being unhappy is too awful, so if you feel like taking him, I'd be only too pleased. I've seen how much he likes you and how happy he is to go walking with you. I'm delighted you're thinking of settling over here. Have you found anywhere yet?'

'To be honest, I only really decided yesterday.' I gave her a brief outline of how things now stood between me and Helen and she reached out a hand to give my arm a sympathetic squeeze.

'I'm so sorry, Dan. Just give it time. You'll get over it.' She managed a little smile. 'If you like I can ask around and see if anybody knows of a place to rent in the area.'

'I'd be very grateful. Thanks.'

That afternoon I decided to do nothing and the best place for this on a glorious sunny day was down by the pool. When I got there, I found that others had had the same idea. Gavin and his girl-friend, Emily, were stretched out on sunbeds and from the unmistakable sound of snoring coming from Gavin, he had just done what he had told me he did so well: he had fallen asleep. I dropped my things on a sunbed a bit further along from them and slipped gratefully into the water. After a wonderful, refreshing swim, I climbed out and settled down on my towel to dry out in the sun. A shadow fell over me and I opened one eye. It was Emily.

'Had a good swim, Dan?' She was standing between me and the sun so I couldn't make out her facial features.

'Just what I needed. What about you two? All well?'

She hesitated and then sat down on a sunbed alongside me. I could see her better now and the expression on her face was troubled. 'We're fine, thanks, just trying to cope with all the uncertainty. Are the police going to arrest somebody sometime soon?' She lowered her voice. 'Gav and I think it might have been Jonah's awful sister. She's such a cow.'

'What makes you think that? Just because she's a bit brusque doesn't make her a murderer.'

'Brusque? She's downright rude. I heard her arguing with Jonah the very first night and I'm sure I heard her threaten him.'

Considering that Jonah had been my height and

Millicent was little bigger than your average lep-rechaun, there was a limit to how threatening she could have been, but I was interested all the same. 'What did she say to him? Can you remember?'

'She called him a lazy pig and said she hoped something bad would happen to him.'

'That's not exactly a threat.'

'Yes, but then I distinctly heard her say, "or I'll do it myself". That's clearly a threat, isn't it?'

'Yes, I suppose it is. Have you any idea what they were arguing about?'

'Money, I think. She kept going on about how she and Serena had to do all the work while he just sat there and preened himself. That's the word she used: "preened".'

'And where were they when you overheard this?'

'In the dining room.'

'And where were *you*? Surely they weren't arguing in front of you.'

For the first time she looked a bit hesitant. 'Gav and I were outside in the corridor.' She hesitated. 'We'd stopped for a little cuddle, to be honest. Anyway, do you think it might have been her?'

'I really don't know.' There was no point letting her think I was too involved. 'The inspector's coming later this afternoon for another sniff around. When I see him, I'll tell him what you said.'

'Sniff around? Do you think that means he's onto something?'

'Again, I really don't know. He said something about a new lead.'

Our conversation was interrupted by a sleepy-sounding voice from further along. 'Hi, Dan. Sorry, Em, I did it again. I'm always falling asleep. You should've given me a kick.'

'You need your beauty sleep, darling. Besides, I've been having a nice chat to Dan. He tells me the inspector's coming back later on.'

'Well, let's hope it's to announce that he's solved the case and he's arresting the killer. It's creepy being here and thinking that there's a murderer among us.'

A few minutes later, they collected their things and headed back to their room, quite possibly for another 'little cuddle'. I lay back and relaxed and couldn't help thinking that a little cuddle would have been rather nice.

Virgilio didn't appear until almost six and he arrived looking apologetic.

'Sorry, Dan, totally swamped today. Some imbecile decided to beat his wife to death with a hammer because he thought she was sleeping with the neighbour. Turns out she was helping the neighbour's daughter with her homework. Sometimes I feel like I'm in the middle of a Greek tragedy with sex and jealousy being the main motivators for some people.'

All the way along the corridor to the dining room with him, I found myself wondering whether the murder of Jonah might also have been a crime of passion. Had his wife murdered him for his infidelities? Had a jilted lover killed him for abandoning her? Had a jealous husband sought revenge for being cuckolded? The possibilities were endless, but I had little time for further conjecture because when we arrived at the dining room door, we got a shock. The plastic tape pinned across the entrance was still there, but the adhesive seals had all been neatly slit. Somebody had been inside. I looked across at Virgilio.

'I came and checked this morning like I do

every day and the seals were intact. Somebody's been in here since then.'

He handed me a pair of gloves and, while I put them on, he opened the door and we stepped between the tapes and went into the room. It looked exactly as I remembered it, except that the wineglass and bottle had been taken to the lab and there were dark patches around the windows where forensics had dusted for fingerprints, but otherwise it was just the same, even down to the few drops of dried blood on the floor alongside Jonah's chair and the folder of letters still lying in front of it. We both made a beeline for the letters and Virgilio waved me on.

'You go. You're the one who speaks English.'

I opened the folder and was just about to start leafing through the sheets of paper when I immediately noticed something and turned back towards Virgilio. 'Somehow I don't think we're going to find anything of interest. The letter that was on top isn't there now.'

'Was it important? Do you think somebody came in here to take it?'

'That's what I don't understand. It was a fan letter, full of glowing praise. I can't remember the name at the bottom but the address was Swansea, I'm sure of that.' I began sifting through the pages and I'd only turned half a dozen before I came across the one I remembered. I lifted it up and waved it in Virgilio's direction. 'Here's the one I saw. Now I come to think of it, I remember the words *truly exquisite writing* and the address is Swansea. I'm sure this is it. Whoever came in here before us must have misfiled it in their haste. What this means is that somebody did exactly what we're doing. They slit the door seals and came in here looking for something among these letters and, for my money, we're both looking for the same thing.'

'The poison pen letters.'

'Exactly. And if that is what happened, we can be fairly sure that this person also wrote the letters and in all probability is our killer, or at least one of them...' I took my time and scanned every sheet but there was nothing here except fan letters, every one of them enthusiastic. Needless to say, Jonah hadn't hung on to any critical ones. As for the poison pen letters, there wasn't a trace. Either they were never here or somebody had taken them. I gave Virgilio a helpless look. 'No sign. Nothing.'

'It's a strange coincidence that somebody chose to come in here just a few hours before us. If they were that worried, why didn't they do it days ago?'

I've never liked coincidences. Time and time again in my working life I had come up against apparently chance events that then turned out to have nothing to do with chance. I racked my brains and the answer came back very quickly. It was almost certainly my own fault. 'Stupidly, I told a few people you were coming and that you were following up a new lead. All right, I didn't say you were looking for the letters but even so...' I could have kicked myself. Talk about a rookie mistake. 'I told Antonio this morning and I told Emily and Gavin this afternoon. Come to think of it, I also told Charlotte last night so it's quite possible that the word spread to all of the inhabitants of the villa. Christ, Virgilio, I should have known better.'

'Don't blame yourself. In fact, in a way, this helps us. If we'd still been in any doubt as to whether somebody from outside might have been the culprit, this proves conclusively that our murderer – or at least one of them – is right here.'

'And, once again, they've almost certainly been able to slip in and out of this room unseen. I suppose we could try checking everybody's movements over the course of today but I doubt if we'll get any surprises.'

While Virgilio was debating his next move, I remembered the gun and ran upstairs to get it. I fished the magazine out of the cistern and dried it before wrapping it and the pistol in a page torn from my old copy of *The Times* and bringing it back down to the dining room, where I handed it over to him.

'Can you do something with this, please? It belonged to the victim.' I went on to relate the events of this morning and he looked gobsmacked.

'You just asked the butler for it and he gave it to you? You English are crazy. He could have shot you.'

'I don't think he's the sort. Besides, I was pretty sure his intentions were towards self-harm, not shooting at somebody else.'

He clearly remained unconvinced but accepted the package and slipped it into his pocket. 'Interesting that the American tipped you off. I wouldn't have expected his kind to be the sort to help the police, even a *retired* police officer.'

'I know what you mean but somehow I like the guy. It may well be that the two DEA agents are right about him but since he's been here he's been nothing but sweetness and light. He did me – and Antonio – a big favour and I owe him.'

'What about the butler? We could arrest him for stealing, and stealing a deadly weapon would give us the excuse to lock him up. That way I get more time to build a case against him and everybody here can sleep more easily. My boss would be happy.'

'We both know you're going to need more than that to prove that he's our murderer, and I genuinely don't believe he is. The more I think about it, the more I'm convinced these poison pen letters are vitally important. And if they were in English, I'm definitely coming around to thinking that the murderer could well be a Brit, almost certainly somebody who's here now. After all, who else would have had the opportunity to get in here today? It has to be one of the guests.'

'Not necessarily just the guests.' Virgilio was checking his notebook. 'Serena Kempton, the one who dresses like a hippy, was in the UK until recently, and the victim's belligerent sister, Millicent, was too. They both work over there, don't they? One of them could have sent the letters.'

'That's true. I was talking to the young couple, Gavin and Emily, this afternoon and Emily's convinced Millicent did it. Apparently they heard her threatening Jonah last week.'

'Nothing new there. We already know she threatened him with a knife before the course started but, without more proof, what can we do?'

'A poison pen letter in her handwriting would do nicely, but where are the letters if they aren't here?'

'Either the victim destroyed them himself or whoever it was who beat us to it took them and has no doubt already destroyed them. We don't even have the envelopes.'

'Envelopes!' An idea suddenly came to me. 'This might be a wild goose chase, but I think I need to talk to Antonio.'

'You think he might know something? I thought you said you couldn't see him as our murderer.'

'No, but he might inadvertently be able to help.' I checked my watch. 'I bet he's in the kitchen helping the cook get ready for dinner.'

Sure enough, Antonio was there and what little blood there was in his cheeks drained away as he saw Virgilio.

'Good evening, gentlemen.' His voice was hoarse.

I decided to do the talking. 'Good evening, Antonio. We were wondering if you might be able to help us.' Oscar got up from his basket and came over to say hello and I was pleased to see his tail wag as he greeted Virgilio. Clearly this dog was a good judge of character.

'Anything, sir... Signor Dan, anything.'

'Your hobby is stamp collecting, isn't it?' He looked puzzled but nodded his head. 'Now, do you ever keep stamps taken from letters that arrive here at the villa?'

'Yes, but only if the envelopes are being thrown away. You see, I soak them in water to remove the stamps.'

Beside me, I could tell that Virgilio had realised where I was going with this. I explained to Antonio what we wanted. 'Maria told me that since the beginning of the year Jonah started receiving letters, almost certainly from the UK. I don't suppose by any chance you kept the stamps from any of them, did you? Please try to remember.' To my delight, he nodded his head.

'I know the envelopes you mean. I started finding them in the bin in Signor Jonah's study. They were letters from England and you have some rather fine Christmas stamps. I definitely kept the first and second of them but from the end of February they reverted to being just ordinary UK stamps and I've got lots of those already.'

'And have you still got those two stamps?' I had to restrain the urge to cross my fingers.

'Yes, indeed. Let me show you.' He grabbed the album from a shelf and set it down on the table. He was clearly very familiar with its contents as he found the relevant page almost immediately and pointed to the second row. 'There, *signori*, those two are the stamps from those letters to Signor Jonah.' He peeled back the protective sheet of clear film and was reaching for them when I stopped him.

'Let me, Antonio. I'm wearing gloves.' Of course, his prints were almost certainly already all over the stamps but it was worth a try, just in case the author of the letters had left one of their own prints on there. I wasn't sure whether soaking the envelopes in water would have removed any trace but I remembered a case where the forensics people managed to get prints off a pistol that had been lobbed into the Thames. Very carefully, I lifted the two stamps out and took them over to the window ledge where the evening sunlight was streaming in.

'Can you see anything?' Virgilio came up behind me and peered over my shoulder. 'There's something written on that one...'

I was also poring over it. Both stamps were nativity scenes and the one on the left only had the faintest series of horizontal franking lines across it, but the one on the right had the same lines but also a small portion of a roundel just visible across the left side of the stamp. It was blurred and meant nothing to me but it was just possible forensics might be able to make something out of it. I pulled out my phone and took a couple of high-resolution photos before turning to Virgilio.

'Why don't you ask your people to see if they can lift any prints off either stamp and I'll send these photos to Scotland Yard and ask if they can get anything for us? You never know.'

We thanked Antonio, who was looking relieved Virgilio hadn't come to arrest him, and we left him with his stamp collection, now minus two. I checked my watch.

'It's half past six. Feel like a beer?'

Virgilio nodded. 'I might as well; I don't think we're getting anywhere with the investigation. Maybe alcohol will give us a bit of inspiration.'

We went through to the seminar room and I helped myself to a couple of cold beers from the fridge. We took them out onto the empty terrace and sat down at a table in the shade. Virgilio leant across to clink our bottles together.

'*Cin cin*, Dan.' He took a big swig of beer and smiled appreciatively before reaching for his trouser pocket. 'God, carrying a gun around in my pocket's uncomfortable.' He pulled the package out and laid it carefully on the table. 'Let's see if we can get any joy out of the stamps but I have my doubts. And, without them, we're stuck, aren't we?'

As he was speaking, my eyes alighted on a news article at the bottom of the torn-off page of *The Times* wrapping the gun. It was headed:

US imposes sanctions on Sri Lankan army chief over war crimes.

A thought occurred to me.

'I wonder if you could do something for me, Virgilio. Could you find out who Serena's girlfriend, Lihini, was? Serena said she died of a drug overdose in Sri Lanka last August. I don't have a surname but hopefully it shouldn't be too hard to trace. And if you can, ask them why she was in prison a couple of years ago. Was it drugs like Serena or something else?'

'You think she might be involved?'

'I honestly don't know, but it's worth a try. After all, we only have Serena's word for it that the woman's dead. Maybe she slipped in here last week with Serena's help, killed Jonah, and slipped out again. The thing is: when I asked Serena if Lihini had enjoyed her stay here last July, she shook her head and said it was a disaster. I'd quite like to know what happened.'

'Okay, if you think it might help.' He pulled out his phone, called the station and gave instructions. After spelling out Lihini's name to his subordinate, he gave another order. 'This Lihini woman stayed here at Montevolpone last July. Check with Immigration to see if there's a record of her arrival and departure. That way you should be able to get her full name and it'll make things easier at the other end. And once you have the full name, check to see if she's been back more recently.'

He ended the call, looked across at me and nodded. 'Okay, that's in hand. I'll call you when I know something. In the meantime, if you have any other bright ideas, do let me know.'

'Bright ideas? I'm clean out of them for now, I'm afraid. I'm seriously considering sitting down with the dog and asking him to tell me what happened.'

* * *

After dinner that night, I went for a walk in the starlight with Charlotte. As we strolled around the gardens, she caught hold of my arm with both her hands and clung tightly to me. It felt good – different but good. We walked in silence for some minutes, enjoying the relative cool and the silence, punctuated only by the background chorus of the cicadas. There was no sign of my four-legged friend, but my two-legged friend provided very pleasant company. When we reached the gate to the swimming pool, Charlotte looked up at me and spoke softly.

'Was the email from your wife bad news?'

'Sort of...' I hesitated before giving her the gist of it. Her reaction was sympathetic.

'So that's it as far as your marriage is concerned? How do you feel?'

'If you'd asked me yesterday morning, I would have said confused and saddened, but today I still feel sorry but somehow almost relieved. At least the uncertainty's over. I can get on with my life again after months in limbo.'

She opened the wicker gate and walked through the tunnel of rosemary bushes towards the water. I scrupulously closed the gate behind us and followed her. Somebody had turned the lights on underwater and this cast an eerie, dappled glow around the sides of the pool. Charlotte walked across to the springboard at the deep end and perched on the landward end of it.

'Come and join me.' She patted the board alongside her and I took a seat. She hadn't left me much space so I found myself pressed tight against her. She resumed her grip on my arm and rested her head on my shoulder. 'If there's anything I can do to cheer you up, you only have to ask.'

I looked across at her, her face illuminated by the blue light from the water and I very nearly gave in to the impulse to kiss her. I told myself that it was the fact that she was a potential murder suspect that was holding me back – assuming I'd read the signs right – but I knew, deep down, that it wasn't just that. 'Thanks, Charlotte. I'll remember.'

She nestled against me. 'I hope you do.' Silence ensued, broken a few minutes later by her. 'So what did the inspector want this time? I saw the two of you sharing a beer.'

'Still looking for clues.' Because of the ongoing

investigation, I avoided any mention of the poison pen letters. 'I think he's finding it hard to put a case together against anybody.'

'Not even the butler?'

'No, not even Antonio.'

'But who else could it have been?'

'Who else indeed?'

Further silence ensued before she broke it with a distinctly cheeky note in her voice. 'Ever been skinny-dipping?'

In fact, I had been skinny-dipping once in my life. It was with Helen in the early years. We were on holiday on the Greek island of Hydra and we had stripped off and dived in late one night after far too much Retsina. The water was very deep so our attempts to cuddle, or more, were thwarted by the very real risk of drowning. Even so, it would have been a fine experience if I hadn't managed to bang my knee hard against a particularly spiny sea urchin as I climbed out. I was in pain for days and even now, thirty years on, I still find little black pieces of sea urchin emerging from my knee from time to time. In consequence – and for other reasons that I was unwilling to explore with her – my reaction to Charlotte's suggestion was probably less enthusiastic than she might have hoped.

'Not after a big meal, thanks. We'd probably drown.'

She turned towards me and grinned. 'Ah, but what a way to go!'

11

TUESDAY

It took me a while to get to sleep on Monday night. This wasn't because of the roast beef and the cook's pretty good approximation of Yorkshire pudding we had been served for dinner, nor was it because I had been reading yet another erotic novel. It was because I had been doing my best to understand just why I was being so hesitant as far as the advances of a very attractive woman were concerned. There could be little doubt: Charlotte was almost certainly up for it – whatever 'it' might prove to be – so why was I still holding back? My wife, soon to be ex-wife, had made clear that things were irrevocably over between us so why hesitate? I'd always thought of myself as a good detective, but I was struggling to make sense of my emotions every bit as much as I was struggling to work out who had killed Jonah Moore.

On Tuesday morning, Serena made us write a thousand words or more on the subject of seduction and it took a serious effort on my part not to draw on recent events in my own life. In the end I wrote a fairly bland piece on the seduction of one of the Medici women by a handsome *cavaliere*, working on the basis that sex in those days was far less complicated than now. Setting it in the past had the added advantage of letting me write the whole thing without once having to agonise over the correct terminology for undergarments. As far as I could recall, they had rarely been worn at all in those days. Finally emerging into the daylight, I was outside on the terrace resting and recuperating with a strong coffee when my phone rang. It was Virgilio.

'*Ciao*, Dan. Some information for you. The Lihini woman is called Lihini Devar. Immigration records show that she flew into Rome on the second of July last year and flew out again on the fifteenth. She gave her address in Italy as Villa Volpone, Montevolpone. No record of her coming back since then, I'm afraid, so that probably blasts the idea of her sneaking in and killing Jonah Moore out of the water. We've sent a formal request to the police in Sri Lanka for information on her background and possible death and we hope to hear back soon. I'll let you know as soon as I know anything. Now the bad news: no fingerprints on the stamps apart from the butler's so we're back to square one.'

No sooner had our conversation ended than my phone pinged to indicate a text had arrived. It was from Paul in London. I had sent him the photos of the two stamps the previous night with a request for him to see if any information might be forthcoming.

Hi, boss. I thought you were supposed to be retired. Once a copper, always a copper! I've passed the photos on to the lab. I'll let you know if they manage to find anything. Enjoy your saucy writing.

I resisted the temptation to send him a caustic reply and finished my coffee before following the others back into the seminar room for debriefing. This proved to be every bit as toe-curlingly embarrassing as I had feared. For a start, Agatha and Elaine had leapt very smartly from the process of seduction to the nitty-gritty and I had to sit there and try not to cringe as the septuagenarians described the act of sex a whole lot better than I could have done. Just where did they get their inspiration?

Things took a turn for the worse when Charlotte produced an account of two people sitting by a swimming pool who then went on to perform a series of acts that I would have had trouble doing when I was in my twenties, let alone in my fifties. What made matters worse were the knowing looks from my fellow students. It was clear that they were firmly convinced that Charlotte and I were now an item – and a remarkably inventive and agile item at that.

Lunch came as a welcome relief and I had every intention of going out for a long walk afterwards when Maria took me to one side.

'You know you were talking about maybe getting yourself a place over here and settling down? Well, I've been doing a bit of phoning around and Signora Leonardo, one of our neighbours, told me she has a little house she'd be happy to rent or maybe even sell. If you'd like to see it, I can give you her details.'

'That would be great, thanks a lot. Did you tell her I'll have a dog?'

'Yes, indeed, and she's quite happy.'

'Terrific, thanks. Now, whereabouts is it, please?'

'It's very close. Ten minutes in the car or you could walk over there in less than half an hour. Why not take Oscar with you? After all, if you decide to go for it, it'll be his house too. She said she's free this afternoon if you want.'

After a brief phone call, the rendezvous was arranged for three o'clock. I collected the bouncy dog just after two and we set off, following Maria's directions. This involved going up the same track I used for my morning runs and then turning to the right at the top and dropping down into the next valley. It was another glorious summer day and the scenery was spectacular, walking past vines already covered in bunches of pea-sized green grapes and between ancient stone walls populated by terrified lizards. Fortunately, there was no sight of any of their legless cousins. I've always hated snakes.

The little house was situated on a slight promontory dominating the valley below and was approached along a winding white gravel *strada bianca* flanked by statuesque cypress trees. It looked like something from a Visit Tuscany promotional video and I was already in love with the place before I even got to it.

The house itself was built of stone, with a sun-bleached, rose-pink, tiled roof. A battered Ducato van stood outside and a lady who was probably in her eighties was sitting on an old bench in the shade, waiting for me. Oscar trotted over, tail wagging, to say hello and I took this as a good omen. I followed him over.

'Good afternoon, Signora Leonardo? My name's Dan Armstrong.'

She shook my hand and introduced herself before turning and pointing at the house with an arthritic finger. 'This used to be the home of our foreman in the days when my husband still ran the farm. I'm afraid they've both passed away now, and I've rented the land to one of my neighbours. I'm too old for working in the fields.'

'What did you grow?'

'The usual: olives and grapes.' She glanced back at me and I saw a little sparkle in her eyes. 'But I've made sure I still get a regular supply of oil and wine. My husband always used to say that our oil was the best in Tuscany.'

By now I was beginning to get used to the fact that almost everybody I met over here either claimed to produce the best oil and wine in Italy – which of course meant the best in the world as far as Tuscans were concerned – or knew a 'little man' who did. The good news was that if I did take this place, it looked as though I would have no shortage of local produce.

'And where do you live, *signora*?'

She pointed across to the right and I saw a fine-looking old stone farmhouse in the middle of a clump of trees halfway up the next hill. 'For now I'm still in the old house but it's really too big for me. I'm probably going to move down to Montevolpone

one of these days. My daughter lives there and she wants me to go and stay with them.' She gave a little sigh. 'The farm's been my home for so many years, it'll be a real wrench to have to leave, but that's the way of the world... now, let me show you around.'

She had already unlocked the old wooden door – not nearly as fancy as the front doors of Villa Volpone but beautiful in its own rustic way – and she led me inside. I stepped directly into a cavernous kitchen-cum-living room that occupied virtually the whole of the ground floor. The ceiling was supported by massive wooden beams, roughly hewn quite obviously by hand, and the floor was made of ancient terracotta tiles, worn smooth by the passage of countless feet over centuries. There was a long table in the middle with sturdy benches on either side and an unexpectedly modern-looking sink and a large fridge freezer against the side wall.

'There's a washing machine in the bathroom at the back of the house and a washing line outside the back door. I'm afraid the cooker's on its last legs but I'll get a new one installed if you decide to move

in. There's no mains gas up here so it's bottle gas.
Are you familiar with it?'

I wasn't, but it didn't look too complicated.
Alongside the elderly cooker was a big red gas bottle, the same height as the Labrador's head, and an
even more ancient rubber hose connected the top
of the bottle to the rear of the cooker. I was glad
she was planning on replacing it. From the look of
the hose, it was an accident waiting to happen.
Still, apart from this, the place looked wonderful to
me. What Helen would have made of it, I wasn't so
sure but, I reminded myself, that no longer
mattered.

It was quite dark in here but I could see large
glazed doors set in an archway in the middle of the
back wall. Signora Leonardo went over, pulled the
French windows open, and pushed the hefty louvred shutters outwards. Light flooded into the room
and I was presented with a spectacular view down
over the vines to the valley beyond. The dog and I
wandered out onto a covered terrace with a rustic-
looking table and four sturdy wooden chairs, all
covered with a thick layer of Tuscan dust. There
was a hint of a breeze under here and yes, I thought

to myself, I could imagine spending a lot of my time out here.

Upstairs there were two bedrooms, both with solid-looking double beds, and a surprisingly modern bathroom. The *signora* explained that the house had its own sanitation system and although there was no mains water up here, the well had never run dry in three hundred years. The views from upstairs were even better than from down below and I could have stood and gazed out of the windows forever. There was no doubt about it: I could see myself living here.

Back downstairs again, the *signora* revealed the monthly rental figure she wanted and I did my best to conceal my amazement. It worked out to less than half what I was paying for my little flat in Bromley and this was a whole house! She asked me when I was thinking of moving in and I had to stop and think.

'To be perfectly honest, Signora Leonardo, I would probably like to move in almost immediately if that might be possible. My course at the villa finishes on Saturday and that's just four days' time. The problem is that all my sheets and towels and things like that are in London and I'd need to go back and bring them over or buy some new ones here.'

'Don't worry about that. Like I said, I need to downsize. I can let you have all the linen you need, and the same goes for pots and pans and cutlery. If there's anything else you need, just tell me and I'm sure I'll be able to let you have it.'

This sounded perfect so I took the plunge. I gave her three hundred euros from my wallet as a deposit and asked if it would be all right if I brought her the balance the next day. I told her I would have to open a bank account and so on but if she didn't mind being paid in cash for the first month or two, I would like to take the house from as early as this weekend. She didn't bat an eyelid and told me she and her daughter would make sure the place was habitable by Saturday afternoon. This resolved my dilemma about my return flight and I decided to move straight in here at the weekend – even if it would probably be little more than squatting at first – and gradually get myself sorted out over the course of the summer.

After the *signora* had locked up and driven off,

Oscar and I sat down in the shade of the terrace at the rear, which I now knew to be called a loggia, and relaxed. The air was distinctly cooler under here although by no means cold and I soaked up the view down over the vines to a jumble of trees at the bottom of the little valley that Signora Leonardo had told me concealed a pool in the stream where it was possible to swim. Even if that turned out to be little more than a paddling pool for the dog, this was an unexpected bonus. I rested my back against the ancient stone wall – the *signora* had revealed that the house was about three hundred years old – and reflected on this monumental change in my life.

Less than a year ago I had been DCI Armstrong of the Yard, working twelve-hour shifts – if I was lucky – and going through the painful final days of an unhappy marriage. Now here I was in this most beautiful part of the world, about to embark on a totally new phase of my life. Here I would be able to relax and write. Maybe this would be the place where I would become another Ian Fleming, living with my faithful dog, tramping around the tracks and paths of the Tuscan hills without a care in the world as my bank balance gradually filled with generous royalties from my critically acclaimed books.

On the other hand, of course, this might be the place where my dreams of literary glory came crashing down around my ears and I found myself floundering in failure. Here I might end up living an increasingly lonely life, cut off from other people by a kilometre of dirt road – a stranger shunned by the local community. I tried to imagine this place in winter, with rain lashing the roof and an icy wind blowing down from the Apennines and chilling me to the bone. My reduced pension – after Helen had probably taken most of it – might not be enough to allow me to buy firewood. It occurred to me that I had seen no sign of heating in the house apart from the huge stone fireplace in the kitchen. In consequence, this might even be the place where ex-DCI Armstrong would be found one frosty winter morning frozen solid like Scott of the Antarctic, or eaten by his faithful, but starving, dog.

I glanced down at Oscar, who was stretched out on the old brick floor, and rubbed his tummy with the side of my foot. 'You wouldn't eat me, would you?'

He opened one eye and licked my ankle, presumably checking to see how I might taste.

Helen had always accused me of being a hopeless optimist while she had always erred on the side of caution, if not full-blown pessimism. For her, the glass was never half empty; it was lying smashed on the floor. Was I being hopelessly optimistic? As far as my literary aspirations were concerned, maybe, probably, but so what? As far as fitting in over here was concerned, I was less worried. Up to now I had been welcomed by almost everybody I had met. There was Tommaso at the bar, the shoe lady, Signora Leonardo, Virgilio and Lina – and I could sense the beginnings of a real solid friendship there – and there were the people at the villa. Assuming that we managed to find the killer and prove the innocence of Maria and Antonio, I felt sure they would also come to be lasting friends. And then, maybe, there might be Charlotte...

Of course, the first thing we had to do was to catch our murderer.

* * *

Back at the villa, I returned a visibly weary Oscar to the kitchen and found Maria sitting in there on her own. She looked up as I came in and I could immediately see that she'd been crying. Wiping the back of her hand across her eyes, she managed to produce a little smile all the same.

'What did you think of the house? Any good?'

'Any good? It's amazing. In fact, I've said I'll take it.' I went over and gave her a little pat on the shoulder. 'Thank you so much. It's exactly the sort of thing I've been dreaming of.'

'I'm so pleased. This area's so nice – very rural but only half an hour from Florence. I'm sure you'll love it here.' She sounded happy for me but still looked distraught.

'Well, as soon as I'm settled, I hope you'll come round to see it for yourself.' I hesitated and then thought, *What the hell*. 'And maybe Antonio might like to come too, just as soon as all this is over.' There was no need to explain what I meant by 'all this'.

'When do you think it will be over, Dan? I feel totally lost at the moment. Things seem to be getting worse and worse.' She wiped her eyes again and indicated I should sit down. I took a seat on the other side of the table and heard the creak of wicker as Oscar slumped heavily into his basket by the fireplace.

'Soon, I hope.' I didn't know what else to say. 'The inspector's checking a few things. I don't suppose you've had any more thoughts about those poison pen letters, have you? For example, even if you didn't see the actual letters inside, can you remember if the address was typed or handwritten?'

'Typed, I'm quite sure of that. The inspector asked me the same question. But as for finding them, I can only imagine that Jonah must have destroyed them. I've looked absolutely everywhere.' She looked up from her hands and the expression on her face was one of sheer misery. 'I don't know if it helps, but I've just discovered something else that's come as a major shock.'

'What was that?'

'I'd forgotten all about the safe. I haven't opened it for ages and it only occurred to me this lunchtime. At the back of the safe there've always been two files of documents, one for each of us. You know, important stuff like birth certificates, degrees, diplomas, that sort of thing. I'd never looked through Jonah's folder before and while I was going through it an hour ago, I found this. He'd put it in a blank envelope and sealed it, presumably so I wouldn't see it.' She got to her feet and went over to the top of the fridge and brought back a large green folder. She extracted a typewritten letter and passed it across to me. 'Not a poison pen letter but definitely not what I wanted to find.'

I took the letter from her and studied it. It was on University of Exeter headed paper and its contents were unequivocal. In March 1999, Jonah Moore hadn't left of his own free will to pursue his writing career; he had been fired. The exact circumstances surrounding his misdemeanours were not specified but the wording was unambiguous.

As a result of your repeated breaches of the staff/student code, we have no alternative but to terminate your period of employment here forthwith.

It was signed by the vice chancellor himself.

Jonah had got the boot. I laid the letter down on the tabletop. 'And he never mentioned this to you?'

'No. In fact he told me he left his job after the success of his first book so as to devote himself fully to his writing. I've just been checking. *Recurring Lies*, his bestseller, didn't come out until 2002. That's three years later.'

'So you had no knowledge of this and no idea why he might have got the sack?'

'No... but...' She hesitated. 'I have a feeling it was probably misconduct with female students.' She gave a heartfelt sigh. 'I'm not blind, Dan. I've known all along that Jonah's been cheating on me. It was the nature of the beast. He just wasn't the marrying kind but, still, in spite of everything, I loved him.' She looked across at me and I could see the tears building up in her eyes again. 'I knew he wasn't a saint, but I still loved him...' Her words dissolved into a sob.

A saint? Far from it. This letter confirmed, if confirmation were necessary, that my first impressions of Jonah had not been wrong. I waited until Maria had collected herself before asking an important question. 'Might there be some woman with whom he's had a relationship more recently? Maybe one with a jealous husband, jealous enough to murder him?'

She didn't raise her eyes from her hands. 'I've been wondering the same thing but I don't think so. He rarely went out any more. I'm sure I would have known if he'd been carrying on an affair. He went to England for a book signing tour last autumn but I went with him so, no, I don't think there's anybody, at least not for a few years.' She looked up. 'I'm sorry.'

'Thanks, anyway. I'm sorry too, but I had to ask.' I tapped the letter with my finger. 'Would you mind if I keep this for now? I'd like Inspector Pisano to see it and I'll get my people back at Scotland Yard to do a bit of digging. I think we'd all like to know exactly what happened twenty-odd years ago, wouldn't we?'

Deciding that there was no time like the present, I went back to my room, photographed the letter, and sent it over to Paul, apologising for the extra burden but asking if he could get somebody to find out just why Jonah had been sacked. I then checked the time, saw that it was half past four, and headed for the car. I drove down to Florence and was in Virgilio's office in less than three quarters of an hour.

'*Ciao*, Dan. Shouldn't you be off having fun somewhere?'

I shook his hand and brought him up to speed on events at the villa. He made a copy of the University of Exeter letter and thanked me for getting Paul to look into it. He then asked me the very question that had been exercising me all the way down here from Montevolpone.

'Assuming for a moment that the victim's misconduct leading to his dismissal involved a woman, are you suggesting that this woman for some reason might be responsible for killing him after a wait of twenty-plus years? It's tenuous, to say the least.'

'I know, but stranger things have happened. At least it should provide proof of his womanising. Besides, his wife told me today that she's always known of his infidelities although she can't think of any recent woman he might have had a relationship with who could have been out to get him.'

'But even if there were such a woman, how

could some random person have got into the villa without being seen by anybody?'

'Unless she had inside help. By the way, any word back from Sri Lanka yet?'

'No, but that'll probably be a dead end as well.' He glanced at his watch. 'I'm desperate for a cold drink. Got ten minutes?'

'Definitely.'

We went out of the *questura* into the late afternoon sunshine and as we walked, I told him about my big decision and described the little house on the hill. He sounded genuinely delighted and assured me that he would guide me through the bureaucratic maze so as to get me sorted out with a residence permit, a bank account, and the all-important *codice fiscale*. Apparently, a tax code was essential here in Italy before doing anything else and he told me that as soon as he had a bit of free time he would accompany me in person to all the relevant offices. I couldn't thank him enough as I had been dreading this part of the proceedings. We celebrated with two ice-cold bottles of alcohol-free beer and by the time we parted I was beginning to get genuinely excited at the prospect of putting down roots over here.

Before going back to the car, I stopped off at a cash machine and drew out as much as I could so as to be able to give Signora Leonardo the rest of her deposit for the house. While I was there, I happened to walk past a top-end hardware shop selling everything from electric bottle openers to the latest must-have for Florentines with money to throw around: your very own mini mill for producing homemade olive oil. There, taking pride of place in the centre of the window display, was a faux-antique metal stand equipped with a series of stainless-steel bolts and screws, designed to hold a leg of cured ham. A magnificent carving knife with a wooden handle protruded from a holder alongside it. Remembering my vow the other day, I went in and asked the price. This kind of place didn't stoop to putting prices on the items in the window. As expected, it wasn't cheap but I felt it somehow represented a physical symbol of my big decision about my future, so I bought it. The next step would be to buy a leg of ham but I thought it best to wait until I had moved in. Besides, I needed to ask around first to see which 'little man' made the best ham locally.

On my way back to the villa, I noticed that the car could do with half a tank of fuel so, to satisfy my curiosity, I waited until I got to Montevolpone and pulled up outside the rather down-at-heel garage boasting the sign *Autofficina Marinetti*. The fuel price on display was a good bit higher than down in Florence but this would hopefully give me the chance to meet Puppo Marinetti, the bosom buddy of Maria's first husband. Unfortunately, I was served by a young lad of maybe sixteen or seventeen and there was no sign of the owner. I engaged him in conversation all the same and told him I was a tourist, visiting Tuscany for the first time. He asked me where I came from and when I told him London, he looked far more interested in that city than his own, but I gradually got him onto the subject of the garage and discovered that the boy's name was Arturo and the owner, Puppo, was his uncle. After paying for the fuel, I drove up to the gates of the villa and phoned Virgilio. He answered straight away.

'*Ciao*, Dan.'

'*Ciao*, Virgilio, it may be unimportant but I was just wondering something. Do you have the statement from the witness who provided the alibi for the man from the garage in Montevolpone, Puppo Marinetti, to hand? If so, can you tell me the name of the witness?'

'Hang on.' There was a brief silence before he came back to me. 'Arturo Negri – why do you ask?'

'Does the statement mention that this lad is the nephew of Marinetti?'

Another few seconds of silence. 'No, no mention.' I heard him give a frustrated snort. 'That's bad. My man should have noted that. So do you think the witness might have invented the alibi to do his uncle a favour?'

'I don't know, but it might be worth double checking.'

'We'll get on it. Thanks, Dan.'

I drove back up to the villa in time for dinner and sat next to Charlotte. It didn't come as a complete surprise – and certainly not an unwelcome surprise – to feel her hand land on my thigh before we had even finished our antipasti.

'Had a good day?'

'Definitely. I've just found myself a house.' This attracted the attention of most of the other diners and I gave them a brief description of the little house on the hill and told them of my decision to settle here in Tuscany. Martin/Mikey of all people was the first to respond, and he sounded decidedly enthusiastic.

'That's great, Dan. I envy you that. You wanna know something? I've been dreaming of doing something like that myself. New York's okay when you're there, but when you come to a place like this you realise there's more to life than just making money.'

This sounded to me a lot like the suspected gangster indicating he was thinking of getting out of the business. For a second, I exchanged glances with Will and read astonishment in his eyes. I hoped Mikey was serious. With the Feds so keen to catch him that they were expending a lot of resources following him around the world, it was almost certainly just a matter of time. It would be tough if he were to find himself separated from his new fiancée by iron bars for the rest of his life.

Agatha also approved. 'I can see you now, Dan,

sitting on your terrace with your laptop, churning out bestseller after bestseller.'

'Keep believing that, Agatha. I need all the support I can get.'

'Any developments in the hunt for our murderer?'

Suddenly an expectant hush descended on the table. I took a long, slow look around at their faces. Assuming my instincts were correct and neither Maria nor Antonio were guilty, the murderer or murderers had to be sitting here among us tonight. It was a sobering thought.

I decided to take a chance and try to flush out the culprits so I adopted a confident tone that I didn't feel. 'Yes, I believe there might be. I saw the inspector a few hours ago and he told me he's just waiting for some information from overseas and then he hopes to be in a position to make an arrest maybe as soon as tomorrow.'

The expectant hush became a stunned silence. In case you're wondering how to tell the difference, it's a combination of sound – or the lack of it – and the expressions on the faces of the people involved that can range from surprise to out-and-out panic.

My eyes surveyed the people opposite me but of course I was unable to check out those on my side of the table. From the lack of reaction from the American contingent of Mikey, Jen, Will, and Rachel, I realised too late that I was definitely sitting on the wrong side of the table. I could just catch a glimpse of Millicent's face but could read only surprise on it, while the others were hidden from my sight except for Emily and Gavin at the far end of the table. He looked genuinely pleased while I distinctly got the feeling I spotted an expression of alarm on his girlfriend's face. It only lasted a split second and I could have been wrong but it was interesting all the same. Did this mean she might be our killer? And if so, why? Not to mention when and how? It was frustrating not to see the faces of the others.

'Well, I think that's excellent news.' Predictably, Agatha was the first to speak up. A second later, Antonio appeared at the door with a tray and she immediately changed the subject. 'I'm delighted the weather's set fair for the next few days.' There was no doubt where her suspicions lay.

The conversation gradually picked up again and

turned to less contentious issues and I wondered if my little announcement would serve to spur the murderer or murderers into action. It was probably a forlorn hope – after all, they hadn't put a foot out of place so far – but I had known it work in the past.

After dinner, I went outside onto the terrace and stared up at the night sky, wondering, yet again, who our culprit might be. If I had spotted something untoward on Emily's face, how could she be involved? Could this be the jealous woman? Although Jonah had been a confirmed womaniser, it seemed unlikely that such a young woman could have got involved with a man twice her age. Of course, such things had happened and continued to happen – not least to Mikey and Jen, who had been across the table from me – but the next question was where and how? She had allegedly been travelling overseas before hooking up with Gavin, while Jonah had reputedly not put a foot out of Italy except for short trips. I was standing there lost in my thoughts when I felt a hand on my arm. It was Charlotte.

'You promised me a date, you know.' She was adopting a mock-hectoring tone. '"Take me out to dinner," he said. "His treat," he said. Promises, promises.'

I turned towards her and smiled. 'You're right and I'm sorry. How about tomorrow night? I'll pick you up at seven. Dress informal, as Millicent would say.'

'I'll look forward to it.'

After a while, the two of us walked through the trees to the bench by the fence and sat down. A few moments later, I felt her hand catch hold of mine and give it a little squeeze. It felt rather nice and I don't know where we would have ended up if it hadn't been for the arrival on the scene of an uninvited guest. Suddenly we were rudely interrupted by a volley of barking. To my amazement, it was Oscar, and he was making a hell of a racket. And his aggression was very clearly directed at my companion. I hastily took him to task. After all, if he was to become my dog, I didn't want him barking at people – particularly people I liked a lot.

'Oscar, calm down. It's only us. You know me and you know Charlotte. Stop it now!'

Reluctantly, the dog allowed me to pacify him and he was soon sitting at my side, pointedly on the opposite side from Charlotte. However, as soon as I returned my attention to my companion, he jumped to his feet and started barking the place down all over again. I laid a soothing hand on his head and ruffled his ears until he shut up before I turned to Charlotte.

'That's weird. He was all over you when he last saw you here. Remember he tried to climb on your lap and soaked your dress?'

'You know what I think, Dan? I think your canine friend might be jealous. You two have been getting pretty close over the past few days. Every time I see you out and about, you've always got a black shadow at your side.'

'Maybe he knows Maria's just given him to me.' I went on to tell her about Maria's allergy and how this had coincided with my desire to get a dog. However, as I talked, I realised that the moment had passed. Romance was no longer in the air.

In the end, she set off alone back to the villa – because the dog steadfastly refused to let her walk with me – and I sat there with Oscar and wagged my finger in front of his nose.

'Listen, my friend, I like you too, and I promise

if you bring a nice lady friend home I won't inter-
fere, but the same goes for me. *Capito*?'

Now that Charlotte had disappeared from sight,
he just gave me a broad canine grin and wagged his
tail. His rival for my affections had been seen off so
he was a happy dog once more.

12

WEDNESDAY

Wednesday began like any other day. I got up at seven thirty and went for a run. The pseudo-Canadians were nowhere to be seen this morning but with their assignment/holiday about to end in three days' time, they probably had other things on their minds, so I set off on my own.

There was no sign of Oscar and I resolved to take him for a long walk that afternoon when I needed to go over to Signora Leonardo's house so I could finish paying her the deposit for my new home. Thought of him reminded me of last night. Oscar's intervention had been as unwelcome as it had been unexpected. Could he really be jealous?

Tonight, when I took Charlotte for dinner and, more importantly, when we returned, I intended to see that my four-legged passion-killer was kept well away from us.

The temperature was already high and it promised to be another scorcher. Emerging onto the top of the hill, I stopped for a quick breather, my thoughts still on what might or might not happen with Charlotte tonight. For a few moments, I felt more like a teenager than a middle-aged man. It had been a long time since I had felt like this and I ensured that my run this morning wasn't too taxing. I wasn't a young man any more after all...

The session this morning consisted of a compare-and-contrast exercise looking at the way erotic writing had progressed over the years, taking in all manner of writers from some very saucy Greeks to Boccaccio and Chaucer and on through D. H. Lawrence to twenty-first century writers. While we were having our mid-morning break, I got a text from Paul in London that made interesting, if inconclusive, reading.

Preliminary lab report is that they have identified the

last two letters of a word in the franking roundel. The bit with the day and date is missing and all they've found are the letters E and R followed by a space so that indicates a place name ending in ER. There are a lot of places in the UK from Chester to Leicester that these letters could apply to, so I'm afraid this probably doesn't help too much. Cheers. PS University of Exeter have promised a response about Jonah Moore by tomorrow at the latest.

I sat there sipping my cappuccino as I reflected on this information. Paul was right: the choice of places ending in ER was broad, but one name did come to mind, and Paul had just mentioned it. I had no idea at this point just how significant this might prove to be. Jonah had spent ten years of his earlier life teaching at the University of Exeter. Might the poison pen letters have come from Exeter? Was there somebody there who still bore him a grudge after so long? Hopefully the report coming later today might shed some welcome light on that. More to the point, was there one of my fellow students who had a connection to the city? I walked to the far end of the terrace where I wouldn't be overheard and called Virgilio. I told him what Paul's text had said and made a few suggestions.

'Virgilio, you might like to check back with the people in the UK who sent you the reports on the course participants and ask them to check any connection with the city of Exeter. They could maybe check births and marriages, schools and universities, as well as employment records. It's just possible one of the people here knew Jonah back then.' I realised, of course, that this would rule out Emily as a suspect. She would have been a babe in arms. Still, one of the others might prove to have a connection.

'Good thinking. Leave it to me. It might take a day or two.'

'No news from Sri Lanka?'

'Not a thing. Here's hoping. You'll know as soon as I do.'

Thought of Sri Lanka led me on to Serena. 'By the way, did you tell me Serena Kempton has been living in Manchester since coming back from Sri Lanka? If so, that's another place name ending in ER.'

He checked the file and confirmed that she had

indeed been living there. Might she be our letter writer? As before, the suspects seemed to be piling up again.

* * *

After lunch, I collected Oscar and we walked up the hill and over the top in the direction of Signora Leonardo's farmhouse. When the little house that would become my home from Saturday came into sight, I saw that the white van was there again, this time accompanied by a blue van with the name of a firm selling *elettrodomestici* on the side. I called in to hand over the balance of the deposit and found the *signora* in the kitchen with two men who were just finishing installing a smart new cooker, hose, and gas bottle.

'Good afternoon, Signora Leonardo, I've come to give you the money I owe you.'

'That's very kind. Have you seen your nice new cooker?'

'Yes, it looks very smart. Thank you.'

One of the men explained how it all worked and gave me a hefty spanner specially designed for connecting and disconnecting the gas bottle. He then produced a card and explained that when I needed more gas all I had to do was to call him or bring the empty bottle down to Montevolpone, where he would sell me a full one. After he and his mate had left, the *signora* showed me the host of cooking utensils, crockery, glasses, pots, and pans now filling the cupboards and produced a bottle of wine – naturally unmarked – and told me I had to try it as it was from her old vineyard, now being worked by a neighbour. It was very good indeed so I asked if I would be able to buy some and she was quick to agree.

While we were talking, I heard noises from upstairs and the *signora* explained. 'It's my daughter, Isabella. She's up there, giving the place a spring clean. Why don't you go up and introduce yourself? I'll look after your dog while you go and see her. My poor old knees don't like stairs so I'll wait down here if you don't mind. She's interested to meet a famous English author.'

I decided not to disabuse her. If she wanted to think of me as a famous author, that was fine by me. I just hoped I would find inspiration up here and manage to complete at least one book so as to justify part of the description. I went up to find a friendly lady probably around my age or just a bit older. I was delighted to see that not only had Isabella cleaned the bedrooms, she had made up both beds with fresh linen and was on her knees in the bathroom giving the place a thorough clean. I was very impressed and most grateful. It was looking as though I wouldn't just be squatting here after all.

Back downstairs, after I had handed over the outstanding balance to the *signora*, she gave me instructions on how to get down to the pool in the stream where Oscar could go for a swim. We shook hands and arranged that I would meet her here on Saturday at noon to collect the keys and begin my new life.

The dog and I followed a narrow path down the hill through yet more vineyards. Trees and bushes along the bottom of the valley marked the course of the stream and it was easy to find the pool the *signora* had mentioned. To my surprise and considerable satisfaction, the pool, while far smaller than the one at the villa, was almost as wide as my bedroom at the villa and from the way Oscar paddled about in it, the water was probably deep enough for me, too, to come here on a hot day. For a few moments I toyed with the idea of stripping off and joining him in the water but natural modesty prevented me, so I just sat in the shade instead, throwing sticks into the pool for the dog to retrieve. This soon developed into a game of skill – not so much on the dog's part but on mine. Each time the happy dog emerged with a stick for me, he would shake himself and the trick was for me to anticipate the shower and take cover in time to avoid being soaked in Labrador-scented water. We both had a lot of fun, which was only interrupted by my phone. It was Virgilio.

'*Ciao*, Dan, I have news from Sri Lanka. The report's just come in.'

'Interesting news?'

'Lihini Devar is definitely dead. She took her own life on the twenty-first of August last year in Colombo, Sri Lanka. She was just twenty-six. It wasn't a drug overdose. Guess how she did it.'

'Cyanide?'

'Exactly.' He sounded impressed. 'Death must

have been almost instantaneous. Her body was found in a back alley by a policeman some hours after her death.'

'Any idea why she did it?'

'Nothing mentioned but one fact has emerged. She was in Welikada prison for five years from age twenty to twenty-five on charges relating to having been associated with the Tamil Tigers. Heard of them?'

'Vaguely. There was a civil war over there, wasn't there? So if she was a Tamil, I wonder if that was why she took her own life, or if it might somehow have been related to our case. Was there an autopsy?'

'No, her death hardly stirred a ripple. As far as the authorities were concerned, she was an ex-con who killed herself. Reading between the lines of the police report, it meant one less potential terrorist so good riddance.'

'Poor kid. Suicide at any age is grim, but twenty-six? Do you want me to try to sit down with Serena now that we have this information? Maybe this might be the stimulus it takes to get her to talk, hopefully to tell us more about why her girlfriend's visit to the villa last year was a disaster.'

'I think that would be a very good idea. Do you want me to come up to Montevolpone or are you happy to talk to her yourself?'

'If you don't mind, I think it might be better if I see her alone in the first instance. She's been looking very stressed. She's obviously been hit hard by Jonah's death and we don't want to spook her. I'll make sure I talk to her later this afternoon or this evening.'

'Okay, well, thanks. By the way, we followed up your idea about the garage owner and his nephew and you were right: the boy was covering for his uncle, mainly because if he didn't, our friend Puppo threatened to sack him.'

'Nice guy. So, does this add him to our list of suspects?'

'Alas, no. It turned out under further questioning that Puppo has been carrying on an affair with his neighbour's wife for the past six months and that afternoon he was with her. She vouches for him but was seriously pissed off that she had been found out. I get the impression that relationship isn't going to last. Anyway, we've given both Puppo and his nephew formal warnings about wasting police time but the bottom line is that we can rule him out.'

'Pity. Sorry for wasting your time.'

'Not at all, it was worth following up. I'm afraid your holiday's turning out to be a working holiday.'

'You know something, Virgilio? I don't mind. In fact, I love it. It's good to keep my hand in and, if it helps you, so much the better. I'll try and talk to Serena as soon as possible. I'll give you a call back just as soon as I've spoken to her.'

By the time we got back to the villa, Oscar was almost completely dry and I was looking forward to a swim myself, but first I had to talk to Serena. After leaving the dog in the kitchen with Antonio, I went through to the seminar room and out onto the terrace, where I was delighted to find her. She was sitting on her own, as usual looking a million miles away. A bit further along were Agatha and Elaine and I knew I didn't want them listening in.

'Serena, I wonder if you could spare me a few minutes to have a talk.'

She blinked and looked up. 'Yes, of course, Dan. Has something come up?'

'I suppose it has. Like I say, we need to talk, somewhere private.'

'Why don't you come up to the tower room? Give me half an hour or so to sort myself out and I'll meet you there and we won't be disturbed.'

'Fine.'

I wondered what she meant by sorting herself out.

* * *

I went up to my room and took a long drink from the mineral water bottle beside my bed before taking a cool shower. It was already past five and I was supposed to be meeting up with Charlotte at seven so, depending on how long my talk to Serena lasted, it was looking as though my swim might have to wait until tomorrow. Even though I had left the window open, it was boiling hot in my room and the air was even hotter when I climbed the stairs to the tower a few minutes later. Serena was sitting there, waiting for me, looking, as ever, as if she was in her own little world. I noticed that she had changed. She was now wearing a stunning golden sari and had put her hair up, almost as though she was on her way to a ball. Incongruously, she was wearing just one pendant earring.

'Hi, Dan, come and sit down.' Although her voice was low and her tone measured, I immediately sensed the tension in the air. I did as I was told and surveyed her for a few moments, waiting for her to speak first. The only sound up here was the cooing of a couple of amorous doves on the roof outside, maybe distant relatives of birds who had lived here back when this had been a dovecote.

'What did you want to talk about, Dan?' Her voice was still studiously level.

I decided to be direct and to the point. 'Why don't you talk to me about Lihini, her death as a result of cyanide poisoning, and exactly what happened here at the villa last summer?'

'I see.' I had been expecting fireworks, maybe indignation, possibly tears, but all I could hear in her tone was resignation.

'Feel like telling me all about it?'

She nodded slowly. 'I was there in Colombo

when she did it.'

'You were with her when she took her own life?'

'No, I was back in our hotel room. She told me she was going out to the chemist's and she never came back. The police told me what had happened next morning.'

'And why did she do it? A young woman of twenty-six, with her whole life ahead of her, why kill herself?'

The answer was a long time coming. When it came, it was delivered in such a low voice – little more than a whisper – that I could barely catch the words. 'She discovered she was pregnant.'

'Ah...' The picture began to emerge more clearly. 'And the father...?' I gave it twenty seconds or so before I supplied what I believed to be the answer. 'Jonah?'

Abruptly, she looked up from her hands and stared straight at me, her eyes no longer blank but filled with hatred. 'Jonah!' The venom in her voice was palpable.

'How did it happen?'

'It was the end of term party. That's what we call the dinner we have here at the villa each year at the end of the summer course once all the course participants have gone home.'

Her tone was remarkably unemotional. She could have been describing an everyday happening. Only a vein beating at her temple betrayed the tumult going on inside her.

'We all had quite a bit to drink and by the end there was only Jonah, Lihini, and me left. I went up to bed while they had a nightcap.' She dropped her eyes and lapsed into silence for a full minute but I didn't prompt her. Finally, she picked up again but the strain in her voice was more noticeable now.

'I still blame myself every single day for going off and leaving her. I was tired, I was a bit drunk, I just didn't think that even an animal like Jonah would stoop so low.' She raised her head once more and the anguish on her face was all too clear. 'He drugged her. I don't know what he used – Rohypnol or something like that I expect – but, whatever it was, it had the desired effect as far as he was concerned. I don't know what time it was when she came up to the room – I must have gone out like a light – but by the time I woke up in the morning she'd collected her things, called a taxi, and left.'

'She didn't tell you what had happened?'

'I didn't get a chance to talk to her.' For the first time I saw tears in the corners of her eyes. 'Things between me and her had been going so well up till then and suddenly she was out of my life.'

'So you followed her to Sri Lanka?'

She nodded. 'Yes, but I had to wait almost a month until Jonah finally got round to paying me before I could afford to buy the ticket. I flew over to Colombo and managed to trace her. She was in a terrible state. It took me a few days but I finally managed to get her to tell me what had happened back in Tuscany and she told me she was late.' She glanced up at me. 'You know, her period was late. She was terrified she might be carrying Jonah's baby.'

By now I had put two and two together. 'What was she going to the chemist's to buy? A pregnancy test?'

Serena nodded again. 'She must have done the test before coming back to the hotel and when she realised she really was pregnant, she took her own life.' For the first time I saw tears run down Serena's cheeks so I backed off and gave her a few minutes. I

stood up and walked over to the window overlooking the garden and the pool and spotted a dark
shape with four legs wandering across the grass
without a care in the world. Unlike this troubled
woman here with me. I was roused from my reflections by the sound of her voice.

'I knew then what I had to do.' I turned to see
her still red-eyed but sounding more resolute.
'Have you ever heard of the Tamils?'

'I know Lihini was a Tamil by birth. That was
why she was jailed, wasn't it?'

'And tortured...' She wiped the back of her hand
across her face and took a deep breath. 'That was
what happened to them, you know. When the government forces caught what they thought was a
Tamil terrorist, they beat them, tortured them, and
did unspeakable things to them. She was lucky to
be jailed, not killed. The fighters – they called
themselves Tigers – knew what would happen if
they were caught so many of them carried suicide
pills.'

'Cyanide?'

'Yes, because it acts so quickly. Some people
wore the little beads filled with poison around their

necks, others sewn into the collar of their shirt and some as earrings. Lihini was a sympathiser rather than a terrorist and she hadn't been carrying any when they caught her.' I studied her closely while she was speaking and saw that she had now removed her earring and her ears were bare. 'From the moment she was released from jail, she always wore earrings.' Her voice was flat now. 'So after her death I spoke to her brother – he's still in hiding from the authorities over there but I knew how to contact him – and he got me a pair. I've been wearing them ever since.'

'But not today.'

'There's no need any more.' Her voice was deadpan.

'And you used one to exact revenge on Jonah?'

'Yes.'

'And then you stabbed him as well.'

She looked up sharply. 'No, I didn't. That's what's so weird about this whole thing. Yes, I poisoned the wine in his glass, but I didn't stab him.' She was gazing out of the window now, almost as though she was alone up here. 'It was so easy. I slipped out of the afternoon session, saying I was going to the toilet. I knew he'd still be in the dining room getting drunk so I went in and perched on the table beside him.' She shuddered. 'Do you know what he did? He put his hand on my thigh and leered up at me. I was disgusted. If I'd been having second thoughts about killing him, these disappeared into thin air and I tipped the contents of the bead from my earring into his wineglass. He didn't notice a thing and less than a minute later he picked it up and took a big mouthful.'

'And he died.'

'He died almost immediately but as he went into spasm, his eyes looked straight at me and I leant forward and told him this was for what he'd done to Lihini. I'm certain he heard what I said, even if he was incapable of reacting. I could see it in his eyes. I watched him die and then I left the room and went back to the session.' Her voice was definitely stronger now. 'And I would do it again if I could.'

'But you're denying that you stabbed him?' I needed to be sure.

'Of course. Why should I stab him? I knew he was dead.' She was sounding more resolute now.

'My intention was to go back to my room, send a message to my mum, and then swallow the contents of the other earring. But nobody was talking about poison. All the talk was of a dagger to the heart so I waited, wondering if this other person might get me off the hook.'

'And now?'

'And now I know what I have to do.' She sounded remarkably detached, resigned. 'Thanks for listening, Dan. I feel a lot better now. I'm not going back to prison, so *ciao*...'

Before I could react, there was a sharp crack as she crushed something between her teeth and instantly jerked back in her seat, her eyes wide open, just staring blindly ahead. A few flecks of white foam appeared at the corner of her mouth and then, almost simultaneously, she fell forward. I caught her head as she fell and cradled it as she slumped to the floor. Gently prising open the fingers of her left hand, I found the remaining earring clasped in it, now minus the central bead. A touch of her pulse told me it was all over.

Serena was dead.

* * *

Why should I stab him? I knew he was dead.

I stopped the playback and looked across at Virgilio. He had already listened to the whole interview once and I had gone back to this point as I wanted him to be sure of what she had said. Two men had just finished zipping Serena's body into a black body bag and were preparing to manhandle it down the steep staircase from the dovecote. He shook his head slowly, still trying to come to terms with what he had heard. I spelt it out to him.

'That's twice she quite specifically denies stabbing him. Given that she had just admitted to murdering Jonah and probably already had the poison-filled bead in her mouth when she told me that, I can't see that she had anything to gain by lying. In my opinion, if she says she didn't stab him, she didn't stab him.'

'I agree. So we now have the suicide of the woman who murdered Jonah Moore but we still don't know who tried to poison him with the oleander mixture or who stuck the dagger into his heart.'

I shared his frustration. 'I was going to ask her about the oleander poison but I didn't have time. But, again, I don't think she did that either. She specifically said that she put the poison in the wine-glass, not the bottle. I don't think there's any getting away from it: we're still looking for at least one other murderer – or attempted murderer – and it has to be somebody in this house.'

'And of course you didn't have a chance to ask if she had been writing the poison pen letters. Maybe they were from her in Manchester like you thought...'

The two of us stood there in silence as the earthly remains of a heartbroken woman were manhandled down the spiral staircase. Yes, she had committed murder but, to my eyes, the responsibility for this whole tragic episode lay with the original victim himself: Jonah Moore. His self-centred and unscrupulous behaviour had directly caused three deaths – one of them his own.

'I really regret not anticipating she would kill herself like that. This leaves us with a number of questions still unanswered, doesn't it?'

Virgilio gave a wry smile. 'Depending on how

badly we want answers. I spoke to my boss on the way out here and you know what he said when I brought up exactly that point? He told me to forget it. As far as he's concerned, the Jonah Moore case is closed. We have a self-confessed perpetrator who has helpfully saved us the trouble of arresting her, so why waste manpower on trying to find anybody else?'

'I can see his point – sort of. After all, the pathologist definitely confirmed that it was Serena's cyanide that killed Jonah so, given that he was already dead, the other would-be murderers could only be charged with attempted murder at best or maybe even just defiling a body or whatever Italian law dictates.' I caught Virgilio's eye. 'Don't get me wrong. I hate cases with loose ends. The fact is that there's at least one person out there who was prepared to murder another human being and if they can do it once, they can do it again.'

'My feelings exactly.' I saw him come to a decision. 'Right, you know what I'm going to do? I'm going to announce that the case is closed. Serena Kempton killed Jonah Moore and that's the end of it. That means my boss is happy and I can stand down the murder team. We'll give everybody back their passports tomorrow and tell them they're free to leave any time they want. You and I both know that at least one other person tried to kill him and, if you're willing, you and I will keep looking. Who knows? Maybe we'll get some new leads when the answers come back from the UK about possible connections with the victim back when he was working over there.'

'I'm with you, Virgilio, but seeing as everybody's going home on Saturday that doesn't give us much time. Hopefully this way whoever did it will relax and they might give themselves away.'

He checked his watch. 'Seven thirty. Your companions will be gathering for dinner about now, won't they?'

Shit... Charlotte! With everything that had happened over the past couple of hours, I had completely forgotten our dinner date. 'Yes, it's just about time for dinner.'

'Then I think the best thing is for me to collect everybody together and make an official announcement. Okay?'

'Definitely, but first I've got to dig myself out of a

hole.' In response to his raised eyebrows, I explained about Charlotte.

'I'm delighted to hear you're moving on, Dan. Good for you. And don't worry about being a bit late for the lady. If she likes you, she won't mind.'

Charlotte was very understanding once she heard what had happened and together we decided to abandon the idea of going out for a meal, at least until tomorrow, and joined the others in the seminar room to listen to Virgilio. She placed herself at my side and pressed against my arm as we listened to him addressing everybody in the room. Antonio and Maria were there as well, along with Annarosa, the cook. In fact, the only occupant of the villa missing was Oscar, but I could always tell him later.

There were mixed feelings when it was made known that Serena had killed Jonah and then had taken her own life. She had been a popular member of the group. Without going into too much detail, Virgilio explained that the death of Serena's girlfriend had affected her state of mind and she had sought revenge on Jonah for whatever it was he had done which had led Lihini and then Serena herself to take her own life. I kept my eyes on

Maria's face while he was speaking but saw only sadness there, not surprise. She might have told me she had loved her husband, but she was clearly under no illusions as to how appalling his behaviour had been. I felt sorry for her but also glad for her sake that she was now free from him. Hopefully she would never again be verbally or physically abused by any man.

The reaction of everybody in the room was one of relief at the news that the murder had been solved and that we were no longer living with a killer in our midst. For me, the difficult bit was trying to work out whether the expressions of relief were inspired by the knowledge that they were all now free from a murderer, or free from suspicion. I did my best to scrutinise all the faces but came away empty handed. If our poison-pen-writing, homemade-poison-serving, dagger-stabbing perpetrator or perpetrators were here among us, nobody was showing any immediate signs of guilt.

I accompanied Virgilio to the front door. Somebody had already removed the tape from the dining room door and the only sign of the police presence was Virgilio's car and driver left outside. We walked down to the car park together. Conscious that there were probably numerous eyes on us, we shook hands formally, as though this really did mark the end of the case and as we did so, I gave him an invitation.

'Would you and Lina like to come for dinner on Saturday? I'd love to show you my new house. Wear old clothes and don't expect too much in the way of food because I'll have just moved in, but it would be good to see you both and to try to return some of your hospitality.' I explained how to get to the house and he assured me they would be delighted to come. His parting words as he climbed into the car were: 'See you then, but I hope to have some news from England before that. *Ciao* and thanks.'

The mood over the dinner table that night was mixed. Of course there was relief but this was tinged with considerable sadness at the tragic fate of Serena. It came as no surprise to hear Agatha announcing loudly that she had no doubt about what had happened to Lihini.

'Rape, it was rape, there's no getting away from it.' She shot a sideways glance at Maria and I followed her eyes. Maria just sat there, hands

clenched on her lap, and stared down at the tabletop. 'I was here last year and it was painfully obvious to me, to all of us, that Jonah was lusting after
Serena's girlfriend. It was repulsive. I'm sorry,
Maria, but I'm quite certain that his actions, and his
actions alone, were the reason why Lihini killed
herself. And now poor Serena has gone to join her.'
There was a break in her voice for a moment. 'Poor
Serena.'

All eyes were now on Maria. Slowly and deliberately, she looked up and across the table towards
Agatha. 'I'm sure you're right, Agatha. Now, if you'll
excuse me, I think I need to be alone.' Her voice
was studiously under control but we could all hear
the deep emotion beneath her words. She stood up
and made her way out of the room, leaving us all
sitting in silence, which was finally broken by an
American voice.

'Lady, you sure know how to say the wrong
thing at the wrong time.' Mikey/Martin was
shaking his head in disbelief as he looked across
the table at Agatha with barely concealed distain.
'She just lost her husband and her good friend, for

Chrissake.' He took a big mouthful of wine and looked away.

For her part, Agatha had the decency to react appropriately. 'I'm sorry... I just felt it had to be said, but maybe this wasn't the time...' To her credit, she then stood up. 'I'm going to speak to Maria. Please excuse me.'

A few minutes later she reappeared, but Maria didn't. Agatha remained unusually subdued for the rest of the meal and nobody brought up her denunciation of the dead man again. Gradually the atmosphere around the table improved.

If I had been giving out prizes for the most relieved person in the room, first prize would have gone, without a shadow of a doubt, to Antonio. He was a changed man. All right, he still looked like Count Dracula, but the pall of gloom that had been hanging over him for so many days had now lifted and there was a spring in his step as he moved around the table, spooning generous servings of Annarosa's homemade ravioli onto our plates. These were filled with goats' cheese, spinach, and Parmesan and they were delicious.

The wine flowed freely and the smiles gradually returned. At my side, Charlotte kept up a stream of conversation to which I did my best to respond while my brain was still trying to analyse the reactions of my companions. Emily at the end of the table looked positively euphoric. A cloud of suspicion was still hanging over her in my mind after that momentary expression of alarm that I had spotted on her face when I had announced that Virgilio was following up a fresh lead. Was her obvious joy caused by the realisation she had just escaped a murder charge?

Millicent didn't look euphoric by a long way but, in fairness, I couldn't really imagine her looking euphoric about anything. Professor Diana and white-haired Elaine were chatting cheerfully about sex toys and Gavin had struck up a relaxed conversation with Will about windsurfing. I had long since abandoned Mikey/Martin as a possible suspect so unless my hunch about a possible Exeter connection with one of the Brits at this table paid off, it looked as though Virgilio's superior was going to get his wish and the case really had just been closed.

The pasta was followed by a marvellous fish

stew with mashed potato and, as a special treat at the end, homemade tiramisu. By the time Antonio served the coffees and put a celebratory bottle of grappa on the table, I was feeling pleasantly full and a bit tipsy. Most of us helped ourselves to some of the clear spirit, which turned out not to be the firewater I had been expecting and was rather pleasant in a seriously alcoholic sort of way. I couldn't help noticing that Agatha and Elaine took about three times as much as anybody else. They must have had iron constitutions.

After the meal, Charlotte and I went out into the garden for a stroll and I kept my eyes open in case Oscar might come bounding up and resume his jealous assault. To be on the safe side, I led her through the wicker gate – which I bolted behind us – and we sat down side by side on a sunbed on the far side of the pool. Here, at least, we were unlikely to be disturbed by the dog. It was dead quiet and with the starlight sparkling on the water, there was a romantic feeling in the air. I wondered if Charlotte felt it.

We had barely settled down when the pool lights beneath the surface came on and the two

DEA agents appeared. Charlotte was soon chatting volubly with Rachel while I settled back on the sunbed and, to my shame, fell asleep. All right, I imagine it was a combination of the events of the day plus the huge meal and too much to drink but as far as a romantic conclusion to the night was concerned, it wasn't quite what I had been anticipating. When I awoke, it was to find it was one o'clock in the morning and I was all on my own, apart from a little cloud of mosquitoes. Charlotte had left me there to sleep.

So much for romance.

Somebody had switched off the lights by now and I made my way back to the villa in the pitch darkness. It came as little surprise to find the front door locked at that hour so I went around to the kitchen and tried the back door. It, too, was locked and my fiddling with the handle must have sparked some sort of guard dog instinct in the Labrador as he started barking loudly from inside. I was bending down, with my lips to the keyhole, desperately trying to get him to shut up when there was a sepulchral voice from behind me.

'Can I help you, Signor Dan?'

'Jesus... Antonio!'

I hadn't heard him coming and the shock caused me to jerk upwards, clonking my head against the hefty old door handle as I did so. I stood up and massaged my forehead while he unlocked the door and the joyful dog came bounding out. I was about to apologise to Antonio for disturbing the household when he apologised to me.

'I'm sorry I locked you out. I didn't realise there was anybody still outside.' I registered that Dracula was now wearing a pair of blue and white striped pyjamas and slippers. Somehow none of the horror movies I've seen over the years ever portrayed the infamous vampire wearing anything like this. 'Can I get you anything, Signor Dan?'

I shook my head. 'That's very kind but no, thanks. I'm sorry I disturbed you.'

'Absolutely no problem. I wasn't asleep. After the momentous news this evening I've been too happy to sleep. It's as if I've just been given my life back.'

'Unlike poor Serena.'

'Yes, poor Serena.'

13

THURSDAY

I woke up with a headache next morning, which had nothing to do with the bang on the head I had received from the door handle and everything to do with alcohol. I stared at myself in the bathroom mirror and gave myself a stern talking-to. I was no longer a teenager and I knew I should try to behave like a grown-up. There was a hint of a bruise on my forehead from the back door handle and a couple of red mosquito bites on my neck. The only saving grace was that Helen hadn't been here to reinforce the message.

If I had shaved, I would probably have looked fractionally more presentable but I decided to head straight out for a very gentle run, hoping I wouldn't bump into Charlotte in this state. To my delight, while jogging slowly through the trees I met an old friend who gave me a warm welcome. At least he didn't appear to mind that his future master was nursing a hangover and looking like he'd been pulled through a bush backwards.

'*Ciao*, dog. Coming for a walk?'

There was no need for an answer and the two of us headed out onto the track and turned uphill. My gentle jog changed to a gentle walk but even so by the time I reached the viewing spot at the top I was streaming with sweat. The good news, however, was that my headache had abated. I sat down on the now familiar remains of the dry-stone wall and studied the view while composing a list in my head of things I had to do. Before Saturday, I needed to buy some supplies for my new house, invest in a few creature comforts like soap, washing powder and, of course, dog food. But before all that, I had two other items to attend to. These were to catch the dagger-wielding would-be murderer and to apologise to Charlotte for falling asleep on her last night. Of the two, the latter was likely to be the more daunting.

Back at the villa, I took a long shower, cleaned my teeth twice, and gave myself the closest shave I could. I then put on a fresh polo shirt that masked my insect bites, dug out my only remaining pair of clean shorts, and went downstairs to face the music. I found Charlotte sitting in the seminar room with a bowl of fruit salad in front of her and Diana beside her. As our eyes met, I braced myself for a steely glare but all I saw was mild amusement.

'Well, well, well, if it isn't the Sleeping Beauty. Did a handsome prince finally kiss you to wake you up?'

'Look, Charlotte, I'm really sorry...'

'Don't worry about it. Yesterday was a tough day for all of us, but for you in particular. Being with Serena when she killed herself must have been awful so of course you're forgiven. Come and sit down beside me.'

I felt a wave of relief sweep over me. 'That's great, thanks. Are we still on for dinner tonight?'

'I am if you are.'

'Definitely. I was thinking about maybe trying

the restaurant in Montevolpone, rather than going all the way back to San Miniato. The guy at the bar says Da Geppo's the best place in Tuscany for grilled meat.'

'Sounds lovely.'

At that moment Antonio appeared with my regular cappuccino and croissants. I hadn't noticed him but he must have seen me and, impeccable waiter as he was, he had anticipated my needs. I sipped the coffee gratefully as I offered him my apologies once more for having disturbed him last night. He actually smiled in response – a real smile, not a grimace or a near-imperceptible twitch of the lips. He really did smile.

'That's quite all right, Signor Dan. Like I said, I wasn't asleep.'

'Well, thanks anyway.' I glanced around. 'How's Maria this morning?'

'All right, I think. She was very distressed last night but she looks and sounds brighter today. You can see for yourself; she'll be here any minute.'

A couple of minutes later she arrived, accompanied by Millicent. Neither was smiling but they both looked less stressed than of late. Maria sat down on the other side of me and laid a gentle hand on my arm.

'I've been meaning to say thank you, Dan, for all you've done to help me... us. This has turned out to be a busman's holiday for you, hasn't it? I hope all your detective work hasn't spoilt the course.'

'Not at all. Like I told the inspector, I've enjoyed going back to being a copper for a few days. I'm glad we managed to find who killed Jonah but I'm sorry how it ended for Serena. With a good lawyer and a sympathetic judge, she could have pleaded that she acted while the balance of her mind was upset by what had happened to her girlfriend and probably got away with a more lenient sentence.'

'Poor girl.' Maria nodded sorrowfully. 'Agatha was right. All this was caused by Jonah.'

'Why did you marry him, Maria?' Charlotte joined in, her tone soft and supportive. 'Couldn't you see what sort of man he was?'

Maria even managed to muster a little smile. 'Who was it who said love is blind? When he was younger, Jonah could be very charming, considerate even. I suppose people change as they grow older.'

'I'm not so sure about that.' There was harder edge to Charlotte's voice now. 'In my experience once a cheat, always a cheat.'

'Have you had bad experiences in your life?' Maria sounded sympathetic.

'Haven't we all?' Charlotte gave a little sigh. 'But at least I was lucky enough to meet a wonderful man. It's just such a shame I've lost him.'

To my surprise, if not everybody's, Millicent weighed in, her tone reflective and unusually poignant. 'Losing someone you love is awful.'

There then followed a long silence. I dedicated myself to my coffee and croissants and decided to keep out of it. As I knew to my cost, loss by divorce could also be painful, but if I had to put them in order of hurt, I suppose I would have to put Charlotte's loss of her loving husband at the top, closely followed by Millicent's poisoned fiancé, followed by my situation with losing Helen. The death of a slimeball like Jonah ranked way further down as far as I was concerned, but, then, I hadn't fallen in love with him and married him... poor Maria.

'I'm surprised none of you know that "love is blind" comes from *Romeo and Juliet*, by the way.' It was almost a relief to hear Millicent return to her more usual caustic mode once more. 'Now then, this morning we're going to be doing a session that will involve you in writing in pairs, so I hope you're feeling suitably creative.' I felt her eyes flick over Charlotte and me for a second. 'The pairs will be decided by me and I aim to split up any existing couples so you all are in the same boat.'

I wasn't sure whether to be pleased or disappointed.

When the session started, I found myself paired with Agatha. Fortunately, today we were expressly instructed to keep sex out of it and to concentrate on creating 'atmosphere'. The thought of sitting down to compose a sexy romp with Agatha would have been scary so I was quite happy with her choice of writing about a pastoral scene in the English countryside. She proposed composing our piece about a pristine, bucolic paradise and I agreed willingly, once I had surreptitiously googled the word 'bucolic' to find out what it meant. As we wrote, we chatted about the events of the last two weeks and I soon discovered that her opinion of Jonah hadn't improved.

'I still don't think he deserved to be murdered, but he was a nasty, vindictive little man.'

I decided against reminding her that Jonah had been a six-footer but picked up on her choice of adjective. 'Why "vindictive", Agatha? What makes you say that?'

'His blog, of course. He could be terribly cruel.'

'He had a blog?' This was news.

'Yes, surely you must have seen it? It's called *The Gospel According to Jonah* and it's the most vicious, vituperative piece of internet bullying I've ever seen.'

This was interesting. If Jonah had had a bullying blog, then who could tell how many people he had offended or hurt over the years? Maybe even somebody who had resented him sufficiently to wish to silence him permanently. When the mid-morning break came along, I dashed up to my room to check it out on my laptop. Sure enough, even just a quick flip through Jonah's last few posts revealed vicious attacks on established writers and downright cruel and disheartening critiques of lesser authors. Agatha was right: he really had been a mean and nasty man.

I was about to return to the seminar room when my laptop bleeped and I saw that I had an email from Paul at Scotland Yard.

Hi Dan

Report from University of Exeter just in. It reveals Jonah Moore was sacked for 'dalliances' with female students, one as young as seventeen. Some left as a result, one might have attempted suicide but it was never proven, and thirteen women in all filed official complaints against him over a ten-year period. If that had been now, somebody's head would have rolled for not chucking him out sooner. They've promised to send me the full list of names ASAP in case any of them mean anything to you. I'll send them on when I get them.

Good luck.

Paul

I checked the report and, like Paul, was amazed that action hadn't been taken against Jonah much sooner. Nowadays he would have been strung up by his balls long before thirteen complaints. It would be interesting to see the names of the complainants just in case any of them corresponded to somebody here now. All these cases had taken place in the nineties, when Jonah would have been in his thirties. A quick calculation told me that, assuming his victims back then would have been in their late teens or early twenties, those same women would now be aged between forty and fifty or so, give or take a couple of years. The only women here with me now who fitted that age profile were Diana and Charlotte, plus maybe Rachel from the DEA if she had ever visited Exeter. Assuming she had never been there and was out of it, that left Diana, who claimed to have been asleep in bed at the time of the murder, and Charlotte, who was at the pool the whole time with Emily and Gavin. Of the two, Diana was the only suspect with opportunity but I hadn't picked up so much as a hint of guilt from her. However, maybe she was a brilliant actress.

I sent an email back to Paul thanking him for all his work and apologising again for bothering him. I then called Virgilio to tell him what the report contained and about the blog, but his sergeant told me he was in a meeting and wouldn't be available until three o'clock. Seeing as I needed to go shopping this afternoon, I decided to kill two birds with one stone and call in on him while I was in Florence.

Downstairs, I helped myself to a mug of tea and surreptitiously checked Diana out. Virgilio had said she was forty-seven years old so she would have been aged somewhere between seventeen and twenty-seven at the time Jonah was in Exeter. There were lines on her face now that wouldn't have been there twenty or thirty years ago, but she was still a good-looking woman. With her ebony skin and bright eyes, she would no doubt have attracted the attention of a predator like Jonah. Annoyingly, I didn't yet have details of the different courses followed by each of the women as that might have helped to narrow it down. Although Diana's chosen subject now was history, it was possible she might have done English, even as a subsidiary, and so have come into contact with him. I decided to keep a close eye on her. I would also be keeping close to Charlotte but that wasn't necessarily because I saw her as a possible killer.

After lunch, I took Oscar for a quick walk, my mind alternating between musing on possible suspects for the stabbing and more pressing practical matters relating to my move to the little house, which would be happening in less than forty-eight hours' time. The first thing that occurred to me was transport. Continuing to rent a car for long would work out far too expensive so I was going to need my own car. Back home in Bromley – assuming the bad boys hadn't nicked it – I had a thirteen-year-old Ford bought at auction last year when I had abandoned the house and the other car to Helen. The Ford had originally been a police car and had done well over two hundred thousand miles so it would be pushing it to expect it to make it all the way over here, fully loaded, without mishap. So another car was a priority and, considering my new home was a kilometre up a dirt road, maybe a 4x4 might be wise.

I decided to keep the hire car for one more week while I got myself sorted here and then fly home. I had given notice to the landlord back in the UK two days ago, so that gave me a whole month before I needed to clear my stuff out. The plan was to get rid of the old car, buy the new car, load all my worldly belongings into it and drive back to Tuscany. A glance at my four-legged friend reminded me of the responsibility he brought with him. I couldn't just abandon him over here while I did all that, so when I returned him to the kitchen, I explained the situation to Maria, who was happy to offer to take him.

'Of course, just leave him with us. And that goes for any other time as well. Antonio will be happy to look after him here if you go away and I like seeing him around even if I can't get too close.'

I located a huge supermarket on the outskirts of Florence and stopped off to stock up on everything from toilet paper to salt and pepper, along with a couple of dozen two-litre bottles of water. One of the disadvantages of living in the little house would be the fact that there was no mains water and I thought it prudent to drink bottled water until I had the chance to get the water from the well tested. After loading everything into the car, I went on into Florence and called in on Virgilio. He greeted me with his usual smile, but this time it was closely followed by a shake of the head.

'*Ciao*, Dan. Nothing new here. Anything from your end?'

I pulled out my phone and read out what Paul

had told me about Jonah's 'dalliances'. He nodded sagely and didn't look surprised. Then I told him what Agatha had said about Jonah's blog and he shook his head ruefully.

'Of course, this now opens the list of possible culprits to any number of disgruntled writers. Any idea if he badmouthed any of your fellow students at the villa?'

'I wouldn't be surprised but I haven't had time to check yet. I'll do that tonight and let you know.'

'So still nothing concrete. At least Serena Kempton's death means I've got my boss off my back, but it would be nice to tie it all up before everybody leaves, and that's the day after tomorrow, isn't it? By the way, how are you getting on with the redhead?'

'Well, I fell asleep in her company yesterday evening so that wasn't a great start, but I'm taking her out for dinner tonight. It's going to be a little bit weird seeing as she's still a potential suspect. Although she's got a rock-solid alibi, she and Diana are the two whose age would put them in line for having possibly been victims of Jonah and his wandering hands.'

'You don't think she's involved, do you?'

'She has neither opportunity nor motive as far as I can see, but then none of them have.'

'I think Professor Diana's the most likely candidate. She and the tall, mouthy one, Agatha Whatsername, could have done it. They claimed to have been in their rooms but can't prove it. No alibis for those two.'

'But no motive either... yet.'

* * *

Before going out that evening, I sat down and checked Jonah's vituperative blog a bit more closely. Along the right-hand side was a list of all the books he had reviewed and in most cases excoriated. I searched through the list but could see no sign of any books by Felicity Farnborough (aka Agatha), or Sabrina Butterfly (aka Serena). I did, however, discover reviews of several books by Fanny Lovesit, Elaine's alter ego.

There were reviews of three of her books, among them *Dying of Love*, which I had read. To say they were negative would be to understate the tsunami of opprobrium and derision heaped upon each of them by Jonah. All right, the one I had read hadn't appealed to me much, but no doubt people who were into that sort of thing would have enjoyed it. I had found it well-written and had felt compelled to turn the pages all the way through to the end. In my opinion, Jonah's review was way off the mark and more a reflection of his bitter and arrogant personality than any serious literary criticism. Assuming that Elaine had seen these reviews, she had every right to feel miffed if not downright outraged. But outraged enough to bombard him with poison pen letters or even lace his wine with poison? Maybe even stick a dagger in him? Suddenly Diana had company on the possible suspect list.

At seven, I drove Charlotte down to the restaurant in Montevolpone. Da Geppo was only a short walk from Tommaso's bar so we stopped off under a parasol in the piazza for an aperitivo first. She had a Campari and soda and I had my usual alcohol-free beer. This wasn't only because I was driving. Tonight, I most certainly did not intend to fall asleep in her company again.

Tommaso came out and demonstrated that the Montevolpone bush telegraph was working very efficiently. News of Serena's guilt and suicide had already somehow filtered through and the town was abuzz.

'You must be relieved. I certainly wouldn't have enjoyed living in a house with a killer on the loose. The Florence police know what they're doing all right.'

'Definitely.' Once he had gone off to serve other customers, I translated for Charlotte's sake. 'He's right: it does feel good to know we're no longer in the presence of a murderer, doesn't it?'

Charlotte nodded. 'Absolutely. Did *you* catch her or was it the inspector?'

'Good old-fashioned police work. Checking alibis, checking back stories, you know, it all adds up.'

'I would never have thought it of Serena. She seemed so quiet, so serene like her name.'

'Appearances can be deceptive. Who knows what's really going on inside other people's heads?'

She took a mouthful of Campari. The deep red intensified the colour of her lipstick and made her look even more desirable. 'Can you guess what I'm thinking right now?'

'That you're hungry?'

'Try again.'

'That you're looking forward to going home the day after tomorrow?'

'It's something I'm looking forward to, but it's sooner than that.'

I suddenly wished there was alcohol in my beer but I took a hasty mouthful anyway. 'Erm, something happening sooner than that, you say? Something happening today, tonight?'

'Bingo. You got it.' She took another sip of her drink. 'Has anybody ever told you you're a very attractive man, Daniel Armstrong?'

I took another slurp of beer, feeling increasingly out of my depth. 'Not for a long, long time and not when they were stone-cold sober.'

'Well, I think you are. And you're bright with it.'

The meal at Da Geppo was very good but I still maintain that the steak I had at Virgilio's house was the best meat I've ever tasted. Tonight, after a starter of salad with raw porcini mushrooms and smoked ham with quails' eggs, we chose to share a mixed grill. This arrived on a huge wooden board and consisted of crispy little lamb chops that we ate with our fingers, coils of spicy sausage, and slices of chicken breast marinated in local herbs, all accompanied by a mountain of tiny roast potatoes. Afterwards, Charlotte chose panna cotta while I settled for a lemon sorbet. We chatted as we ate and as we chatted, a funny thing started to happen.

What started it off was a comment she made about her complexion. I was gallantly telling her how much I liked freckles when she shook her head and told me the downside to having skin like hers.

'Even smothered in factor fifty, I can't stay out in the sun for more than a few minutes at a time. Do you know? I can even get sunburnt when I'm underneath an umbrella.'

I commiserated with her, but all the time the thought going through my head was how come she had spent the whole afternoon of the murder down by the pool with Emily and Gavin? First, from what she had just told me, this sounded like the very last thing she would have done and second, if this had been the case, why hadn't she returned from her afternoon in the sun looking bright red? I remembered her looking a bit pink, but nothing more than that. No sooner did I find myself going down this line of conjecture than I could almost hear Helen's words ringing in my head: *You just can't take people at face value. You're always questioning, questioning, questioning.*

I did my best to relegate any suspicions of my charming dinner companion to the back of my mind but it was a forlorn hope. Only a few minutes later, as the waiter brought us our coffees, another thought occurred to me. She had told me she worked for a printing firm in Bridgwater and I couldn't help letting my thoughts dwell on the fact that the last two letters of the name of that town were very familiar. Could she be the author of the poison pen letters and if so, why? What reason might she have had to do something like that? Or worse?

All this combined to make me suddenly hesitant to take our fledgling relationship to the conclusion she might well have been indicating and to which I had been looking forward – albeit with trepidation. What if she really was our poisoner or even our stabber? Maybe she had only been cosying up to me all along so as to keep me sweet and to learn how the investigation was proceeding. In fact, that would go a long way towards explaining why such an attractive woman had demonstrated such interest in me. Yet another flash of realisation came to me: every time she had sat down alongside me or stood beside me or accompanied me anywhere, she had always asked – tactfully and unobtrusively – how the inspector had been getting on. This thought was immediately followed by the recollection that she had been the first person I had told about the inspector's impending visit on Monday and this had resulted in somebody cutting the tapes and entering the crime scene. Was I in the presence of a wannabe killer?

My mind was racing as we drove back up to the villa. I had come out this evening suspicious of Diana and Elaine but now was I really suspecting Charlotte as well? Was this what paranoia felt like? It couldn't be her, I told myself firmly. She had a cast-iron alibi. She had been at the pool in the company of two complete strangers: Emily and Gavin. Both of them had confirmed that they had been there for two solid hours and Emily had produced the alibi before anybody else last Tuesday afternoon. It was almost as though she had been preparing it. But why would Gavin and Emily lie for somebody they didn't know?

There was only one logical explanation.

When we got back to the villa, I suggested a walk in the park and Charlotte seemed happy to agree. She clung on to me as we strolled down across the lawn and into the trees, following the path in the starlight as far as the bench by the fence where we sat down side by side. I was trying to make up my mind how best to say what I needed to say when we were joined by a very noisy companion. Needless to say, as Oscar spotted Charlotte, he started barking the house down all over again.

It was as I was gradually calming him down that I had my epiphany. Suddenly I realised what he was saying. He wasn't barking out of jealousy. Could it be that the only living witness to what had gone on in the dining room last Tuesday was telling me who the culprit was? I stroked his head and looked across at Charlotte. Suddenly I felt sure I had made the logical connection. I could just make out her facial features and I studied them closely as I popped the question.

'Emily's your daughter, isn't she?'

Charlotte jumped as if she had been stung and this set the dog off all over again. It took a full minute before I managed to pacify him once more. She hadn't responded yet so I asked again.

'It all happened at Exeter university almost thirty years ago, didn't it? And that's why you decided to stab Jonah.'

I saw her eyes glint in the starlight. 'What on earth makes you say that?' She was blustering; I could tell.

'I have a witness who's told me what really happened last Tuesday.' The fact that the witness was a Labrador was something I chose to leave out. 'In case you're under any illusions, I've requested birth, marriage, and academic records from the UK along with a list of the thirteen women who filed complaints against Jonah. It was you, Charlotte, and we both know it.'

She made no reply so I took a leap of faith and pushed a little more. 'Emily was born as a result of an affair you had with Jonah, wasn't she?'

'Affair? It wasn't an affair.' Her voice was rising in pitch. 'It was rape. He got me drunk. The first thing I knew about it was waking up in the bushes outside the hall of residence with half my clothes ripped off.'

'Did you go to the police?'

'Of course I went to the police and to the university authorities but I was banging my head against a brick wall. The university wouldn't even listen to me and what help did your lot give me? None at all. The alcohol in my blood convinced them that I only had myself to blame. Do you know what they said, those bastards?' Her voice was more level now but the emotion in it was plain to hear. '"Be more careful next time, love." Love! Love had nothing to do with it.'

'But why wait until now to get your revenge?' A long pause followed and I wondered if I had pushed her a bit too far but, finally, she answered. This time her voice had dropped to little more than a whisper.

'When I discovered I was pregnant, Jonah denied any involvement and left me to my own devices. I had to give up my degree course and if it hadn't been for the support of my parents I'd have been completely lost.' Her face was pointing at the ground by this time and her voice remained low. 'Richard, my husband, knew the full story. I met him five years after Emily was born and we married a couple of years later. I told him the whole sad story before we got married. After all, there I was with a little child who had no father. He told me Jonah wasn't worth it and managed to help me get over it. I owe Richard everything: my job, my happiness and my sanity. When he was so brutally taken away from me last year, I was completely lost all over again.'

I listened closely. My guess had been right but I had no sense of elation. Charlotte's tragic story effectively ended whatever story she and I might have been building together. Jonah had done it again.

'How come you ended up here?'

'It was pressure from Emily, really. I had told her all about her real father when she was a teenager but she had never been interested in contacting him. In fact, after hearing the story, I think she detested him as much as I did. But one day last autumn, quite by chance, I saw an advert in the paper for a book-signing taking place in Bristol for Jonah's new book and for some reason I decided to go and see what he was like and if he remembered me. Part of me wanted to go in there screaming at the top of my voice, telling everybody what a scumbag he was.'

'Did Emily go with you?'

'No, I didn't tell her about it and just went on my own.'

'And what happened?'

She looked up. 'What happened? Nothing happened, that's what. He didn't recognise me and even when I told him my name, my maiden name, he still didn't react. Can you imagine how I felt? How can you forget the mother of your child?'

She was crying now and I gave her some time before repeating my original question.

'So how was it you decided to come here? You mentioned Emily.'

She blew her nose and wiped her eyes before continuing. 'They were handing out leaflets at the book-signing event advertising this creative writing course to be hosted by Jonah. Emily came down to see me a few weeks later and saw the one I'd brought home. When she saw who it was, she convinced me to sign up for the course and come over and have it out with him, try to get some sort of closure. She said she'd come along as well to add a bit of support.'

'But why didn't she just come as your daughter? Why the secrecy?'

'That was her idea. I could tell she was dreading meeting him and she wanted to be able to stay in the background if he and I ended up having a massive row. Besides, she knew Gavin would be interested in doing the course.'

'And Gavin was happy to go along with the illusion?'

'Gavin still doesn't know I'm Emily's mother. They only hooked up together a few months ago and they've been abroad a lot. The first time I met him was here last week.'

'And what did Emily think of her father when she met him for the first time?'

'She told me he made her skin creep.' For a second or two I was reminded of the look of repulsion I had spotted on Emily's face as she had first set eyes on her father on the first night here.

'And the afternoon of the murder, did she know you were going to speak to him?'

Charlotte shook her head decisively. 'No, I didn't tell her. She and Gavin were fast asleep. I just waited until they were both sleeping and slipped off. When I came back a couple of hours later, Gavin was still snoring.'

'But Emily was awake, and she realised you'd gone to see Jonah that afternoon?' Charlotte nodded and I continued. 'And you told her what you'd done and asked her to provide you with an alibi?'

'I had to tell someone. I took her to one side, leaving Gavin fast asleep, and I confessed it all to her and she was appalled. I was as well, with myself. She knew I'd been planning to have it out with Jonah, but that was all. And I meant it, honestly.' She looked up towards me and I could see tears glistening in her eyes. 'I didn't go in there to kill him. You need to believe me. I went in there to spell out to him how he'd ruined my life and that I was going to tell his wife the whole thing and spoil his life for him in return just like he had done to me.'

'So why stab him?'

There was a long pause before she answered. 'Frustration, I suppose. When I got in there, I could see he was already dead. His eyes were wide open and he was totally unresponsive. I now know that Serena had poisoned him but at the time I just assumed it must have been a heart attack. Anybody could see he was an overweight alcoholic and something like that would have been almost inevitable. The thing is, I'd built this scene up in my mind for so long, I felt cheated. It was so unfair that he could just pass away in the blink of an eye without realising the destruction he'd left in his wake. Because of him, my whole life changed forever. I lost my hopes of getting a degree and becoming a teacher. I was transformed from a happy university student without a care in the world to a single mother, scraping to make ends meet.' There was a catch in her voice but she refused to start crying again.

'So you stabbed him out of frustration, even though you knew he was dead?'

I saw her nod. 'It was a moment of sheer, stupid frustration. I took his precious knife – the symbol of his overbearing conceit – and stuck it in him, thinking this would release me from the burning hatred I'd been carrying with me all those years, but all it did was turn my stomach. I ran up to my room and was violently sick. Then as the reality of what I'd done began to sink in, I had a sudden thought that I'd probably left my fingerprints on the handle of the dagger so I hurried back down and wiped it clean. This made me feel sick all over again and I had to rush to my room a second time to vomit. I spent ages up there crying my eyes out before finally going back out to the pool.'

'And that's when you asked you daughter to lie for you?'

She nodded miserably. 'To be honest, I feel guiltier about that than about sticking the dagger in Jonah.'

'And the poison pen letters?'

'What poison pen letters?' There was no mistaking the bewilderment in her voice. 'What do you mean?'

'Somebody sent him poison pen letters before he died. Are you telling me that wasn't you?'

'Of course not. Maybe it was Serena?'

'Maybe it was.' Of one thing I was now almost

certain: from her reaction, Charlotte wasn't the author of the letters.

'And can I take it that you had nothing to do with any attempt to poison him?'

She was looking baffled by now. 'No, of course I didn't. Surely that was Serena, wasn't it? Like I told you, I had no intention of killing him. I wanted him to suffer, the way I'd had to suffer: inside. The man was a callous, heartless beast.' Her voice was heavy with outrage.

'He certainly wasn't a good man, that's for sure.'

'So what happens to me now?' She paused for a good long while. 'I don't suppose you could just forget this conversation, could you?'

I'd been asking myself the very same question ever since she had started telling her story. I felt sorry for her and even more angry at the callousness of the dead man, but when all was said and done she had stuck a knife into another human's heart. There are some lines people should not cross and to my mind this was one of them. The fact that this would forever sever any romantic links we might have been forming between us was not lost on me but I had no choice in the matter. I couldn't live with the knowledge that I had tacitly condoned such a brutal act, however understandable the motivation behind it might have been. I knew I had to tell Virgilio but I resolved to do my best to plead for clemency.

'I'm afraid I can't do that. But what I will do is to tell him you came to me and volunteered this confession of your own free will and that I believe you – and I do – when you say you knew Jonah was already dead when you stabbed him and the pathologist's report supports that. Get yourself a good lawyer and I'm pretty sure the worst you could be facing is a charge of violating a body or whatever they call it over here. I'd be very surprised if you don't get away with little more than a suspended sentence.'

She gave a heartfelt sigh. 'Thank you, Dan.' I saw the starlight reflect in the moisture in her eyes. 'By the way, in case you start wondering, I meant it when I said I liked you. I could have seen this relationship developing, you know. You'll make some woman very happy one of these days.'

'I very much doubt that. My track record on that front isn't good.'

14

FRIDAY

Charlotte was taken away for questioning but later released on bail. She didn't return to the villa. Emily collected her mother's things on Friday and she and Gavin headed off to a hotel somewhere. I went down to the car to see them off. Gavin, for whom all of this was clearly a massive surprise, gave me a bemused smile as he saw me.

'What a mess!'

I nodded in return and looked over at Emily. 'Try not to worry too much. She'll be okay, I'm sure. I told the inspector I firmly believe she had no intention of killing Jonah.'

'She told me. Thanks, Dan, I can't apologise

enough.' She was close to tears. 'Bringing her here was my idea. I thought it might give her some sort of closure after all these years. If I'd thought for a moment that it might have all ended up like this, I'd never have dreamt of doing it.'

'I'm sure you wouldn't.' She might have been telling the truth or it might have all been an elaborate act, but there was nothing to be gained in taking it any further. When all was said and done, her life had been blighted enough by Jonah and his callous behaviour. 'Promise me you'll keep a close eye on your mum from now on, will you? I like her and she deserves all the support you can give.'

'I promise. And thank you, Dan.'

I subsequently heard from Virgilio that the public prosecutor was apparently still scouring the statute books to see what charge, if any, might be levelled at Charlotte. Certainly, it looked as though anything as serious as attempted murder wasn't on the cards. After all, we already had the pathologist's report saying Jonah had died up to an hour earlier and you can't murder somebody who's already dead. I hoped she would get off without a custodial sentence. How she would pick up her life again when all this was over was in the lap of the gods and I wished her well in spite of everything that had happened.

Friday saw the conclusion to our course and there was a subdued atmosphere over lunch. Compared to only a few days ago, there were now four empty places at the table and it soon emerged that there would be four more by the evening.

Over a cold seafood salad and fresh asparagus from the garden, Mikey/Martin announced that he and Jen would be leaving that afternoon. They intended to head south to continue their holiday although they gave no details as to where they were planning on going next. It was obvious to me that wherever they went, Rachel and Will from the DEA would also go, so by the evening there promised to be just a handful of us left.

At the end of lunch, as I was standing on the terrace with a coffee, I felt a large hand on my shoulder and turned to find Mikey/Martin standing there.

'I came to say goodbye, Dan. It's been good knowing you.'

'And you. By the way, I've been thinking about

something you said. When I told you I was going to settle down here, you sounded quite serious about making a change in your life.'

'It's very tempting. I admire you for having the balls to do something so radical.'

I glanced around but we were alone. 'You did me a favour as far as Antonio and that handgun were concerned and I told you I owed you for that. Let me try and repay that debt now. You probably don't want my advice but here it is anyway. I've seen you and Jen together and it's clear how happy you make each other. Promise me you'll take a few minutes to imagine what life would be like for both of you if you were separated for years and years.' I looked him square in the eye. 'From what I hear, you're living on borrowed time. They're out to get you and they will... Mikey.'

His eyes narrowed and I braced myself for the punch that never came. Instead, I found myself enveloped in a bear hug that almost lifted me off my feet before he stepped back, still gripping my shoulders. 'You're a good guy, Dan. Thank you.' His tough face creased into a smile. 'DEA agents stand out a mile and I'd already worked that out for myself. I've kind of grown to like Rachel and Will but I'm tired of having those guys on my back. Maybe you're right. I promise I'll give it some thought. You look after yourself now, Dan, and thanks again.'

I was down at the pool an hour later, trying to remember how long Helen had always insisted Tricia and I should wait before going swimming after a meal when the two DEA agents appeared. They, too, were leaving, as I had expected.

'Michael Cornish and his lady have moved on and we'll be following close behind.' Will grinned. 'As long as he doesn't locate the tracker we fixed to his car. Congratulations on cracking the case here.'

'What about you two? Are you going to break the news to your bosses that you're a couple?'

Rachel nodded. 'First thing when we get back.'

'Well, good luck with everything. Enjoy the rest of your lives together and if you're ever passing, come and look me up.'

'Enjoy your new life in Tuscany.'

As there were so few of us left for dinner that night, Annarosa gave us a real treat: oysters followed by an omelette made with artichoke hearts and smoked ham, and then a rich wild boar stew, allegedly made from a marauding boar that had been shot by the neighbouring farmer the other day after demolishing half of his vineyard by ripping up the vines with its tusks. The wild boar's loss was our gain. It was delicious, accompanied by fried porcini mushrooms and roast potatoes. To drink, Antonio opened bottles of the local white fizz and some expensive Villa Antinori red wine and Annarosa rounded off the meal with home-made ice cream and fresh strawberries, served in a delightful meringue case.

At the end of the meal as we sat back and sipped our coffees and while Agatha and Elaine knocked back liver-crippling quantities of grappa, I made one last effort to discover the identity of the person who had put oleander poison into the wine bottle. After all, anyone in the room with me now could have done it. Both Agatha and Diana had written about similar plant-based poisons and Jonah's crushing critiques of Elaine's books provided a possible motive. Assuming Maria and Antonio were out of the equation – and I did – that only left Millicent and she'd arguably had not only motive and opportunity but also experience of poisonous plants. I started with a simple question.

'Have any of you ever experimented with do-it-yourself poisons?'

Diana was the first to respond, with a slightly embarrassed expression on her face. 'To be quite honest, I did once. I followed a recipe – can you say "recipe" for poison? – from the internet and managed to produce a potentially lethal gooey liquid made from crushed yew berries. It was remarkably easy.' She glanced over at me and smiled. 'It was for my book, you see. I always like to try out things first before I write about them.'

Considering that she had told us her book also contained a plethora of weird sexual acts, I wondered just how far she was prepared to go in her search for authenticity, but I didn't comment as she carried on.

'The problem I had was what to do with it once I'd made it. Seeing as I wasn't going to poison anybody or anything with it, I didn't know how to get rid of it. I thought of flushing it down the toilet but then wondered if it might somehow get into the water supply. I considered throwing it into the sea but then I found myself thinking that the fish might eat it and then people might eat the fish and die. I was getting quite worked up, I'm afraid.'

'So what did you do with it? Have you still got it?' Agatha sounded fascinated and I soon found out why. 'Wouldn't that be a super idea for a murder mystery? A writer makes her own poison and then it falls into the wrong hands and she gets blamed.'

Diana nodded vigorously. 'All those sorts of thoughts were going through my head so in the end I burned it.'

'You burned the poison?'

'Yes, I lit a bonfire and poured the poison into one of those plastic trays the chicken Kiev from M&S comes in and put it on the fire. The poison gradually evaporated away before my eyes and then the plastic tray finally caught fire and voila. All gone.'

I threw the question out to the floor once again, just in case. 'None of you other ladies ever tried your hand at brewing your own poison?'

'Of course not.' Agatha fixed me with her eagle

eye. 'Why the questions, Chief Inspector? I thought that was all done and dusted.'

I decided that a little white lie might be in order. 'No, this is for my book. I've been reading about the Medici and there was a lot of poisoning going on over here at that time. Just curious.'

'The thing about poisons...' All eyes turned towards mild-mannered Elaine, who hadn't spoken up yet. 'You need to be sure you know the right dose. There's no point giving somebody a litre of poison when a few drops would do. Also...' She very deliberately looked across the table at me and I swear there was a twinkle in her eye. 'Not every poisoner sets out to kill. Some people don't deserve to die but they do deserve to be made to feel very poorly so they learn their lesson.'

I met her gaze. 'And what sort of lesson might that be?'

'Humility, kindness, humanity... that sort of thing.' She paused for a moment. 'Some people can be so very cruel.'

'They certainly can. Of course, a simpler method of teaching people a lesson is to confront them, either face to face or by letter.' I deliberately stressed the final word but she didn't rise to the bait. She just sat there with a little sphinx-like smile on her face.

I gave it another few minutes and then came up with an apparently innocent suggestion. 'You know I'm settling down over here, don't you? Well, I thought I'd give you all my address so we can stay in touch. If any of you come over again, do pay me a visit. In fact...' I tried to sound as casual as I could, as if the idea had only just occurred to me. 'Why don't we all exchange addresses?'

This suggestion was met with universal approval and Millicent produced an A4 pad and passed it around before going off and making copies for everybody. As I was finishing the last of the grappa Agatha had insisted on pouring into my glass, I let my eyes run down over the addresses, particularly the last two letters of the place names. Millicent was Warwick, Diana Bristol, Agatha Littlehampton and so, I thought, was Elaine. But then I looked more closely. Her address was in fact a village near Littlehampton called Lyminster, and the last two letters of the name leapt out at me. Could it be? After her little homily on poison doses, it wouldn't have surprised me, but there wasn't a shred of proof.

The previous day, Agatha had organised a whip-round and had bought Millicent and Maria presents with the proceeds. It was a pity so few of the original course participants were now left but this didn't stop her standing up and proposing a vote of thanks worthy of a Greek orator to the half-empty room, thanking both of them for what had been a very useful writing course. I joined in with the applause. It had been an interesting two weeks. She made no mention of Jonah or of Serena and went on to give thanks to Antonio and Annarosa for providing such wonderful hospitality, before Elaine then surprised me with a bulky gift wrapped in paper and with a bow on top. This was apparently a housewarming present for me from her and I was genuinely touched. She slid it across the table and smiled benevolently.

'Every time you see it, you can think of me, Dan.' And she winked.

The present was a healthy-looking oleander plant in a pot.

ACKNOWLEDGMENTS

Thanks to my lovely editor, Emily Ruston, and everybody at Boldwood Books for their faith in me and my whodunnits. And warmest thanks to my friends who took the time to read and comment on the original manuscript and who definitely helped improve the book: Elaine Brent, John Dearden, Judy Hands, and Tricia Willey. Thanks to you all.

MORE FROM T.A. WILLIAMS

We hope you enjoyed reading *Murder In Tuscany*. If you did, please leave a review.

If you'd like to gift a copy, this book is also available as an ebook, digital audio download and audiobook CD.

Sign up to T.A. Williams' mailing list for news, competitions and updates on future books.

https://bit.ly/TAWilliamsNewss

ABOUT THE AUTHOR

T A Williams is the author of over twenty bestselling romances for HQ and Canelo and is now turning his hand to cosy crime, set in his beloved Italy, for Boldwood. The series will introduce us to to DCI Armstrong and his labrador Oscar. Trevor lives in Devon with his Italian wife.

Visit T.A. Williams' website:

http://www.tawilliamsbooks.com

Follow T.A. Williams' on social media:

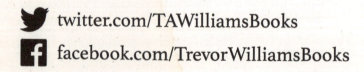

twitter.com/TAWilliamsBooks

facebook.com/TrevorWilliamsBooks

ABOUT BOLDWOOD BOOKS

Boldwood Books is a fiction publishing company seeking out the best stories from around the world.

Find out more at www.boldwoodbooks.com

Sign up to the Book and Tonic newsletter for news, offers and competitions from Boldwood Books!

http://www.bit.ly/bookandtonic

We'd love to hear from you, follow us on social media:

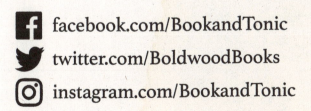

facebook.com/BookandTonic

twitter.com/BoldwoodBooks

instagram.com/BookandTonic